Compleet Bear

A Fantasy about a Bear and Baseball

Jack Graybill (handwritten signature)

Jack Graybill

TATE PUBLISHING & Enterprises

Published by Tate Publishing & Enterprises, LLC
127 E. Trade Center Terrace | Mustang, Oklahoma 73064 USA
1.888.361.9473 | www.tatepublishing.com

Tate Publishing is committed to excellence in the publishing industry. The company reflects the philosophy established by the founders, based on Psalm 68:11,
"The Lord gave the word and great was the company of those who published it."

Book design copyright © 2009 by Tate Publishing, LLC. All rights reserved.
Cover design by Tyler Evans
Interior design by Joey Garrett
Based on illustrations by Gina Soldi Burns

Published in the United States of America
ISBN: 978-1-60799-939-3
1. Juvenile Fiction / Sports & Recreation / Baseball & Softball
2. Juvenile Fiction / Animals / Bears
09.10.02

Written for Dad, with whom I watched
countless Phillies games on TV.

Contents

Part Four: Reach for the Bronze and Conclusion

Epilogue: "Whatever Happened to ... ?"

The Characters

Clint and Ginny Bruedock: Owners of a farm in West Tennessee

Clara: Clint and Ginny's daughter

Ronny: Clara's teenage son and Compleet's playmate, friend, and advisor

Meade and Alice Fountlund: Summer visitors of the Bruedocks

Compleet Bear (a.k.a. Roger): Black bear extraordinaire

Doc Heelem: The Bruedocks' family doctor

Mitch: Scout for the Tenn Nine

Clyde: Manager of the Tenn Nine

Joe Wathersmythe: Principal owner of the Tomtowne Tenn Nine

Spencer (Spitz) McOystre: Ballplayer and Compleet's roommate and close friend

Kristy: Ronny's love interest

Mushie: Trainer for the Tenn Nine

Robbie and Max: Scouts for the Chum

Fred Miltones: Principal owner of the Cuspin Heights Chum

John Boslerts: General Manager of the Cuspin Heights Chum

Sal Frogertee (Frog): Manager of the Chum

Dwight Hofenpfeiffer: Commissioner of In-The-Sea Association

Jury: Hitting coach for the Chum

Stunkie Fonkules: Cuspin paparazzo

Matti Gimcrack: Office temporary on Troefield's West Side

Dolly Dampling: Waitress

Debbie Drumsticke: Second waitress

Lolly Lental: Third waitress

Helen Achts: Desk clerk at the Three C's Hotel

Mai Tai: Helen's Siamese cat

Wilmont (Willie): Bartender on Troefield's West Side

Honey B.: Compleet's love interest

Lance McCrewl: Judge at Compleet and Spitz's hearing

Dan Cuff: Brawler at Tailors Station

Marvin Smytes: Second brawler

Elmer (Dutch) McOystre: Spitz's dad

Julie: One-time fiancée of Spitz

Billum Ghraye: Left fielder on minor league team in Texas

Yodel Beisst: Chum fan who had dispute with Montvue

Abee: Beisst's pet aardvark

Vache Montvue: One-time owner of the Cuspin Heights Chum

Charles and Carly: Julie's children by her first husband

Tom, Terry, and Tracy: Cubs of Honey B. and Compleet

Morgan (Dutch) McOystre: Spitz and Julie's son

Animals on the Farm

Lame dog (Slo-Mikey), deer (Autumn), mallard ducks
(Quack, Quacker), Arabian camel (Desert), llama
(Andy), coyote (Coty), beaver (Carpenter), pheasant, rac-
coons, and a bear (Roger, later named Compleet)

Ballplayers

Tomtowne Tenn Nine: Donny, Compleet Bear, Spitz
McOystre, Dusty Plain, Tad, Pedro, Vern, Eric, Motsie
Mangrove, Juan Aragoone, Beau Hummle, Joey Ghurtz

Cuspin Heights Chum: Compleet Bear, Spitz McOystre, Claude Hammer (Ham), Emile Jean Pierre Fri (French Fry), James Nicholas Gathorin (Jimbo), San Diego Santana (Santa), Jack Frumme (Drum Drum), Gary Payoly (Payday), Philip Unterfuss (P.U.), Amo Amas (Amat), Frank Jammache (Jammin), Greg Grumpet (Gee Gee), Bule Penn, Walter Muffint (Muffy), Tony Splinterrs (Rail)

Balflint Batfish: Gunsten Gonzalez (Killer Kong)

Horstead Haddock: Al Rutherum (Long Ball)

Prumfort Porgies: Elroy Speedbal, Dig Deeper

Gallsun Goldeye: Gene DeeRouch (Dee Rock)

Part One:
Farm with a Bear in Residence

Tragedy ... Then a New Life

Can a bear live with humans? Must he always apologize for his differences? Can he overcome scandal, insults, and reproofs in his baseball life—become a sports legend? Sometimes make-believe mirrors events in real life. This is one of those stories.

Clint and Ginny Bruedock were an energetic, pleasant couple, the kind that put others at ease. They were always willing to do more than their share, always available if the neighbors needed them, and always thinking that tomorrow might be a better day than today. The two lived on a farm in West Tennessee with their daughter, Clara. The land wasn't the best, but then, it wasn't the worst either. The couple made a better than average living from their crops—corn, soybeans, wheat, tobacco, turnips, peas—and the few pigs they slaughtered from time to time. Their orchard gave them, in season, apples, peaches, pears, plums, and cherries. There were berry patches on the south end of the farm. Much of the year, the couple maintained a roadside stand, and they sold at the local market every Saturday.

They loved the land, and they loved their animals. In the first years they had two horses and a mule, a few cows, a steer, pigs, chickens, and three cats. A lame dog showed up; since no other farmer wanted him, the Bruedocks took him in. The dog and Clara quickly took to each other and were usually seen together. She named the dog Slo-Mikey.

Clara grew up, got married, and moved to another state. Her departure left a gap in Clint and Ginny's life, but it was soon filled. One fine day in late fall a wounded deer wandered onto the property and lay down, near death. Ginny was an RN and removed the lead shot and nursed the deer back to health. She called the deer Autumn. Friendly and gentle, the deer quickly fit into the established routine on the farm. So delighted were the Bruedocks with Autumn and Slo-Mikey, they decided to take in other animals in need.

Over the years, they added two raccoons, a beaver that was always stopping up the stream that ran through the property, mallard ducks, a pheasant, a llama (which they got from a petting zoo that folded), a coyote (which Clint rescued from a trap), and an Arabian camel (which they bought from a traveling circus that was hard up for cash). It may surprise you, dear reader, to know that the animals got along tolerably well with one another and rarely annoyed the neighbors. At night the wild animals of size were kept within a fenced area not far from the orchard and had access to sheds if they wanted shelter. During the day all the wild ones but the coyote could roam about the farm, and on the occasions they wandered beyond the farm, they were quickly rounded up by one or more of the Bruedocks. The coyote was restricted to a large fenced-in pen with trees, bushes, wild flowers, and grass. Ginny and Clint knew their neighbors wouldn't fancy seeing a coyote in a crouched walk close to their chickens and other fowl.

Because Clint and Ginny were so well liked in their part of the county, no local hunter asked to come onto their property. And signs posted by the Bruedocks told strangers their animals were not for shooting, only for seeing.

Clint and Ginny got on in years, as we all do. Their daughter divorced, and she and her teenage son Ronny returned to the farm. She took back her maiden name. Clint and Ginny were sorry the marriage hadn't worked out but were happy Clara and Ronny were with them. They welcomed younger hands, especially on a farm that had so many animals that needed care.

A Cub and No Mom

Clint and Ginny were making their visitors from New Jersey feel at home. They were the Fountlunds, Meade and Alice. Ginny and Alice had met in college, become good friends, and continued to keep in touch after graduation. After Alice married Meade, the two scheduled a trip to West Tennessee every summer to see the Bruedocks.

One evening after supper, Alice handed Ginny an article from Newark's *The Star Ledger* and said, "I know you, Clint, Clara, and Ronny love animals, so I cut out this article to read. It's about a bear."

The bear was a male cub that had lost its mom when she was run over by a car at night. The driver was rounding a curve, saw the bear in front of him, and couldn't stop in time. The cub was being cared for at the Highlands Habitat Shelter in northwest New Jersey, a short distance from the spot of the accident. The area where the accident took place had woods and few people. A lot of bears, deer, and small animals called the area home.

Near the bottom of the article was a picture of the cub and two of the staff. Someone at the shelter had named the cub Roger. He was a black bear, a yearling, with black to dark brown hair, a little tail, cute standup ears, and a sad face.

Ginny stared at the picture. Then she passed the article to Clint, who handed it off to Clara, who gave it to Ronny. After all had read the article, Clara was the first to comment. "In his picture he looks so sad, and so ... so lost."

"I guess that's how people—and animals—look when they lose a ma or pa," said Ronny.

Ginny and Clara both spoke at once. "Do you think we might—" They stopped in midsentence and started to laugh when they realized they were thinking the same thing.

"Couldn't we adopt him and raise him on the farm?" asked Clara.

"You're talking about a bear," answered Clint. "That's a wild animal, and wild animals are unpredictable. No, the cub would be cute and playful; but cubs grow up, and then they can be a danger."

"I read that black bears aren't nearly as mean and unpredictable as grizzlies," said Ronny. "Take Desert and Coty; they get along well enough. No one is afraid of them."

"Yes, Ronny, I know," said Clint. "But a camel and a coyote aren't nearly as strong and aggressive as a bear. I won't take the responsibility."

Clara walked over to her pa and put her arms around his neck. She said in a soft voice, "I'll gladly take responsibility. And if I ever think the bear is a threat to anyone—animal or person—I promise I'll find a new home for him in a zoo or make sure he's returned to the wild."

Clint looked into his daughter's eyes. Those pleading, dark brown eyes of hers had won him over so many times. Ginny smiled. "Clint, I think we have you outnumbered."

"Ginny, you too? You think we can handle a bear on the property?"

"Yes I do. We'll have to make the fencing stronger and perhaps extend it in some places. And we should post signs warning that Roger may sometimes act in unpredictable ways. The signs should emphasize that no onlooker should feed him. We'll have to build a cage to keep him in. But I think if all four of us pitch in, Roger will be happy with us, and we'll be happy with Roger."

"I'm so glad you said that, Ginny," said Alice. "I told Meade I was pretty sure you would want to adopt Roger after I showed you the article."

Letter and a Long Wait

A few days after Meade and Alice said their goodbyes and headed back east, Clint sat down at his desk and wrote a friendly letter to the Highlands Habitat Shelter. He told the shelter he and his family had read a news article about the cub and wanted to adopt him. He wrote a little about each member of the family and said every Bruedock had been around animals and knew a lot about their care. Listing every domestic and wild animal on the farm, he told under what circumstances the lame dog, deer, two raccoons, beaver, ducks, pheasant, llama, coyote, and camel had found a new home.

If the shelter would allow the Bruedocks to adopt the cub, he promised to take it to a vet for regular checkups, never exhibit the animal for profit, and make sure the cub would not harm any person or beast. At the end of the letter, Clint wrote he would pay to ship the cub to Tennessee or, if need be, he would go to New Jersey to pick up the bear. And he would donate money to the Highlands Habitat Shelter at least once a year.

Then the waiting began! After a week had gone by, Clara and Ronny said they were worried the shelter had turned down Clint's request. Clint and Ginny disagreed. Certainly the shelter had many animals to care for. Perhaps it was short on staff and hadn't the time to meet to talk about the letter.

"Give them another week," said Ginny. "I'm sure we'll hear from them."

Another week went by and still no answer. All four began to worry now. Clint decided to give the shelter a call then changed his mind. "It's the right thing to let those people handle the matter in their own good time. We'll just have to wait and hope."

A third week went by and no letter from the shelter. But in the middle of the fourth week, when the mail truck stopped at the Bruedock farm, the mailman put a letter with the shelter's logo on the envelope in the mailbox.

The letter was from the executive director of the shelter. He apologized for the delay in answering. The small staff and many volunteers had been especially busy and recently had to minister to five new arrivals at the shelter: three raptors that had been wounded by lead shot, a red fox that had an ugly gash in one of its feet, and a skunk that had been badly bitten by a much larger creature (judging by the teeth marks). A weasel in their care had dug a hole under a fence and had led three volunteers on a merry chase before they recaptured it. A bobcat that had been at the shelter for two months had scratched a volunteer, leaving deep marks.

"See," said Ginny, "there *was* a good reason they took so long to answer Clint's letter, in fact, a lot of reasons!"

Clint started to read the rest of the letter to himself. "Gran'pa," said Ronny in a loud voice, "don't read to yourself!"

"Good news," said Clint, and he smiled a wide smile. "No, it's g-r-e-a-t news! Everyone at the shelter enjoyed reading about our collection of animals." Clint skipped a few lines. Then he read, "It is the policy of the shelter to release the animals back into the wild when they are healthy again or, in the case of orphans, when they are big enough to get by on their own. The cub in question might be considered a special case. Although he is a yearling, he won't be able to take care of himself for some time."

Clint stopped reading out loud again. "Go on, Pa!" said Clara. "Tell us what else he wrote."

"Well, the staff believed me when I said we had the experience necessary to raise a cub. They had a long discussion about whether giving us the cub would be the right move. The bear would need supervision, love, and proper accommodations. When he got older, he would resent being held in captivity. The staff took a vote and decided, by a narrow margin, the cub could stay with us until such time as he got unmanageable. The staff would then decide the next step. We would be required to send a report to the shelter from time to time. And ... "

Clint kept on reading but said nothing. "And what, Pa?" asked Clara, almost shouting. "Do they want money?"

"No, they don't mention money. But they want letters of recommendation from our neighbors, and they want them to grade us on how well we take care of our animals. They also want close-up pictures of the animals."

"Why the pictures?" asked Ronny.

Ginny answered, "A picture can tell a lot. Do the feathers or the hair look healthy? Does the animal look well fed? Does it look contented? Are the eyes sad, do they show an interest in the surroundings?"

"We can do what they ask," said Clara. "I think Roger is in the bag." Clara smiled. "I mean, I think Roger will soon join our little family of animals."

"I think you're right," said Clint. "And when he gets too big for us to manage ... well, we won't think of that now. We'll take one thing at a time."

Within the next week, seven families that lived near the Bruedocks sent seven letters to the shelter saying what good people the Bruedocks were and how much they loved their animals, wild and domestic. All the comments in the letters were glowing. No one had ever seen any Bruedock mistreat an animal. The animals on their farm were always clean looking and appeared to be content. When any of the wild ones had gotten through the fencing that surrounded the farm and wandered onto a neighbor's pasture or crop land, one or more of the Bruedocks had promptly retrieved the animal—or animals—and made repairs to any broken fencing on the neighbor's property. If the animals had damaged crops, Clint always offered to pay for the damages.

Ronny took the close-up pictures, some of which were amusing. Two of the mallards, Quack and Quacker, posed on Desert's back, an odd combination for a picture since mallards don't live in the hot desert. Ronny put sunglasses and a red scarf on the llama, which he had named Andy, and a conical hat and a bow tie on Coty. Near the beaver's lodge, Ronny posted a sign that read, "My house is on the water, but I like it that way," and got the sign, the lodge, the beaver, and the dam all in the picture.

Soon after, the Bruedocks received a letter from the shelter that said the regular staff and volunteers had carefully read the letters of recommendation and had laughed at Ronny's photos. Roger would soon be theirs. The shelter would pay two volunteers to drive Roger to Tennessee in a hitch-up used to transport horses. It would take the volunteers two days to drive the long distance between western New Jersey and West Tennessee. On the road, the volunteers and Roger would stay overnight at an RV campground.

Bear on the Bruedock Farm

It was June 26. In later years, Clint would always remember the date and celebrate it as if it were as important as, say, Clara's or Ronny's birthday. This was the date when the Bruedocks first set eyes on Roger. Many of the neighbors, including all those who had sent letters of recommendation, moseyed over to the

Bruedock farm to welcome the black bear. Some brought their babies and cameras. Two little girls carried American flags. A young boy had a drum attached to his belt. An older girl kept a sign high over her head that read, "Western Tennessee Welcomes R-O-G-E-R! You are now one of us!" Every word was in a different color.

When the volunteers in their cab and Roger in the hitch-up came into view at the head of the Bruedocks' driveway, the neighbors and Clint, Ginny, Clara, and Ronny all started to cheer and wave their hands. Cameras clicked, the drum let out a *bum bum bum*, the two flags waved in the late afternoon breeze, and the sign bobbed up and down.

Roger was reluctant to leave the safety of his hitch-up, but the volunteers didn't want to disappoint the welcoming committee. They had no choice but to pull the cub from the hitch-up by a collar placed around his neck and a rope fastened to one of his legs. They tried not to hurt him; it was slow and difficult business. Roger had been treated royally at the shelter; now he was frightened. The noise made by the crowd alarmed him, and he didn't know the people or the place. The cub expelled air through his nose. It sounded like h-u-m-p-h. He stuck out his upper lip!

Ginny was the first to realize something should be done and quietly asked the neighbors to greet Roger and leave. There would be other days to observe him. Some waved at the cub, some said "Hi, Roger" or "Glad to have you as a neighbor" or "Hope you will like it here."

Soon the only people in the driveway were the two volunteers, Roger, and the Bruedocks. Clint invited the volunteers to supper and insisted they stay with the family overnight before they began their long journey back to New Jersey. Roger was allowed to get back into the hitch-up, the only place in his surroundings he recognized. He was fed and watered, and in the early evening one of the volunteers and Ronny took turns leading the bear by a rope attached to his collar on his first walk around the farm. They made sure the cub kept a good distance from the other animals. The volunteer gave Ronny some information about black bears and tips on how to make a cub feel safe and loved.

The cub seemed to observe everything—the buildings, the animals, vegetation. Every now and then he gave a soft hum in a high voice. The volunteer said that meant the bear was enjoying the walk. Ronny thought the cub was short for a yearling. He came up to the middle of Ronny's thigh. The volunteer said the cub's height was normal for his age. The bear would add height, muscle, and fat for another three years.

During the night, the volunteers and the Bruedocks took turns looking in on the cub to make sure he was safe and to see whether he had quieted down. They shouldn't have worried. The cub was exhausted from the long trip and the excitement caused by his arrival at the farm. He slept soundly all night until the cock crowed a little before the first light of day.

The Bruedocks built a big, outdoor cage for Roger among some tall bushes and near the stream and woods. The cage was half hidden from view so the cub would have some degree of privacy and would be shielded somewhat from unfamiliar noises from such places as the big barn and the machine shed. Roger's new family made sure he had plenty to eat and water to drink, and they were conscientious about keeping his cage clean. In the cage they put various objects the cub could examine, move around, or play with: a couple of small logs; two large, worn basketballs; a tire with the tread gone; a beat-up wheelbarrow; a bundle of corn stalks; and some corncobs.

They took turns visiting him or working near his cage so that during the day he was hardly ever without a human nearby. They always talked to him in a quiet, friendly voice. Twice a day, one of the Bruedocks attached a long leash to the leather collar that the volunteers had put on the cub and took him for a walk around the farm. The long leash allowed each Bruedock to give the cub ample walking room. But Ronny didn't need a long leash. For a reason known only to Roger, the cub took an immediate liking to the teen and walked or bounded along quite close to him, sometimes deliberately bumping up against him.

Maybe the cub sensed Ronny's confidence. The teen was athletic with developed biceps and strong hands, and he feared nothing. Once, he grabbed a cow that was considered the most ornery on the farm by the neck and wrestled it to the ground after two of his school buddies dared him. He had a steady look. Some of his female admirers at school became embarrassed when he looked at them with his clear brown eyes. His face was handsome with fine features. His light brown hair extended down almost to his shoulders. Clint and Ginny thought his hair should be as short as his male friends', but Clara told them he was just going through a phase. It was best to let him have his little clash with convention. He was a good son and grandson with a big heart. That's what mattered.

Ronny told the other members of the family he wanted to be the first to pet the cub and, at a later date, play with him. He wouldn't engage in play until he was sure the cub thought of him only as a friend, or perhaps another cub! The petting part was easy. Ronny learned that Roger liked to be stroked across his back. He moved his hands slowly so the cub wasn't surprised by his movements. Then two weeks after the petting began, Ronny started to wrestle with the cub, and immediately the two got into a routine. When Ronny started to put on his protective equipment, Roger grunted in approval. The stroking and soft words, followed by wrestling, were about to begin!

All cubs are playful and enjoy contact, a preparation for fighting as adults. Play periods—always in the outdoor cage—proved to be great fun for Roger and sometimes a peril for Ronny. The cub was quite strong for a yearling. He often caught Ronny off guard and knocked him to the ground. Roger was well proportioned and quick. His eyes were bright and knowing and seemed to anticipate Ronny's every move. Ronny always wore a heavy jacket, thick pants, gloves, and a catcher's mask he had borrowed from his school's baseball coach. Since he was a second baseman, he had no catcher's mask. With his sharp claws, Roger often tore Ronny's jacket and pants when they wrestled. Clint filed the cub's claws, but they still posed a danger. It was three weeks before Ronny felt safe to discard the catcher's mask and gloves.

Soon after, Clara began playing with the cub, although she never roughhoused like her son. Clint and Ginny liked to stroke Roger, but they said they were too old to wrestle with anyone, let alone a frisky black bear.

Freedom and Restrictions

The domestic and wild animals on the farm didn't take to Roger at first. Some hid when he approached; some turned and quickly walked away. Others more or less ignored him. Ronny observed how cool they were to his new friend and said to himself, "In time, the animals will get used to him. He's so friendly; he's sure to win them over."

During the two walks a day, Roger learned a lot about the farm. He took an interest in everything: Clara's milk pail and stool; Clint's grinding stone and the tobacco juice he spat to "oil" it; Ginny's basket of eggs she collected twice a day from the henhouse, the pies she placed on the window sill to cool, which always sent out an irresistible, delicious smell; the big tractor, which made such a racket when it moved; Ronny's baseball glove and bats and balls; the trees with tall trunks good for climbing; and the berry bushes.

And the animals! Roger paid special attention to the animals, both familiar and unfamiliar: the birds in their many sizes and colors, the butterflies with their beautiful color patterns, the salamanders and frogs and turtles and mice, the camel with the hump on its back, the beaver that swam under water, the llama with the long ears and long neck, the weathervane rooster atop the big barn that never came off its perch. There was so much to smell and touch and see—so much to learn!

I guess, dear reader, there was nothing Roger didn't show an interest in! In his eagerness to inspect everything, he would pull hard on his leash, and on occasion all but drag a Bruedock behind him. The family soon learned if he started to get out of hand, all they had to do was speak to him with a sharp tongue, and he seemed to understand he should stop pulling.

It was the middle of August. One afternoon Ronny said to his ma, "I think Roger needs a little more freedom. He seems to get a little bigger every day, and he's becoming more and more restless. It's getting harder to keep him on the end of a leash. He's not really bad. Like a child, he just wants to explore."

That evening in the parlor of the farmhouse, Ronny and Clara talked to Clint and Ginny about the cub. Ronny said it was unnatural to cage a wild animal and deprive him of his freedom. "He needs to get out on his own and explore. It's in his nature."

"And who will see that he stays within the confines of the farm?" asked Clint.

"I think all of us should help whenever we can," said Clara. "My job ties me up part of the week. Other times, I'm free. Ronny can help after school some days and on holidays and vacations. On the weekends, Ronny and I can take the load off you and Ma," said Clara, looking at Clint.

After a long discussion about responsibility and freedom and limits, the four agreed Roger should be allowed to roam the farm during the day, provided someone was free to keep him in sight and monitor his actions.

Someone always took the cub back to his cage a short time before dinner or a little after dinner and sometimes stayed for a while and talked to him. The family didn't want Roger wandering about the farm at night, climbing over fences and getting into trouble, scaring animals and people, and keeping the Bruedocks from a good night's sleep.

Like a young child who resists going to bed, the cub tried to postpone his trip back to his cage. Sometimes he would attempt to hide when he knew it was time to go back. Sometimes he just lay down on the grass or dirt and refused to move until the Bruedock in charge commanded him to get up and follow.

As may be expected, Roger got into hot water with one or more of the Bruedocks almost every day. After all, he was still a cub. Although all bears are naturally curious, Roger must have been the most curious bear of all time. He loved to smell anything that had an odor. He loved to open anything that had a lid.

He loved to root out anything partially buried. He loved to paw or chase anything small that moved, and he loved to eat ants— big ants, small ants, red ants, black ants, sugar ants, carpenter ants. It didn't matter. The sting of red ants didn't matter. Some humans can't resist chocolate; Roger couldn't resist ants, as an appetizer, a dessert, or a late-night snack.

But it was the farm animals, domestic and wild, that he found most interesting. Wild animals love the chase. Roger got great pleasure from chasing the chickens, the cats, cows, ducks, the pheasant, llama, and deer; that is, when none of the Bruedocks were watching. He never ate any of the above, but the thought may have crossed his mind. He usually had a full belly, and that may have saved many a life, especially a feathered one. He left Slo-Mikey alone because he was aware the dog couldn't run. He thought it no fun to chase an animal if it couldn't try to get away.

Sometimes Roger would slip away from the member of the family who was trying to keep a close watch on his whereabouts. Then he would look for adventure, often seeking out the beaver (named Carpenter by Clara) and Coty, the two wild ones he most liked to annoy. The beaver was easy to locate, since he was either at his dam or lodge or nearby. Roger loved to splash in the stream, which was a short distance behind his cage. The stream flowed at a good rate and contained small fish. Roger loved to try to scoop up fish. It was in his blood. The small fish were a tasty snack between the meals provided by the Bruedocks.

The cub had great fun knocking apart Carpenter's dam. On most occasions the beaver was no match for the growing cub, but he always put up a fight, showed his teeth, and mouthed off. When the beaver was in a bad mood and fought particularly hard, Roger would back away. After climbing up the bank, the cub would shake himself almost dry and stretch out in the shade of a tall tree or under a warm sun, and nap. And forget about Carpenter until another day.

Coty was fun to chase because he always gave Roger a good run around the pen. The cub gained entrance by climbing a tall sycamore nearby and dropping into the pen from one of the branches that extended over the fence that enclosed the area. The coyote disliked the cub immensely. He didn't like to play games with a bear, and he didn't like to get all tired out running from one end of the pen to the other, and he didn't like it when the cub got too close and knocked him over. His hair would shoot out along his back and neck. He would show every tooth in his mouth and snarl something awful at Roger and *snap snap*. In turn, the cub would make a popping sound with his jaw, slam a paw on the dirt, and stretch to his full height as a show of strength. Then he would get hold of the same branch he had dropped from and in short order bound away, looking for other amusements, which he always found.

The animal the cub learned to stay away from was Desert. Camels are intelligent. The females are gentle and hard workers; they will go to great limits to please a good owner. But Desert was a male, and males can be temperamental. And all camels have a particularly smelly cud they can spit on the unwary.

When the two first became acquainted, Roger would pretend he was charging Desert and pull up short before he reached the camel. The cub enjoyed his make-believe, but the camel wasn't amused. After enduring fake charges a few days, Desert met a charge by extending his neck, regurgitating his food, and spitting his stinky cud at Roger's face. The cub dropped to the ground and tried to wipe off the cud. But part of it stuck to his face and the rotting smell was overwhelming! He got up, rushed with all speed to the stream, jumped into the middle with a big splash, and put his head under water to wash off the rest of the cud and get rid of the odor. After that incident, Roger never bothered Desert again.

A Bear and Baseball

One late afternoon, when Ronny and Roger were walking near the stream, Roger stopped and grabbed a large stone in his right front paw, stood up on his hind legs (as bears sometimes do), and with a sidearm motion threw the stone across the water and hit a tree. Ronny was dumbfounded! He had never seen the bear hurl anything. He even allowed himself to imagine that Roger deliberately hit the tree.

"If this doesn't beat all," Ronny said out loud. He looked at the bear. "Where did you learn that trick?" Roger, on all fours again, looked up at Ronny and stared.

Ronny reached down to the ground, picked up a stone, and handed it to the cub. Roger took it and, as before, threw it across the stream and hit the same tree. *This is no accident,* thought Ronny. The day before, while the bear was upstream looking for fish, Ronny had thrown some stones across the stream, and some had hit trees. *He must have been watching, and learned to mimic me in just one day! And he hit the same tree twice on two throws!*

Ronny couldn't get over what he had seen Roger do. Since baseball was Ronny's sport, he thought he might teach the cub how to throw a baseball, and maybe more.

The next day Ronny hurried home from school, completed a few chores, and got out some baseballs and a bat. With Roger in tow, he took the baseballs and bat to an area near the big barn. Over the next three hours, he taught the cub how to hold a baseball and throw it at the side of the barn with the same sidearm motion the bear had used throwing the stones. He taught the cub how to hold a bat with his right paw while on all fours, get up on his hind legs with the bat, and swing at a ball with two paws. At first Roger missed most of the balls, even though Ronny threw them underhanded and with little speed. But by the end of the three hours he was hitting many of them.

Excited with Roger's progress, Ronny decided to do more. The following day after school, he selected a spot of ground south of the bear's cage and marked off a diamond with four old, beat-up bags he got from his baseball coach. Ronny made dirt lanes between the bases and put chalk marks along the first and third base paths. He encouraged Roger to chase him around the bases. Ronny always ran inside the lines, staying on the dirt. Good at imitating, Roger soon learned to stay on the dirt and near the chalk lines. The next day Ronny hit balls to the cub in the outfield and taught him how to catch a ball with his teeth. He gave the cub ample opportunity to hit, and, in just a few days, Roger was hitting balls out of the infield.

Ronny invited his girlfriend, Kristy, over to see what he had taught the cub. She was thirteen, the same age as Ronny, and went to the same school. She lived about a half mile south of the Bruedock farm, on the road that went by the Bruedocks. She was a brunette with a pretty face, good figure, and lovely hands. She was a bit shy and felt uneasy being around the cub, even though Roger was non-threatening. She was impressed with all that Ronny had taught Roger.

Her visit was brief because she had a big test the next day and wanted to review her notes. Kristy was a straight-A student, one of the things Ronny liked about her. Some of his close friends chose to date girls that weren't as smart as they were. Ronny preferred to date girls that were as smart as he was, or smarter. He liked talking to them; they always had interesting things to say.

Ronny was so proud of the cub's newfound talent and his quickness in learning that he held a small exhibition for the three other members of the family. Clint, Ginny, and Clara knew Ronny was teaching the bear baseball, but they were not prepared for what they saw. Roger ran the bases behind Ronny, batted a baseball about 150 feet, caught a ball with his teeth, and threw it with a sidearm motion. Ginny and Clara were amazed and thrilled. Clint's reaction was somewhat different.

Although Clint was pleased with what Roger had learned, he reminded Ronny that farm work came first. Clint was saving money so he and Ginny could send their grandson to college in a couple of years. But when they had finished paying the bills each month, there weren't many dollars left over from farm sales to go toward Ronny's college fund. And Clint and Ginny were slowing down.

Ronny couldn't help. He was kept busy with his studies, practice and games with his school ball team, and farm chores. Clara's part-time job at a convenience store near Tomtowne didn't earn much. She could save only a small fraction of her wages for her son's education.

Ronny wasn't sure how to answer his grandpa. Clint saw his confusion and said, "Ronny, I couldn't be more proud of you and what you have taught Roger. I know you work hard around the farm. It's just that, well, Ginny and I and your ma want to make sure you get to college. Farms don't pay much; they never did, not for the small farmer. Farmers remain farmers because they love the land and the life it offers, but that love doesn't pay the mortgage or the grocery bills or the taxes or the many other expenses. Listen to me. Go to college and afterward get a good-paying job and save. Then if you want to buy a farm, you'll have money in the bank to keep up with the payments, and you'll have training in some skill or profession so if the farm fails, you won't go down with it."

Ronny loved Grandpa Clint and always listened to what he had to say. But he couldn't put Roger out of his mind. It seemed the cub was always ready to play ball or wrestle with Ronny. And he was so smart! He said to himself, "I think I could teach Roger to do almost anything."

Tenn Nine's Unusual Fan

When the weather was warm, Clint and Ginny often watched TV on their screened-in porch. Clint followed the Tomtowne

Tenn Nine baseball team. The Tenn Nine was a double-A farm team of the Cuspin Heights Chum, and the games were shown on satellite TV.

Sometimes Clint and Ginny were out on the porch and had to attend to some chore or some other necessity and left the TV on. One evening Ronny was in a great hurry to get back to the house to call Kristy, and he didn't close the lock on the gate of Roger's cage all the way. I told you, dear reader, how very curious Roger was, and how smart Ronny thought the cub was. Sometimes Roger would bat the lock with his paw so it would swing from side to side. On this particular evening, he did just that. But he noticed the lock looked different, and it didn't swing to either side. He examined it closely, and in less than two minutes he figured out how to get the lock off the gate.

The door swung open, and Roger was out into the night in seconds! Such freedom! The stars looked brighter, the night deeper, and the lights in the farmhouse gave off a warm glow. He bounded toward the house and up to the porch. The TV was on, and Clint and Ginny were nowhere in sight. On the screen were the Tenn Nine and the visiting team. Roger soon realized that what he was watching was a game something like he and Ronny liked to play.

Much of what he saw made little sense to him. What were the two people doing behind the batter, one bent over and looking over the shoulder of the one that was squatting? And why were they each wearing a mask, like the one Ronny used to wear when the two of them wrestled?

Although it was confusing to Roger, the play on the field was so interesting he watched the game until he heard Clint and Ginny's footsteps. Not wanting to be seen, he quickly ran away into the dark. But he was not content to go back to his cage. He roamed the farm for about two hours until he got tired and decided he had seen enough for one glorious night.

In the morning after breakfast, Ronny walked to the cage to let Roger out. The cage door was open. "Well, what's this?" asked Ronny out loud. He saw the lock on the ground near the gate, picked it up, and examined it; it wasn't broken. "I guess I didn't close the lock all the way," he muttered to himself. "But why is it on the ground?" He looked at Roger, lying curled up in a corner of the cage, his eyes wide open. "So...you got out during the night," said Ronny, looking at the cub and smiling. "Good boy, Roger. You came back to the cage by yourself, good boy." He went over to the cub and gave him a big hug.

Ronny told Clara, Clint, and Ginny what had happened. All of them were as surprised as Ronny that Roger had returned to the cage of his own free will. "Roger is real special, that's certain," said Clara.

"He's real special, and he's darn clever," said Ginny. "He knew if he didn't return, Ronny would get mad at him and maybe keep him in the cage all day."

Clint said, "Roger's smart, but he's not *that* smart."

"Then why did he return to the cage?" asked Ginny.

"So he wouldn't miss his morning meal. Nothing is more important to an animal than food. He probably was out all night and got back only a few minutes before Ronny showed up to open the cage."

That evening after dinner, Clara walked Roger back to his cage. When she tried to attach the lock to the gate, Roger put his paw in the way. The cub became agitated and made a popping noise. Clara was startled and a little afraid. She shouted Ronny's name, then Clint and Ginny's. Ronny came on the run and got to the cage before the other two. He heard the popping sound.

"Why is he upset?" asked Clara nervously. "What is that strange noise he's making?"

"I don't know," said Ronny. "Maybe he's telling you he wants out again, like last night." Ronny stroked the cub across his back to calm him. "I wonder if there is something more to it than just being outside the cage."

"What do you mean?" asked Clara.

"I'm not sure."

When Clint and Ginny joined Ronny and Clara, Ronny told them the cub had kept Clara from closing the lock and made a noise he had never heard before.

"He wants us to do something. Why don't we let him out and see where he goes?" suggested Ronny. "I think he's on a mission."

"On a mission?" repeated Ginny. "What kind of mission?"

"I don't know. But maybe if we let him out, he'll lead us to … to somewhere," said Ronny. "Can we, Gran'pa?"

"Well, I guess we can. But I don't know if it will do any good. He'll just get into trouble."

"I'll stay right behind him," said Ronny as he pushed the gate wide open.

Roger didn't need urging. He raced toward the farmhouse, and the Bruedocks started after him. Although none could run as fast as the cub, Ronny wasn't far behind. Roger stopped when he reached the screened-in porch and stared at the TV. It was on, and the Tenn Nine team was warming up before the start of a game with the Montsonny Monarchs. Ronny soon caught up to the cub but stopped a few feet behind him. The bear seemed not to notice him and kept staring at the TV.

"I get it!" Ronny exclaimed. "He came here to watch baseball! I can't believe my eyes!"

The other three got to the farmhouse out of breath and sweating. "My word," gasped Ginny. "How … that … bear … can … run!"

Clara couldn't run because of her asthma, but she walked fast and made good time. "If I tried to keep up with him all day," said Clara, breathing heavily, "I could lose five pounds easy."

"What's he staring at?" asked Clint.

"He's watching the Tenn Nine get ready to play, Gran'pa. I think he's figured out that what they do is like what he and I do when we play with a ball and bat and run the bases."

"I find it hard to believe he understands what he's looking at," said Clint.

"I think he understands more than we give him credit for," said Clara. "Ronny may be right, Pa. The cub sees a connection. Is that being smart or what?"

"Whoa, wait a minute!" said Clint. "Aren't you assuming too

much, Clara? Roger may be clever, and he certainly is inquisitive. And, like some animals, he imitates well, but he *is* a bear."

"Have you ever heard of a bear that likes to watch baseball on TV?" asked Ronny, half smiling. That broke the solemn mood; everybody started to laugh.

Roger's concentration was broken momentarily. He looked at everybody laughing and then looked back at the TV.

"Gran'pa, just think!" said Ronny. "This bear may be one in a million. I mean, he just might be smart enough to learn the rules of the game. That is, if his mind can absorb that much."

"And what about work around the farm?" asked Clint. "I told you it comes first."

"I know, Gran'pa. And since you talked to me, I've been working extra hard. I hope you've noticed."

"Yes, I have."

"Then let me try to teach him more than he knows now, a lot more. Maybe I could get up earlier and work with him before my morning chores. Or maybe we could work together after dark. If I shined the tractor light on the diamond, we might have enough light."

Ginny asked, "Do you want to exhibit him and make money?"

"No, Gran'ma. Gran'pa promised the people at the shelter we wouldn't do that. Of course, we all could use extra cash money, but Roger wouldn't be happy performing in front of strangers. He's very happy as things are, and we should keep it that way."

Nobody said anything for a while. Clint broke the silence. "I don't know what this will lead to, but okay. Let's give Ronny a chance to work with Roger. I have one request. Keep this little experiment among ourselves. If the neighbors knew one of us was trying to teach a cub how to play baseball, well, I don't think I could show my face among my friends."

"It's a deal," said Ronny. "Nobody but us four will know our little secret."

"And Roger!" said Clara. "And Roger!" said the other three in unison, amid the laughter.

The game with the Monarchs was about to begin. Clint had a

chore to do and was about to turn off the TV. Ronny asked him to leave it on. The cub and Ronny stood outside the screened-in porch and watched the game from beginning to end. Ronny used his hands to try to explain to Roger what was happening on the field. And after each play, he talked to him as if he were talking to a youngster who could understand what he said. When the last out had been made, Ronny went up on the porch and turned off the TV, then walked Roger back to his cage. The cub didn't resist. In his own way, he seemed to understand Ronny had done something special for him. Before Ronny had a chance to close the gate, Roger rubbed his head back and forth on Ronny's leg.

"I know, Roger, it was fun watching baseball, right?" The cub shook his head up and down. "If I didn't know better, I'd say you were telling me you agreed."

Bear Baseball

In the weeks that followed, Ronny started his day extra early and ended it extra late, all for the benefit of Roger. The cub didn't mind; it meant he could spend more time outside his cage. And just as important, he and Ronny could have fun playing baseball.

Ronny never did any exercise too long. He wanted to keep up Roger's interest, so he worked out a routine for the cub: twenty minutes batting practice, fifteen minutes running the bases and trying to steal, ten minutes laying down bunts, fifteen minutes catching flies and scooping up ground balls, ten minutes throwing to the bases from center.

Roger couldn't slide, and Ronny didn't want to force him to do something that was unnatural to him. So he taught him how, at the last second, to roll into a base. This created a lot of dust that worked in Roger's favor. Often Ronny wasn't sure exactly where the cub was and missed the tag. Another problem was catching. Ronny was afraid if Roger caught hard-hit balls all the time with his teeth, in time he would break some teeth or get them out of line, which could cause tooth problems. So he taught Roger how to use his chest to stop the ball and quickly cover it with his paw so it wouldn't fall to the ground. After a catch, Roger would use the sidearm motion, which Ronny had taught him, to relay the ball to the infield.

The exercises the cub got the most fun out of were running the bases and hitting. The cub was so fast because he was young and muscular and because he got power from four legs, not two. Ronny would stand on second base and Roger on home plate. On a signal, the bear would start to circle the bases, and Ronny would take off from second. Sometimes the cub would be almost at third when Ronny was about to cross home plate.

One of Roger's problems running the bases was his claws, which were long and curved. He dug into the dirt to gain speed, and in short order the base paths had ruts. And he often tore a bag while rounding it. Ronny never scolded the bear when he damaged a bag or tore up the bath paths. Instead, he cut the cub's nails often and replaced the bases as needed. During the fifteen-minute session on running, Ronny usually smoothed out the base paths with a rake every four or five minutes.

As to the bear's hitting, my, how he could drive a ball! Such power in the legs of a youngster! When he became good at swinging the bat, he often hit balls high and far. Ronny estimated that some of the cub's hard-hit balls traveled 250 feet. The playing field, which Ronny had measured, was close to 200 feet from home plate to the line of bushes near the bear's cage. Ronny had to guess at the distance if a ball was hit beyond the bushes and Roger's cage.

Ronny thought it very important that Roger see as many games as possible on TV so he could observe how players behaved in game situations. He wrote to the Tomtowne Tenn Nine and asked for a schedule of their home games. When someone in the sales office sent him one, Ronny posted it on the bulletin board in his bedroom. He checked it often to make sure he and the bear didn't miss a game. The two would stand outside the screened-in porch, and sometimes Ronny would get a chair if he got tired of standing. On the porch, Clint and Clara often watched the games. Ginny wasn't a fan of the Tenn Nine; in fact, she didn't follow baseball. She preferred to read or knit or crochet. Sometimes she joined them anyway because she liked to be with the family.

Every Saturday afternoon, if it didn't interfere with a Tenn Nine home game, an activity at school, or work on the farm, Ronny scheduled an extra practice and enlisted the help of the rest of the family. Ronny usually pitched, Clint got behind the plate, and Clara played short outfield. Since Ginny could neither field nor hit well and had trouble moving about with any speed, she became the cheering section. During most of each practice, Roger batted. Whenever he got a hit, he would run the bases and sometimes practice rolling into a base. When he played center field, Clara would pitch, and Ronny would hit balls to the cub.

Clara, Clint, and Ginny were certainly pleased with how well the cub had learned how to play the game. At each practice they went out of their way to praise and encourage him and to compliment Ronny for being such a good teacher. They were amazed at Roger's power at the plate, considering how short he was when standing on his hind legs. His speed in the field and on the bases was remarkable. Running the bases, the bear always left a cloud of dust behind him! From dead center, he could race to midleft or midright field to catch a ball and hardly raise a sweat.

A Name Change

Clint liked to rename familiar words to add a little color to his speech. To him, plow was "soil turner," honey was "drip gold," automobile was "gulper," and so on. One of his favorite made-up words was "complete" to describe someone who had the ability to do almost any job to perfection. "That farmer sure is complete!" he would say to Ginny to describe a neighbor who got the most from his land and the most work from his animals. He thought Ronny was almost complete. He worked so hard around the farm, and he had taken a cub under his wing and made one heck of a ballplayer out of him. Clint had no doubt that within a few more years Ronny would indeed be "complete."

One Saturday afternoon, after a practice in which Roger did especially well hitting the ball, running the bases, and playing his position in center field, Clint said to Ginny on the walk back to the farmhouse, "You know, Ginny, I never did especially warm up to the name Roger."

"It's the first time I've heard you mention it. Why tell me now? Roger's been Roger so long I don't know if I could feel comfortable calling him by any other name."

"Remember I told you I thought Todd and Zeb were such good farmers they were complete?"

"Yes, but what does that have to do with Roger?"

"I was thinking earlier that Complete would be a better name for Roger. I know he's not really complete yet, but give him a year or so and he will be."

"C-o-m-p-l-e-t-e is a funny name for a bear!"

"I know, but he's wild about baseball, and Complete is a good baseball name. It suggests confidence and the ability to get things done."

"Are you feeling all right, Clint? Complete isn't a name. I don't know anyone named Complete."

Clint said, "I don't either, but that doesn't matter. The name is right for him, but the spelling is wrong. It should be spelled C-o-m-p-l-e-e-t. That's more like it sounds, phonetic like, as in sweet, feet, or meet."

"Well, if you have your heart set on changing his name, talk to Ronny about it. But until you both agree on a change, I'll continue to call Roger, 'Roger'."

Clint did talk to Ronny about it. Like Ginny, Ronny was used to calling Roger, "Roger."

"I don't know, Gran'pa. I kind of like Roger for a name. When we got him, he was called Roger."

"Would you mind if I called him Compleet once in a while to see how he reacts?"

"No, of course not," said Ronny.

In the next two weeks, Clint called Roger "Compleet" so often the name seemed to take life. Clara liked the new name, and Ronny was warming up to it. Even Ginny let slip the name "Compleet" once when she was talking about him. Gradually, everyone got used to calling Roger by his new name.

The only one confused by the name change was Roger, that is, Compleet. When Ronny began calling him Compleet, the cub hardly took notice. But he soon realized Ronny always looked at him when he said the name. Since he wanted to please his good friend, the cub decided he would answer to the name.

A Time to Mature

I would like to do a time jump, dear reader. All young living things—dogs, horses, whales, birds, trees—need time to mature. And so it was with Compleet. He was still a yearling, still growing.

So let's leave him on the farm for another year and a half before I take up the story again. I shall comment briefly on these eighteen months, which included two New Years, two hibernations, and a spring.

Hibernation was a special concern of the Bruedocks. They knew it was an important part of a bear's year, and Clint and Ronny decided they would help make Compleet comfortable during the months he would be sleeping. The two dug out a large area next to a group of trees not far from the bear's cage. In it they put two big logs and leaves, grass, moss, ferns, vines, and tree and shrub bark. The cub watched as Clint and Ronny worked on their special project. When he felt the time had come, he instinctively pawed the area to prepare it as a den for hibernation.

During the cub's first winter sleep, Clint sometimes heard a popping sound and something like a moan coming from the den. The first time he heard the commotion, he thought he should investigate. But he changed his mind. *In the wild*, he thought, *no one would look in on a bear that was restless. It's best to let him fight whatever demons he has.*

After each of the cub's long sleeps, when the earth had started to warm and vegetation appeared, Ronny and the bear would get the diamond in shape and begin their baseball workouts. Every week, every month, the cub kept getting better; his timing at the plate improved dramatically. He had a natural patience, which he used to his advantage. Refusing to swing at bad pitches, he rarely struck out.

Ronny continued to give advice to the bear on mechanics, using his hands to illustrate. Compleet was always attentive and seemed to understand. Since the two interacted so much, it was natural they became the best of friends. When not practicing baseball, the bear often sought out Ronny so he could be near his teenage friend and tutor. Clint, Ginny, and Clara often saw the two walking together along one of the dirt roads on the property.

Compleet became something of a farmhand. His increased strength allowed him, with some effort, to lift bales of hay and heavy bags of grain. Whenever a farm wagon or light machine got stuck in deep mud, Compleet, with help from others, would lean against it with his muscular shoulders and move it back onto solid ground. Clint especially appreciated the bear's presence. When the bear noticed Clint was having trouble lifting, he would nudge him and do the lifting himself. At harvest time, Complete did the work of two men. And he hardly broke a sweat.

Of course, he missed his mom and sister and thought of them at odd moments. But the farm worked its magic on him. It was a healing influence. He found rural living a quiet life, a good life. The smell of the orchard and the fields, and the heavy odor of tobacco drying in the barn, were good smells to Compleet. He looked with anticipation for the silver catkins of the pussy willows along the stream, one of the first signs of spring. Sometimes he thought he heard the wheat heads talk to one another as they swayed in the summer air. He looked forward to the changing seasons: the green and blossoms of spring, the hot days and field work of summer, the cool breezes and muted colors of fall. The bear was happy and relaxed spending his hours and days with the Bruedocks and the farm animals. He imagined staying on the farm forever and growing old. This was home to him now, a place where he felt warm and needed. This was where he wanted to be.

Turning Pro as a Solution

Sometimes a single event takes on a deep meaning in life and clouds over everything else. It requires our full attention and action of some sort. Such a happening occurred on the farm one cloudy weekday morning when Clint got his right sleeve caught in a motor he was trying to fix. The sleeve pulled his hand into the whirling center. Trying to free the caught hand, he mangled two fingers on his left hand before he managed to turn off the switch by leaning on it with his elbow. Blood quickly covered both hands; the pain was intense. The right hand was smashed and looked like it had been hit with a sledgehammer.

He yelled to Ginny, and she came running. Clara was at work, and Ronny was at school. Compleet heard Clint yell and knew he was in trouble. He saw Ginny run toward Clint faster than the cub had ever seen her run. He followed her, but kept at a distance.

Clint was standing by the motor with his arms dangling and blood dripping onto his overalls. He couldn't hold back the tears. "Why did it have to be my hands, Ginny? Why?"

"Let's get you to a doctor quick," she said quietly. "Then we can talk about it." To stop the bleeding, she tore off the bottom part of her shirt and wrapped the strip tightly around the right arm above the elbow. It was a makeshift tourniquet, but it stopped most of the bleeding. As best she could, she bandaged both hands.

Clint saw Compleet standing nearby, as if he were waiting for someone to give him instructions. In spite of his pain, Clint thought of the safety of the cub and said to Ginny, "Put the bear in his cage before we leave."

The cub had seen the bloody, mangled hands and had heard

Clint's sobs. Animals react to human sounds, and crying some-times subdues them. He quietly followed Ginny to his cage. She talked to him in a soft voice and stroked his back before she locked the gate.

At the clinic, the doctor admitted Clint to his office right away. He stopped the bleeding, cleaned out the wounds, put new band-ages on the hands, and gave Clint a tetanus shot. Doc Heelem didn't have good news. Clint's right hand and two fingers on his left would have to be almost completely reconstructed, bones set, ligaments and tendons reattached, tissue replaced, and more. Clint would need two operations, maybe three, and rehab. "Your hands will never be one hundred percent, but plastic surgery can get them looking good again. It will take time and money. I know you people don't have insurance. I'm sorry. I'll try to keep costs as low as I can."

Clint and Doc Heelem had known each other a good many years. Clint was confident the doc wouldn't overcharge him and would line up a good surgeon. Still, each operation would be expensive, and what about rehab? What if he needed that third operation? In the meantime, how much use could he get out of his hands?

Clint looked down at the floor and heaved a long sigh. Heelem put a hand on his shoulder. "Take heart, Clint. Surgeons can do so much more nowadays than they could when you and I were young."

On the ride home from the clinic, Ginny and Clint hardly said a word. It was as if the doc had given them a sentence of doom. Ginny was there when Ronny got off the school bus at the junction of the highway and the dirt road that passed the farm. She hardly ever met him when he got off the bus since the highway was some distance from the farm. He figured right away something bad had happened.

"What is it, Gran'ma? What's wrong?"

When she told him about Clint's accident, he almost cried. They hugged, and Ginny told him Clint was strong and would bounce back, not right away but in time. Back at the farm, Ronny put his arm around his grandpa and let the tears stream down his cheeks. When Clara got home and learned of the accident, the color left her face. Since she had lived on a farm most of her life, she knew accidents to farm workers were common. She knew that an injured worker was only half a worker. Her pa should hire someone to help him, but would he? He had always liked being his own man. He probably would accept help from the family, but how much more could the family do?

Midway through supper, Ronny blurted out, "I'll quit school and work full time here on the farm. And when Gran'pa has the use of his hands again, maybe I'll go back to school."

"That's out!" said Clint in a stern voice. "Everyone is working hard to get enough money to send you to college. I'm surprised you would talk about giving up the chance to get good learning just because I injured my hands. No! The family can get through this crisis if we all think this out and don't lose our heads."

"But Pa," said Clara, "the hospital and surgeon's bills will be high, and rehab too. Where will the money come from?"

"Your ma and I have a few bonds we can cash in. We'll borrow if we have to. Let's wait and see how high the bills are. Don't you fret over my bad luck. Let me do the worrying for all of us."

Ronny quit the school baseball team but didn't tell Clint. This gave him more hours to help out on the farm. He told his coach about the accident, and word soon spread that the Bruedocks needed help. Most of Clint's neighbors came up to him after church, at market, or stopped by the farm to offer some of their time, a couple of hours each week, a half day every second week, and so on. Farmers usually don't have much cash money on hand, but they have a mountain of goodwill to spread around and strong backs. Clint could hardly keep the tears back when he received offers of help. At first he said thank you, but he didn't need help; the injury was minor. One look at the bandaged hands told everyone otherwise. He finally came around and accepted all offers. He thought, *If one of my neighbors were hurt, I'd be one of the first to offer help.*

It was true. The year before, someone whose friendship he valued had shot up his foot in a hunting accident. The foot had to be amputated. While his friend was waiting for a prosthetic foot, Clint went to his farm every other day and spent hours helping out.

For a time, conditions improved now that Clint had help. Ronny found he could put in long hours of work on the farm and still find time to play baseball with the bear. Clint's first operation went well, but the bills, as expected, were high. He and Ginny cashed their bonds and also took out a small loan. But there was the second operation and rehab to consider.

Just when they thought their circumstances might worsen, Ginny and Clint received some encouraging news. The second operation had gone well. The surgeon was optimistic and said another operation wouldn't be needed.

Ginny started driving Clint to rehab, which meant going to Memphis two times a week for treatment. At first all seemed to go well. The trips to Memphis were time-consuming, and traffic was usually heavy, but Clint noticed improvement with each visit. But after a few weeks he hit a plateau, and his condition showed little or no gain. The traffic began to wear on both Bruedocks. And the bills kept coming. How much more could they borrow and still be able to meet payments? Would they have to sell off land or rent to a tenant farmer? Was it possible, could it happen, could they lose the farm? The worries mounted. The future seemed filled with dark clouds and very little sun.

A Great Happening

Ginny had always looked up to Clint, who was eight years older. He was very smart and had always showed confidence in a crisis. His thick head of wavy hair, rough features, and knowing smile had attracted her from the first. But now he was changing. The confidence wasn't there. He looked haggard; he was losing weight. He couldn't remember where he had put things or what he was supposed to do next. He seemed overwhelmed.

Then something unexpected happened. It was so unexpected and special that, well, dear reader, it's hard to believe it really happened. But it did.

40

BRUEDOCK
FARM

I had mentioned to you that Ronny always talked to Compleet during practice. In fact, he talked to him on every occasion the two were together. It was as if the cub were his indispensable buddy and not just an extraordinary bear he was fond of. He knew Compleet couldn't understand what he was saying, at least he thought he couldn't. But he liked to pretend the cub could follow his conversation.

One evening during practice, Ronny had his back to the bear and without thinking said, "Bring the ball here. I want to show you how to get a better grip on it." Normally he would face Compleet, say what he had to say, and use gestures to make his meaning clear. In this instance, he forgot to do that, but in the shake of a leg the cub was handing the ball to Ronny.

"Thanks, Compleet," said Ronny. Then he realized he hadn't looked at the bear when he spoke. "What!" he exclaimed. "You understood what I said!" He reconsidered. "No, no, it's not possible! How can you understand language? You're good at bear language, grunts and popping sounds, but not English." Compleet just stood there and looked up at Ronny.

Not satisfied with what he had said, Ronny was determined to find the truth. He fixed his eyes on Compleet and said, "Stand by the bushes behind your cage, and I'll see if I can throw a ball that far." He gave no gestures, and he didn't look in the direction of the cage. Sure enough, Compleet immediately loped to his cage, which was some distance from the diamond, and continued to a clump of tall bushes. Then he stopped and turned around and waited.

"It's a miracle!" shouted Ronny. He was so excited, he threw the ball over the cub's head and almost into the stream. "Bring it here, Compleet!" shouted Ronny. Dutifully, the cub did just that.

"Come on, you big beautiful bear," said Ronny. "The family has got to know!"

The two ran at top speed toward the farmhouse. Clint, Ginny, and Clara were together on the porch watching TV. Putting his face next to the porch screen, Ronny gasped for breath and said, "You'll never believe it, but it's true!"

"Never believe what?" asked Clara.

"Compleet, he understands what I say!"

"That's because you gesture when you talk to him," said Clint.

"No, no, he understands language," said Ronny, with emphasis on the last word. "I had my back to him when I spoke. I told him to bring me the ball so I could show him how to get a better grip. And he brought it to me! I didn't use gestures!"

"Ronny, bears don't understand language," said Ginny. "There must be another explanation."

"No, this bear understands me! Look, someone tell him to do something that's a little complicated."

"All right," volunteered Clint. He looked away from the cub and said, "Compleet, look in Ronny's back pockets and see if he has a baseball hidden inside."

In seconds, the cub was pawing Ronny's two back pockets, trying to find a ball. He gave up only after Ronny pushed him away after he ripped one of the pockets.

"Well, are you satisfied?" asked Ronny.

Clint hesitated. "I ... I guess. Are you sure there's no other explanation?" He sighed and said, "It's something no one would believe. *I* find it hard to believe!"

"It's true, Gran'pa. The bear understands us. It's a miracle! He learned language just like a child learns language, through association and repetition. If that's not a miracle, I don't know what is."

"It would be a miracle," said Clint, "if the cub could dig up a pot of gold." Clint laughed, and Clara and Ginny joined in. But not Ronny; this was new ground. This was huge, totally rad, awesome! This was cooler than cool!

In the weeks that followed, Ronny not only worked with the bear to better his ball skills, he also taught him a lot of new English words. The nouns were easy because Ronny could often point to the object on the farm or point to the object in a book. Pronouns were a bit harder, and verbs harder than pronouns. Ronny introduced Compleet to only a few dozen verbs and often used gestures. Idiomatic expressions and many adverbs and some adjectives were the hardest to teach. But the cub was very patient and very attentive. Ronny knew when Compleet understood a word. The blank expression on his face turned to a bright look. Then Ronny would say the word four or five times so the cub was sure of the pronunciation.

A New Language for Two

Although Ronny was pleased with the progress Compleet was making, he realized something was missing. The cub's vocabulary was growing, but he couldn't talk back. The conversation was one-sided. Bears haven't a voice box like humans. And their talk consists of only a few sounds. Ronny knew this. *But maybe, maybe*, he thought, *I could teach him sign language. If he can learn English words, he should be able to learn sign language.*

The trouble was, Ronny didn't know sign language. So he decided to do something about it. At the first opportunity, he got on the Web and ordered some books on the subject. When they arrived, he stayed up late every night for weeks studying the language. Then he began to teach the signs to Compleet.

At first the cub didn't understand what Ronny was trying to do. But after a few lessons he caught on. Since sign language is manual, it proved to be a lot of fun for both. But it also turned out to be hard work for the cub. A bear's paw isn't shaped like a human's thumb and fingers, and the claws are an impediment. But Compleet persevered and made progress in cupping his paws and separating his claws and moving his arms, that is, his front legs, as required. He even got fairly good at special facial expressions, and mimicking. But his paws weren't made for something as delicate as signing.[1] Ronny learned to read Compleet's messages, but someone else who used sign language would have been dumbfounded at the rough way the cub made his signs and probably would have given up trying to make sense of them.

Ronny didn't tell anyone about his new experiment. The timing wasn't right.

Ginny, the "Stopper"

While Ronny and Compleet continued their lessons in secret, Clint continued to have problems. The rehab seemed to go on and on, and the bills never seemed to end. He began to withdraw from the rest of the family. The others tried to cheer him up. Ginny prepared his favorite foods. The family tried playing parlor games, but he was too absentminded to follow along. Ronny taught Compleet some tricks to entertain Clint. Nothing worked.

Then Ginny said she might give up retirement and go back to work. As a registered nurse, she knew she could find work in Tomtowne or Memphis or Nashville. It meant commuting, but she said she had done it once, and she could do it again. Clint frowned when he heard her suggestion. He said she was too old to take on the rigors of day-to-day nursing.

But it wouldn't have been the first time (or the third or fourth) Ginny had intervened in order to save a situation or rescue a family member. Clint was the backbone of the family, but Ginny was the "stopper," someone who prevents a situation from getting worse and eventually gets everything back to normal. In the first years of their marriage, she had often volunteered to work extra shifts at the hospital to keep the family afloat while Clint was struggling to make a go of farming.

When they were more financially secure and had started a family with the birth of Clara, they thought the hard years were behind them. Clara was a beautiful child with thoughtful eyes; smooth, delicate hands; a constant smile; and well-proportioned figure. But when she was five she contracted whooping cough and later was troubled by asthma attacks. Ginny cut back on her nursing schedule and frequently took time off to nurse her daughter. There were mad dashes to the clinic or the hospital when Clara's asthma became especially bad. Many a night—at the hospital or at home—Ginny stayed up holding Clara's hand, trying to comfort her as she gasped for air.

Ginny and Clint had kept her out of kindergarten but later thought she had recovered enough to enroll her in first grade.

Early in the school year she got the chicken pox, and then allergies began to upend the routine of daily life. She was allergic to so many things. Bee stings posed a danger, especially since she lived on a farm. Tomatoes, strawberries, and eggplant gave her an itch and a rash. If she tried to eat sunflower seeds, her throat turned acidic. If she tried to eat a peach or cherries, her mouth swelled. When the pollen count was high, she went through the house gasping for air. Her sinuses were often inflamed. Her asthma attacks were a constant worry. She missed so much school, her teacher wanted to hold her back and have her repeat first grade.

Ginny scheduled a meeting with Clara's teacher and pleaded with her to let Clara advance with her class. If held back, she would be seven years old and still in first grade. She was a smart child and could make up the work. Ginny would tutor her. The teacher smiled, commented on the close bond she had with her daughter, and relented.

Ginny was right. Clara did catch up with her classmates. By the end of the second grade she was recognized as one of the brightest students in the class. But most important was the impact the years of stress had on Ginny, Clara, and Clint. Rather than cause dissension in the family or create constant gloom, Clara's problems had brought the three closer together, made them stronger. They had struggled as one and got through the worst of times.

Clint's Proposal and the Bear's Counter

A few days after Ginny suggested she might return to work, Clint called the three members of the family together and announced he would sell off a section of the farm so they would have money for his rehab, no matter how long it took, and money to pay unpaid bills from the two operations. He said he didn't want to sell, but there was no other answer.

He stopped talking, looked down at his thin, red, scarred hands, and looked up again, with moist eyes, at Ginny. Taking a deep breath, he began again. "I wouldn't be the first in the family to sell off some of the farm. My great-granddaddy did it, more than once. He never worried about anything. He said life was too short to spend sleepless nights and good energy worrying. When times got tough and money scarce, he just sold off a few acres. I wish I could be like him, always with a smile and relaxed. He saw promise in every rising sun. And he always had a story of interest to tell."

Clint paused. Then he chuckled. "He said he used to sit in the kitchen during the winter months when there wasn't much to do and annoy the womenfolk. ... I'm sorry none of you got to know my great-granddaddy."

It was true about his great-granddad living free and easy and selling off a piece of land as needed—but not his granddad or his dad. Neither one sold off a single acre. And if Clint sold a piece of land now, it would be so much easier to sell off another piece later on and then another. Ginny, Clara, and Ronny were of one mind. They told him there were other ways to make ends meet. It was almost unholy to sell part of the farm, no matter how small a part. They said too many family memories were here on the property, in the good earth, the very air.

But Clint would not be swayed; he would sell land because he had to. His land was fertile enough; there were several people he knew might be interested in buying. He couldn't go on accepting help from the neighbors. Then Ginny wouldn't have to go back to work, and there would be money for Ronny's college.

The next day, before they began baseball practice, Ronny told Compleet what Clint intended to do. He told the cub not to worry. He was sure his grandpa wouldn't sell off the section that included the bear's cage. The cage was near the stream, and he would never sell land too near the stream or sell off part of the woods on the other side.

During practice Compleet seemed sluggish, and his mind wandered. He missed hitting many of Ronny's pitches. On one long hit, he didn't touch second on his way to third. He stopped at the bag, although he could easily have made it home before

Ronny ran to home from the outfield. In the outfield, he dropped two balls in a row. Realizing the cub had his mind elsewhere, Ronny decided to end the practice early. Compleet collected the balls and put them in a burlap sack. He pushed up against Ronny's side, led him to a tree, and motioned him to sit down.

By this time, Compleet could converse fairly well using sign language. He told Ronny, in disjointed sentences, that Clint shouldn't have to sell off part of the farm. Clint had always been kind to him. He had never hit him or even scolded him. Clint and the rest of the family had allowed him outside his cage during the day, which meant he could become part of the daily life on the farm. In short, Compleet owed Clint and the rest of the family a lot, and he had an idea how he might help.

Ronny was surprised by this last remark. "How can you help?" he asked.

The cub mentioned the Tenn Nine. He and Ronny had watched enough games outside the screened-in porch to know that the club needed some new faces. They were stuck in last place, and their center fielder was, well, he was pretty bad.

"What are you trying to tell me?" asked Ronny, his voice getting louder. "*You* playing ball in center field with the Tomtowne Tenn Nine?"

Compleet nodded.

"Are you out of your mind? You're a bear, and bears don't play on pro teams, and they don't play on amateur teams. In fact, they don't play on any team anywhere. They only perform in circuses or attract crowds in zoos. It can't be done. Besides, there's a lot to the game I haven't told you about. There's more to it than hitting a ball, running the bases, and fielding. There are problems like selecting a savvy agent, getting a good roommate, adjusting to long bus rides and bad food, and more, and these problems all have to be addressed. It's not your world, Compleet. Take my word for it."

The cub persisted, *What's an agent?*[2]

"Well, an agent looks after a player and makes sure he gets a high salary and other perks."

Perks?

"Yes, like special privileges, a no-trade clause, a signing bonus, an option for a second or third year."

You could do all that for me.

"Me? I wouldn't know how to start. If I asked a scout to come to the farm to look at a prospect and told him he was going to watch a bear, he'd laugh me right out of the county."

Don't tell him I'm a bear.

"But, Compleet, when he sees you, he'll know!"

Yes, but if you get him here, maybe you can talk him into watching me play.

"Compleet, this conversation is crazy! No scout in his right mind would think of trying to recruit a bear."

We must try everything we can to help Clint. We can't let him down. I can't let him down.

Ronny said nothing for a while. He kept staring at the cub, as if trying to figure out how a bear could come up with such a way-out idea. Then he said, "Compleet, you have more guts than any human I ever knew." He paused again before he continued. "If I try to get a scout out here and it doesn't work out, you must promise me you won't bring it up again."

I promise, Ronny.

Making an Impression

The next day, Ronny called the office of the Tomtowne Tenn Nine and got someone to agree to send a scout to the Bruedock farm to see a "really hot prospect," as Ronny worded it. Then Ronny cornered Clint, Ginny, and Clara, and told them he had called the ball club.

"It was Compleet's idea."

"I don't understand," said Clint. "How do you know?"

"I can communicate with the bear using sign language. I learned enough signs to get by and taught them to the cub. I didn't tell you this before because, well Gran'pa, you've had troubles on your mind."

"You should have told us, Ronny," said Clara. "This is amazing! Now the family can find out, through you, what the bear is thinking."

Ginny said she would like to know about Compleet's life as a cub before he came to the farm. Clint said he'd like to know when Compleet was aware he understood English. Then he asked, "But why did he want you to get in touch with the ball club?"

Ronny answered, "He has this crazy idea the Tomtowne club will hire him. He wants to give all the money he makes to you, Gran'pa, so you don't have to sell any land. He says he owes us a lot and thinks he can help this way."

Clint was touched by Compleet's concern and generosity, and so were Ginny and Clara. All three knew no team would consider hiring a bear. But because Compleet was so intent on doing this thing, they agreed with Ronny he should have the opportunity to perform for the scout, that is, if the scout would stay once he saw the "really hot prospect" was a bear.

Two days later, a scout with the Tenn Nine showed up at the farmhouse in the early afternoon. Clint answered the door, introduced himself and Ginny, and invited the scout to sit with him on the screened-in porch. Ginny went looking for Ronny, who had taken off a half day of school so he could organize the event and talk to the scout on behalf of Compleet. Ronny was hitting balls to the cub when Ginny showed up. She shouted to Clint to send the scout to the diamond. She had been baking and needed to return to the farmhouse. As she passed the scout, she pointed to Ronny and Compleet and walked away before he could ask why a bear was standing next to the youngster. She muttered to herself, "Mister, are you in for a surprise!"

Ronny saw the scout approach and dropped his bat. "Hi, my name's Ronny."

"Afternoon, son, I'm Mitch." The two shook hands. "You this hot prospect I was told about?"

"No, not me, mister. That's the hot prospect." Ronny pointed to the bear. Compleet was standing on his hind legs, trying to look tall and human-like.

"Son, I came all the way out here to see a ballplayer. I'm not in the mood for funny business."

"It's true, Mr. Mitch, this cub knows his baseball; he can play with the pros. I know he can."

"I don't get paid to watch bears play ball. They belong in the woods or catchin' fish in a stream, not on a ball field."

"Please, Mr. Mitch, please. My gran'pa smashed his hands in a motor, and we need money real bad to pay the bills for the surgery he's had and for rehab. Please, just give Compleet a chance to show you what he can do. I'm asking you, please."

"Complete? That's the cub's name?"

"Yes, and we spell it C-o-m-p-l-e-e-t."

"It's an odd name." Mitch put his hand to his chin. "Son, I can't ask the Tenn Nine manager to give a tryout to a bear. I'd be fired on the spot."

"I don't want you to get into trouble. I just want you to spend a little time watching the cub play. If you think he can be of help to the team, I'll go with you to the tryout and try to smooth things with the manager."

Mitch stared at Ronny. He seemed like a nice kid, and he had a good face. He was asking for a few minutes, no more. Mitch looked down at his watch. "Kid, I'll give you and the bear five, maybe ten, minutes of my time, tops. Then I gotta be on my way. I have another prospect to look at, and I know for sure he's human."

"Thanks, Mr. Mitch. Thanks loads. That's all I'm asking, a chance to show what the bear can do."

First, Ronny threw pitches to the cub. Hitting the ball was Compleet's strongest point, and Ronny wanted to impress Mitch right off. The bear hit the second pitch high in the air and far, maybe 310 or 320 feet on a line from home plate. Mitch's jaw dropped. Rarely had the scout seen a young prospect hit a ball that far and that high. It was a drive that anyone on the Tenn Nine team would have reason to be pleased with.

Mitch gave the cub his full attention, not for five or ten minutes but for over an hour. He watched Compleet hit ball after ball far beyond the bushes that lined center field. He saw the cub run the bases faster than he had seen any ballplayer on the Tenn Nine run bases, and catch a baseball on his chest, then quickly release it with a sidearm motion. It looked awkward, but it worked well. He saw the cub throw from center field to home on the fly and on target. And he saw the bear lay down four or five respectable bunts.

At one point, Mitch wanted Compleet to do something over again. He thought he had to tell Ronny what he wanted the cub to do. "You can talk to him. He understands what you're saying," said Ronny.

"What? Now I've heard it all," exclaimed Mitch, "a bear that understands English!"

At the end of the session, Mitch went up to Compleet who was on all fours, looking up at the scout. Mitch studied the cub's well-developed physique. "I don't know how I'm gonna do this, but I'll get you your tryout."

Mitch saw the bear raise and lower his paws, turn them and shape them, and sometimes use his arms (front legs). "What's he doin' now?" asked Mitch.

"He's using sign language to tell you how thankful he is. He says he won't let you down."

"I'm lookin' at a bear that knows what I'm sayin' and can use sign language? Have you got a kid in a bear costume? Are you makin' fun of me?"

"No, no. He really *is* a bear. He talks to me by signing. I taught him how. He's real! You can touch him; he won't hurt you."

"I'll take your word for it. But I won't be surprised if Clyde, he's the manager, throws a punch at me when he finds out I scouted a bear."

"Why not tell him all the good things and don't say he's a bear until the end of the conversation?"

"I gotta think about what I'm gonna say. Clyde's got to see this freak of nature." Realizing what he had just said, he apologized to Ronny. And to Compleet!

"Apologizing to a bear!" he said to himself. "I can't believe I just apologized to a bear!"

The Tomtowne Tenn Nine had an off day the following Monday. Ronny told Mitch he would ask his grandpa to go with him and Compleet to the ball park for the tryout. Ronny, who was now 15, would drive. He had a learner's permit but needed a licensed adult in the car.

"Nine sharp, kid. I want the bear to get in a good practice. It's supposed to be real hot. Maybe it'll start to warm up early. If it does, the ball will have good zip."

Ronny didn't like taking off a full day of school, but he knew he had to be there with the cub to see that everything went right.

Clyde the Skeptic

Mitch didn't see the prospect he had mentioned to Ronny. He was too excited about the bear. In the car he wrote out his report, using the notes he had scribbled down. On his cell phone he called Clyde. He talked fast so he could get in everything he wanted to say before Clyde had a chance to ask embarrassing questions.

"Clyde, this is Mitch. I got a prospect you gotta see. He can hit the ball, I'd say 340–50 feet, circle the bases like the wind, and throw home on the fly from the outfield. And he's still a kid. He's kind of short but has muscle. You won't believe this youngster. I scheduled him for a tryout on Monday at nine. I know you don't like to come to the ball park on your day off, but this prospect is real special."

"If this kid is all you say he is, I wanna see him. Tell me more. How old is he?"

"Well, I don't know, but I know he's not full growed."

"You didn't ask him his age? Mitch, you're slippin'. Did you talk to his parents?"

"No, I was too excited. I filled out my report and then called you."

"Mitch, if the kid is underage, we gotta talk to the folks. A lot of things have to be settled."

"Well, you see, Clyde, there's a special problem with Compleet."

"Complete? The kid's named Complete?"

"That's right, Compleet, spelled with the two *e*'s together. It has a ring to it, don't it? It makes a statement."

"Maybe it does, maybe not. It's a name I never heard. What's this problem you mentioned?"

"Are you sittin' down, Clyde? I think you should sit down first before I go on."

"All right, I'm sittin' down." Clyde was still standing, but he said he was sitting to humor Mitch.

"Compleet is … different. I mean *real* different."

"Hey, any youngster that can hit a ball 350 feet, and do all those other things you said has got to be different."

"No, I mean … well, he's not exactly human."

"What are you sayin', Mitch? He's not a werewolf, is he?" Clyde laughed.

"No, no. He's not a wolf. But he's a … he's a—"

"Out with it, Mitch. Spit it out! Is he a troll? Has he got pointed ears? Does he have eight toes on each foot? Out with it! I've got a lot of business to attend to before I go home."

"No, it's none of them things. The fact is, Clyde, Compleet is ... he's a bear."

"He's a what?"

"He's a bear, but he bats and throws standin' up; he can understand language, and, get this, he uses sign language to communicate with Ronny, his buddy. Ronny will be at the tryout."

"Mitch!" shouted Clyde into the phone. "Are you on the bottle again? I told you, one more time, and you're fired!"

"No, honest Clyde, I been dry goin' on six months now. It's true what I said. Everything I told you about the bear is true. You got to see him to believe. And he plays center field. Hear me? You know we need help in center. Donny's gone from worse to zero. This Compleet may give the team the lift it needs. You know, someone new, someone different. And attendance could pick up. The Tenn Nine can't keep goin' with attendance so low and the team the way it is. This deal's got angles, Clyde."

There was a long pause on the other end. "Mitch, you listen, and you listen hard. I'm gonna be at the ball park Monday morning just so I can give you a swift kick and tell this bear and his trainer to go back to the zoo or wherever they came from. You got that, Mitch?"

"I got it. Then you'll definitely be at the park Monday at nine?"

"I said I would! Now hang up so I can calm down and get my work done!"

"You won't regret it, Clyde. I promise you, you won't regret it." Mitch put down the phone. Sweat was running down his face, and he was breathing heavily. "That's the longest ten minutes I ever spent on the phone," he said to himself.

Tryout with the Tenn Nine

Monday morning was a good time for a tryout. The sky was bright blue with only a few wisps of clouds. The temperature was climbing. There was a wind of some size, and it was blowing toward the outfield, a hitter's wind. Clint, Ronny and the bear showed up a half hour early. Mitch arrived a little later and talked calmly to Compleet, in case the bear had the jitters. But it's hard for a human to read the mind of a bear. No one knew how Compleet felt, not even Ronny. Fact is, the cub felt more energized than nervous; he wanted to get going. He wanted to show everybody what he could do, and he knew he could do a lot.

Clyde was there, of course, and three of his staff to help evaluate the cub. The principal owner was there. He had sworn to Mitch he would never sign an animal to a contract, but he showed up because he was curious. Mitch had been so excited when he had spoken to him. The owner wanted to know why he was making such a fuss over a bear. He had never seen bears do better than a few tricks in a circus.

Clyde had asked a few of the regulars on the team to show up so he could put some men on the field. When he told them the tryout was with a bear, they all laughed hard and long. But Clyde said he'd give each player a hundred dollars cash and pay for transportation and a meal. Minor league players don't make much money; seven said they'd be there. Clyde put two in the outfield, three in the infield, one on the mound, and one behind the plate.

On cue from Clyde, the bear ambled up to home plate to hit a few. The first pitches to him were a revelation. The Tenn Nine pitcher was so much better than Ronny. The fastballs were coming in at 90, 92, 95 miles per hour. And in succession, he saw a curve, slider, sinker, and cutter. Ronny had thrown fastballs and sometimes a curve; his pitches were soft and easy to hit.

Normally, a pitcher will throw some easy balls during a try-out, and he won't mix his pitches too much. But the pitcher was annoyed he had to face a bear, and a youngster, no less. He was determined the cub would not get much to hit.

Compleet watched the first balls go by and refused to take a swing. He was looking for pitches that were to his liking. Mitch and Clyde moved about uneasy. "Why don't he hit?" asked Clyde. "Does he want an invitation?"

When the cub saw a fastball, not too high and not too low and over the plate, he swung and got all of it. The ball hit below the scoreboard in left, bounced twice, then rolled toward the foul line. There was a player in left, but since there were only two outfielders, he was playing halfway between left and center. He couldn't get to the ball until it had almost reached the foul line. Compleet dropped his bat and started toward first. No one had told him to run; he was supposed to stay in the batter's box and hit pitches. But his blood was up; he wanted to run. He reached first while the left fielder was still chasing down the ball. He was past second when the fielder wound up to throw. And he arrived at third well before the ball got to the bag.

"My, oh my," exclaimed Clyde, "how those legs of his move!"

Mitch, who was standing near Clyde, said, "I told you he runs like the wind."

From that moment until the end of the tryout, Compleet had the eyes of everybody in the park. All marveled at the youngster's hitting, his speed on the bases, and his ability in the field. There was little he couldn't do well, and his mistakes were minor. Ronny was proud of the bear's performance. He had never seen him so sharp at the plate, and he had never seen him run so fast on the bases.

When Clyde called an end to the tryout, he had some words with the principal owner and walked over to Compleet. He leaned over and gave him a tap on the shoulder and said he had done real well. He told Ronny the owner wanted to talk to the two of them in the clubhouse. Clyde invited Clint to join the two. Clint thanked him but said, "No." He turned to Ronny. "The bear is your protégé. I want you to talk to the owner. You're old enough; it will be good training. I'll be in the car or close by if you need me."

Historic Signing

The owner's office was a small room. Almost everything about the minors is small. Locker rooms are small, the stands don't hold too many people, budgets are modest, and salaries are middling. Teams don't have the money to build big, fancy offices with plush chairs and thick rugs and fine-wood paneling on the walls.

Behind a desk sat Joe Wathersmythe, the principal owner. He was dressed casually with his shirt open at the neck. A man in his mid-thirties, his tanned face had few wrinkles and showed confidence. He was smiling. He introduced himself to Ronny and Compleet. Ronny sat in a chair near the desk. Although the bear was offered a seat, he declined and stood on all fours since he found it most comfortable. The truth is, he had never sat in a chair! Mitch and Clyde were also in the room. A stenographer and the office manager were seated near the door.

"I was very impressed with what I saw this morning," said Wathersmythe, looking at Ronny. "We'd like to sign your man, ah, I mean, your protégé. But there are a lot of questions that need answering."

"I hope Compleet and I can answer them all," said Ronny.

"Yes, I hope you can, but I'm not sure." He stared at Compleet for a few seconds and turned to face Ronny. "Like, what about when the team is on the road? Where will the cub sleep? I don't think any hotel or motel will allow a bear on the premises."

"Well," said Ronny, thinking hard, "he could sleep on the bus or maybe in a tent away from everyone. I'm sure your people can work that out."

"And meals? Does the cub eat at a table?"

Ronny smiled, and Compleet shifted a leg uneasily. "No, he eats off a plate I give him. On the farm I put the plate on some cardboard in his cage so the area he eats from is clean. Again, your people will have to see he has a place to eat that is sanitary and in a location that won't disturb others."

"The biggest question is whether the league will allow him to play."

"I can't answer that," said Ronny, "but his signing would certainly make headlines and that should help attendance. I think Compleet would be good for baseball. You know, like the black player who broke the color barrier. For Compleet it would be, uh, the animal barrier."

Wathersmythe thought for a minute. Then he said, "Let's do it this way. I'd like to sign the cub to a contract today, and then I'll contact the other owners and tell them what I've done. Hopefully they will agree I did the right thing. I'll schedule a meeting with the league head and see whether he'll give me permission to put a bear on the roster."

Ronny said he hoped Mr. Wathersmythe would be successful.

The next order of business was salary. The owner began to dangle some numbers in front of Ronny, who answered, "I was hoping for something a little higher. Compleet doesn't need money, but my gran'pa does. He and my gran'ma are the owners of the farm the cub lives on."

Ronny told about the accident, the unpaid bills for surgery and rehab, and Compleet's plan to help as much as he could. The owner said he admired the bear for wanting to help. "Usually humans help bears, instead of the other way around. Well, I guess I can go a little higher."

Wathersmythe gave a number; Ronny countered with a still higher figure. Wathersmythe gave a slightly lower one, and Ronny agreed to it. Soon the office manager was handing Ronny a contract. He read it hastily and said he would have his grandpa sign it. "He's waiting for me in the car … I'll be back shortly."

Ronny saw his grandpa standing under a tree near the car. When he reached him, he handed him the contract and spoke briefly about the meeting. Clint took time to read the contract line by line.

"It looks okay. I'll sign," said Clint.

Both parties agreed the checks would be made out to Ronny's grandfather since Compleet couldn't read or write, and he didn't have a bank account.

When everyone had left the office, except Wathersmythe and Clyde, the owner leaned back in his chair and said, "Clyde, I wonder what's going to happen. Will the league say yes? If so, will the bear become a regular or will he fold under the pressure?"

"Wish I could look in a crystal ball and have the answers starin' at me," said Clyde.

"I know one thing." Wathersmythe laughed and looked at a photo of his wife and kids on his desk. "If the bear gets to play, either I'll be remembered as a genius or the biggest chump in the history of baseball."

Yes from the League

On the ride back to the farm, Ronny noticed his grandpa was more cheerful than he had been in a great while. Clint said, "I wasn't there when you talked to Mr. Wathersmythe, but I'm sure you handled yourself well. I'm real proud of you, Ronny, and how fast you're becoming a man."

Ronny continued to work out with the cub every day and kept telling him how good he was and how he deserved a chance to play with the Tenn Nine. They waited for Clyde or Mitch or Wathersmythe to call. A week went by and no phone call. But on Wednesday of the second week, Ronny got a call from Wathersmythe. The owners had agreed that the bear's signing might be good for the team and the sport, but the league head was dragging his feet. He said there was nothing in league rules that prevented an animal from playing, but he was skeptical about the public reaction. He would have to confer with others before making a decision.

Ronny told Compleet what Wathersmythe had said. *Why would people be against my playing baseball if I'm good enough? Does the league always follow the public's lead?*

"I really can't say, but you must think positive. Think of a dip in the stream behind your cage, your favorite food, a brisk wind across your back. Think of fans cheering after you make a great catch in center. If you think bad thoughts, they sometimes come true."

In the days that followed, Compleet tried to think only good thoughts. He imagined himself in center field catching hard-hit balls that almost cleared the fence. He imagined hitting an easy double and stretching it into an inside-the-park home run. He imagined hitting a homer in the bottom of the ninth with two outs and the bases loaded to win the game.

Did his good thoughts somehow travel to the league office and influence his future? No one can say, but when Wathersmythe finally called Ronny back, the news made the teenager smile. The league head had given the go-ahead, and Wathersmythe wanted Compleet in the lineup as soon as he could get his things together.

Actually, there wasn't anything to get together. The cage, of course, would stay on the farm. Bears don't have wardrobes, and they don't collect knickknacks or keep family albums or piles of books and magazines or stacks of DVDs. Compleet owned no iPod. The only thing he had to do was say goodbye to the Bruedocks. That seemed like it would be easy, but it wasn't. Everyone got sentimental. Clint and Ginny had tears in their eyes.

"I can't get over the fact," said Clint to the cub, "you're doing this to help pay my bills. I don't know what to say."

Compleet answered, *Just wish me good luck, Mr. Bruedock.*

Ronny relayed the message. "All the luck in the world, Compleet," said Clint. "And for heaven's sake, call me Clint." And he gave the cub a big hug; dare I say it, dear reader, a bear hug.

Clara and Ginny gave him hugs and going-away gifts. Ginny had knitted him a sweater with the words "Tenn Nine" across the front and "Compleet" on the back. It fit him rather well, which surprised everybody except Ginny, who knew how to measure someone for clothes from a distance. She had baked him a berry pie, which he gulped down after he was out of sight of the farm and on his way to the ball park. Clara handed him a baseball cap she had bought a few days earlier. It was green and white, the Tenn Nine's colors. She had cut out letters and sewn them above the brim of the cap. The letters were of different colors and spelled out Compleet's full name, that is, Compleet Bear.

Because he was going to drive Compleet to the ball park, with his grandpa in the passenger seat as the licensed driver, Ronny didn't give the cub a hug, and he didn't get emotional. But later, when he went with the bear to the team locker room, he leaned over and put his arms around the cub's neck and held on tight and kept telling him it would work out, and he would make the family proud. They all would come to see him play as often as they could manage it.

Part Two:
Tearing Down the
Animal Barrier

A Different Kind of Ballplayer

After Ronny left, Clyde gave Compleet a uniform with the number seventy-six. But the cub pushed it away and pointed to the sweater he was wearing, the one Ginny had given him. He kept pointing to it with his paw.

Clyde said, "Okay, so you wanna keep the sweater on. It's not regulation, but I guess you would look silly in a regular uniform. I see the sweater's got the team name and your name on it. Now all we need is a number. Do you like seventy-six?"

Compleet reached up, grabbed Clyde by the arm, and pointed with a paw to a calendar that was hanging on the wall. "What about the calendar?" asked Clyde.

Compleet pointed to the fifteenth day of the month. Although the cub couldn't read, he had learned to recognize numbers. "Number fifteen?" asked Clyde. "You wanna wear number fifteen?"

The bear nodded. "I guess you have a reason," said Clyde, who then looked at a chart with a list of players and their numbers. "Yep, the number's available. I'll get someone to pin it on you good and later sew it on."

Soon Compleet had the number fifteen pinned to the back of his sweater. Why fifteen? It was Ronny's age, and Ronny was the person he loved the most, the one who had taught him everything he knew about baseball. Every time he put on his sweater to play ball, the bear told himself, he would look at the number and think of Ronny.

Trouble from the Start

All the fuss about a uniform and a number made the cub late joining the team for pregame warm-up. He put on Clara's cap, which he thought was a good match with Ginny's sweater, left the locker room, and found his way to the dugout and playing field. At first he enjoyed getting some exercise and being around the other guys. The players were relaxed and joked with one another. No one talked to him, but he didn't care. He thought maybe they were shy about talking to a new teammate, especially since the teammate was a bear.

The truth is, many of the players resented Compleet. "Has the owner gone nuts," asked one, "putting a bear on the team? Next thing, we'll have a gorilla playing third!"

"How do you talk to a bear that's sittin' next to you?" asked another. "Do you growl at him?"

"If he gets a hit and later scores, do you give him a slap on the shoulder or do you scratch his back?" asked a short, stocky player.

"What's this sweater business?" asked one of the pitchers. "How come we can't wear sweaters or sweatshirts or T-shirts in the game? How come he can wear whatever he wants?"

"Who's gonna be his roommate on the road?" asked one of the two catchers on the team. "If it's gonna be me, that's when I quit the team, guaranteed!"

"Do bears snore?" asked a right fielder. "Do they sleep on top of the covers or under? Maybe they sleep under the bed."

The players seemed more interested in talking about the cub than getting in a good warm-up. Some of the comments were funny but most were nasty. Compleet had overheard some of the talk and realized the team didn't want him around. Did they see him as a threat?

Then someone with a big build and a raw voice, a face older than the fresh, smooth faces on the team, spoke up. "All right, guys, that's enough. If you don't like havin' a bear on the team, keep it to yourself. The cub's done you no harm. Let's concentrate on practice." After that, the players stopped the nasty remarks and got back to hitting and fielding and playing catch.

The older player with the big build and raw voice was Spitz McOystre. After his little speech, he went over to the cub and said, "Hey, kid, don't let 'em get you down. They'll come 'round. Give 'em a little time to get used to you. You know, it's not every day a bear joins a baseball team." The cub looked up at Spitz and gave a grunt. He was glad someone had taken his side and was trying to be friendly. He tried to look pleased, but he was too sad to put on a good face.

A short time after warm-up ended, the Tenn Nine took the field, and the game started. The team was playing the Norville Knights, who were currently in first place in the North Division. The Tenn Nine was in last place. Compleet was in the starting lineup in center field, batting seventh.

On the ride with Ronny and Clint from the farm to Tomtowne, the bear had thought about his first game. He would field without making an error, get two, maybe three, hits, drive in three or more runs, and win the game in his last at bat. Alas, dreaming is what we hope will happen. It often doesn't work out that way. He was in a real game now, and he couldn't concentrate. The nasty remarks he had heard came back into his thoughts again and again. *Do bears snore? Maybe they sleep under the bed. How do you talk to a bear? Do you growl at him?*

He struck out his first at bat and later made an error in the field. He lost his confidence! He had two chances to drive in runs and failed. He was miserable. He thought, *Maybe it wasn't such a good idea to try to join the team. I was happy on the farm; I'm not happy here.* The Tenn Nine lost the game 4–1. The cub was glad none of the Bruedocks had been in the stands.

Tears and Errors

Until other arrangements could be made, Clyde decided that Compleet should sleep in the team's locker room and take his food—mostly fish—out in the alley that ran behind the scoreboard. Clyde didn't want fish smells stinking up the lockers.

When the fans had left the ball park after the 4–1 loss, the bear walked slowly toward the alley, found a place beside a mound of trash, and tried to keep out of sight. His misery was so deep he didn't want to be around anyone. Presently, Clyde, with a package under one arm, appeared at the head of the alley. The sky was dark; the new moon was hidden by clouds. Clyde kept stumbling as he walked. The only light in the alley came from a dim security lamp high up on a pole next to the back wall of the stadium.

At first Clyde couldn't find the cub. But the bear accidentally kicked some trash with a leg, and the noise led Clyde to the pile. "Oh, there you are," he said, a bit startled. "I've been lookin' for you." He glanced at the mound of trash, and then looked up and down the alley. "Sorry, bear, there ain't a better place for you yet to sit down to a meal, I mean, uh, to get some grub."

Clyde opened his package and held up a good-sized trout. "Lookee here, this fish I got on Front Street, in the seafood store I go to regular. Looks mighty temptin'! And here are some nuts; all I could get were peanuts. That's about it. Ah, maybe tomorrow I can do a little better." Compleet kept looking at Clyde with a face that showed no expression. He loved trout, but at this moment he wasn't thinking of food. His mind was filled only with sadness.

"Well, bear, I guess there's nothin' more for me to do, so I'll be gettin' on home. See you tomorrow, and maybe things will go right for you." Clyde left the trout and peanuts on top of the package and quickly walked away when it started to drizzle.

Compleet only picked at his food. Later, he walked to one of the doors at the entrance to the stadium. Clyde had told him which door to look for. It would stay unlocked and open slightly so the bear could get to the locker room. But the door was shut and locked. Compleet examined every door he could find, but all were shut tight. Did a guard or maintenance forget to leave that one door unlocked and open? Did the wind blow it shut? Did a ballplayer, when exiting, see the door ajar and close it?

Compleet had no choice; he returned to the alley and the mound of trash, curled up, and tried to get comfortable. The drizzle now turned to rain; there was occasional thunder and lightning. From a ramshackle house not far away, the bear heard the strains of a melancholy, pretty song. The thunder made it hard for the cub to hear all the words. "... My tears ... I add them to the rain ... how can I explain ... a sad time, a bad time, the nighttime, no right time." Compleet looked in the direction of the music. A soft light shone from a lamp near a window left slightly open. Rain pelted down, and streams of water ran along the bear's long snout and onto the ground. The bear had a wistful look, and his eyes were red. Not since that night of horror so long ago had he felt like this, as if no one in the wide world cared, as if no one could even acknowledge he was a being with emotions and wants, someone that wanted a place alongside others.

The bear's performance in his second and third game was worse than in his first. He had no hits and two errors in the second game and no hits, three strikeouts, and two errors in the third game. The fans had packed the ball park for each of the bear's first three games. No one had ever seen a bear play baseball. Some romanticized his role on the team. They expected to see the cub perform miracles, bat .350 or .375, and get the club out of the cellar.

With Compleet playing so poorly, many of the fans started to turn on him. They concluded he was just an ordinary bear and a mighty poor baseball player. It was all a hoax. Management had signed him just to get more fans to come to the games.

The fourth game was a real trial for the cub. The fans booed him when he ran out to his position in center field, and they booed him when he came to the plate. When he made an error in the second inning, they booed him, and when he later caught an easy ball for an out, they cheered and laughed as if it were a rare event.

Compleet saw the looks on the faces of the fans and heard the boos. He thought, *The people are here to support the team. What good does it do to make someone feel bad? I'm trying, but I just can't get it together. I can't concentrate. I'm not helping the team at all.*

In the dugout, none of the players would talk to him except

Spitz, who tried to cheer him up. It didn't work; Compleet was in a deep depression. Spitz decided to wait until after the game to try to get him out of his gloom.

In the fourth inning, the bear made a throwing error that let in two unearned runs. His bad play rubbed off on the team, and the game went from bad to horrible. No one on the Tenn Nine got a hit from the fourth inning on. In the top of the fifth the team committed six errors, and a parade of pitchers gave up seven bases on balls, made two balks, threw four wild pitches, hit three batters, and allowed five steals. And the hits! There were so many singles, doubles, and home runs it was hard to keep count. The TV announcer said it must be a record of some sort. "Call it the lousiest half inning ever played by a pro team!"

The score at game's end: Knights, 32 and Tenn Nine, 1. Only a dozen diehard fans, who perhaps were looking for a record comeback, stayed to the last out.

The Bruedocks had seen all four games on TV; Ronny had invited Kristy over for games three and four. They all felt bad for the bear, especially after the lopsided loss in game four. Ronny called the clubhouse after the game, but the player who answered the phone couldn't locate the cub, and he didn't know Compleet's address.

"I'll write him a letter and mail it to the team," said Ronny to the family and Kristy, "and tomorrow if I have time I'll call the Tenn Nine office and get his address. I know he'd like to hear from us. I'm sure one of his teammates will volunteer to read our letters to him."

Ronny sat down at the desk in the parlor and started to write, telling Compleet how much everyone on the farm missed him. He had tried several times to call him after his first game with the team, but the clubhouse phone was always busy. He said he knew the cub could do better at bat and in the field. He just needed to get his confidence back. But if the bear decided not to stay in baseball, he could always come back to the farm. This was his permanent home. The welcome mat was out 24/7.

The other members of the family, and Kristy, added comments. Ronny sealed the envelope and said he would put it in the mailbox for delivery.

Spitz in Charge

After game four, Spitz pulled Clyde to one side in the locker room and spoke in his raspy voice. "We gotta get the kid on track. He's pullin' the team down with him."

"Somethin' better's got to happen," answered Clyde. "I should have benched him today. He ain't doin' nothin' right."

After a few seconds of silence, Clyde put a hand on Spitz's shoulder. "I need your help. Think you can straighten him out?"

"Well," answered Spitz, thinking hard, "how's this? Let me bunk with the kid and eat with him and talk. If he has a friend, a good friend, maybe he'll bounce back. It could happen."

It hadn't been settled who would room with Compleet. Since the series with Norville had been in Tomtowne, the players had families and houses or rented apartments to go to. But where could Compleet stay? The wind had been the culprit the night the bear had been locked out. Clyde fixed the door so it couldn't lock on the cub. Still, Compleet had only the locker room and an alley to call home.

The team was going on the road in two days. Where would the cub sleep? What would he eat? With team money, Spitz bought a tent big enough to hold him and the cub, a tarp, large canvas, and for himself an air mattress, two pillows, a light blanket, a down comforter, and sheets. He stocked up on food for the bear, all kinds of nuts, dried and canned fruit, greens, fish, especially salmon and trout, and jars of honey. He got hold of a supplier of meats who agreed to ship deer meat to the team regularly. He sent the supplier the Tenn Nine's schedule so he would know where the team was playing on any given date. He bought a couple of big ice chests.

The first stop on the road was Burgeston. Compleet occupied two seats on the bus so he could lie down, which was the most comfortable position for him. Because he had never been on a bus before, he almost got motion sick. He gradually got accustomed to the sway but hated the stale air and kept the window next to him wide open. When he wasn't snoozing, he looked out the window; he especially liked seeing woods, which reminded him of his first home in the northwest corner of New Jersey. And he liked looking at the animals in the fields, by the road, and in the towns. He saw dogs, cows, horses, mules, pigs, a few sheep and goats, squirrels, and a lot of birds. He wondered whether all of the animals were happy. He knew the birds were because their singing was so pretty. *It must make them feel so alive when they sing*, he thought. *If only bears could sing, instead of grunt.*

He saw crowds of people in the towns they passed through. He mused, *Where are they going? Are they searching for food? Where are their young ones? They should be within sight so the moms can guard them from danger. What's that? Smoke coming out of a high, brick pile? Why don't the people near it run away? Smoke means fire, and fire is dangerous. It can cause pain, and it uses up everything around it!*

Cars and trucks zoomed by. *The road is so noisy*, he thought. *The forest is quieter and so much prettier. No one is in a hurry unless he's chasing a meal or being chased.* It was a new, mysterious world to him, a world so different it made him uneasy.

In Burgeston, Spitz set up the tent in a field next to the motel where the team was staying.

The Mind Game

In the afternoon of the first day in Burgeston, Spitz told the bear he wanted to talk to him about something important. Their game was at night. Spitz said they had time. He cleared his throat and began.

"You know, kid, there's more to the game of baseball then what you see on the field. There's the mind game and it's very important; sometimes it wins games."

The bear looked at Spitz with fixed eyes. "It's kinda like tryin' to outfox a fox. You know the fox is clever. So you try to be cleverer then he is. It's the same in baseball. You know the other team's good and might beat you. Your job is to be better and beat them. And how do you do that? By playin' good ball and by gettin' into the mind of your opponent. Like I just said, the mind game's important. That's what I gotta teach you."

Spitz took a deep breath. He wasn't a teacher; he was a ballplayer. But somehow he had to get his message across to the bear. "In the games in Tomtowne, you got upset 'cause the guys on the team made bad comments 'bout you, and 'cause of the boos. That's the mind game at work! Don't you see, kid? Some of our players resent you and don't want you to succeed, and some fans were upset 'cause your play was so lousy. And the fact they was upset made you upset."

Compleet was listening to every word. He wanted to ask questions. *If only Ronny were here!* he thought.

Spitz came to the point. "And how do you deal with all that? If you wanna win in baseball, you gotta go with what's happenin' on the field. You gotta ignore all the negative stuff, put it behind you, and concentrate on what's in front of you: the shift they got on you, the next pitch, the base runner startin' out on hit-and-run or tryin' to steal. You gotta be so perfect the other team's a little afraid of you, feels a bit inferior. That's the mind game. Play like you can't lose, can't make errors. Play like you can catch any ball hit to your field, no matter how deep or shallow. Play like you already won!"

Spitz put emphasis on the last word and held onto it until the sound died away. To Compleet, this mind game was a new idea, something he had to think about carefully.

Spitz summed up. "Remember, do your very best, concentrate on what's in front of you, and always, always keep your eyes on the ball when it's comin' at you. Forget the negative. Sometimes you gotta be thick-skinned."

It may have been the longest speech Spitz ever made. He had a dry mouth at the end and sweat was rolling down his cheek and onto his neck. He stared at the bear. Was that something like a smile on the cub's face?

If Spitz had known sign language or could have read the bear's thoughts, he would have been pleased with the cub's reaction. *I got you, Spitz. I know now I can't let the bad things upset me and ruin my game. I got to look straight ahead, ignore the boos, the bad talk. I got to believe in myself. I got to believe I can do what's expected of me. I know from your talk you will stand behind me. Anyone willing to give up a comfortable bed and a roof over his head to sleep with a bear, to eat with a bear, and talk to a bear has got to be a decent fellow. Thanks, Spitz, for being a friend.*

T he bear's turnaround was about to happen. Spitz's talk did it. It gave the bear answers, and that's what he was searching for. Mind you, the change didn't happen in an instant. Good things take time to develop—like a great bird with a huge wingspan at the edge of a lake, about to fly away. It juts out its wings and lifts them almost in slow motion and rises a little off the ground. Then it flaps its wings more, a little faster, and gradually, little by little, with great energy, it lifts itself up into a bright, clear sky. The great bird didn't rush; it took its time, time to get up to a bright sky where there are no limits and all things seem possible.

Turning It Around

The Burgeston team was called the Bears. Compleet thought it was funny a baseball team had the name Bears. After all, everyone on the team was a human!

He was nervous and uncertain before the game began. Would the fans boo him? Would he get a hit, play in the field without error, drive in runs? Then he mused to himself, *This is silly! Why worry? I can only know the answers when the game starts. Relax, Compleet, relax!* And he did.

The fans packed the stands, and they were easy on him. They

were more curious to see how a bear played baseball than trying to unnerve him. No one booed.

During the game he kept telling himself to concentrate and do his best. *Have confidence, Compleet. You know you can play this game. Just keep in mind what Spitz said.*

He caught or fielded cleanly every ball hit his way. He went two for four at the plate, walked once, and immediately stole second. With a chance to drive in a run in the seventh, he flied out to end the inning. The Tenn Nine lost the game 4–3, but the mood in the clubhouse after the game was upbeat. It was as if a great dark cloud had lifted and let in some sun.

Players had been surprised at Compleet's good play at bat and in the field. Maybe the owner was right in signing him. Maybe he could help the team get out of the cellar. So what if the team lost this one? Every ballplayer knows the maxim: If you don't win today, there's always a game to win tomorrow or the next day.

There were three more games with the Bears. The Tenn Nine won the last two. In the latter, Compleet stole home in the fifth, and the game ended 1–0. In the dugout and in the clubhouse, players started to talk to him. It was nothing important, just the small talk that helps players get through the minutes and the hours. But to Compleet it was big talk because it meant he had been accepted by the team. Everyone knows how important it is for elephants, wolves, ants, and bees—indeed, all living things— to be accepted by their own. So imagine how happy Compleet felt to be accepted by humans.

The road trip now became a sign of great times ahead. In Mullersburg the team won all three games. In Haggenside they took three of four; Compleet had two steals in game three and made a spectacular catch in right center. The team took two of three in Jimmick. The cub had a triple and scored two runs in game two.

Last stop on the road was in Musters Mine against the Mammoths. A team to watch, they were currently in second place in the North Division. The Tenn Nine was still in the cellar but playing great team ball. Could the players keep it up and get ahead of one or two teams in the standings? It was a four game series, and the Tomtowne team took all four. In game three, Compleet threw out two Mammoths at the plate. In game four, he hit for the cycle—triple, single, double, home run. His average was now .339. He was hot, and so were a number of his teammates. Spitz McOystre had raised his average to .277. His RBI total was 19, and he had seven doubles and one home run. Compleet was as proud of Spitz's numbers as Spitz was of Compleet's.

Victory was in the air. For the team, baseball was fun again. Most importantly, the team was out of the cellar and in fourth place in the standings.

On the bus ride from Musters Mine back to Tomtowne, the bear was bright-eyed, optimistic, and anxious. But he was thinking of more than the team and its new place in the standings. He was going home, and that meant he would see the Bruedocks. Ronny had written often to him, and Spitz had read the letters to the cub. Ronny promised that all four of the family and Kristy would attend the first game when the team returned. Since the home stand would be long, he hoped to see Compleet in action in a number of games.

A Home Stand to Remember

The first home game was against the Chalkmon Cruisers. The Bruedocks were seated high up in the stands, hoping to get a good view of the bear in center. The ball park was jammed. Good news travels almost as fast as an 18-wheeler. All Tomtowne was abuzz with the fine play of the Tenn Nine, and especially Compleet, on the recent road trip. Fans easily forgive past sins; they came to the park not to find fault with the cub but to praise him.

During pregame practice, the bear looked for the Bruedocks and saw them waving wildly at him. In answer, he shook his head up and down. It made him feel good to have his family in the stands. His mom and sis had receded further in his mind. Someday, perhaps, he would put up a small monument in their honor. His mom had been a good mom. He and his sister had shared so much fun. But that part of his life was over. We are all forced to live in the present. He was lucky the Bruedocks had wanted him.

The game was close; both pitchers were throwing strikes and forcing the batters to hit a lot of ground balls. In the third inning, Compleet threw out a runner trying to score from second on a single to center. The Bruedocks cheered so loudly the cub was sure he heard some of their voices. In the fifth, the Cruisers scored a run on a single and a double. In the bottom of the seventh, the Tenn Nine catcher singled, and Compleet hit a home run that cleared the scoreboard in left. Spitz estimated the ball traveled 360 feet! The cheers were deafening! A chant began in the left field bleachers: "We got the team, we got the bear, aimin' for first, we're on a tear." The bear had to come out of the dugout twice. In recognition, he touched the cap Clara had given him. His two-run homer held up, and the Tenn Nine won 2–1.

Afterward, the cub, with Ronny's help, had a long talk with the Bruedocks and Kristy. The bear located Spitz, and everyone went to a nearby drive-in for snacks. Compleet had a hamburger (plain, no bun, a lot of ketchup) and ice cream. Everyone was surprised he liked ice cream, which he got all over his face. He told Ronny it wasn't as delicious, filling, and smooth as honey, but it was soft, cold, and sweet, and he liked it.

The home stand was a huge success. Tomtowne took the series from all five visiting teams. The Bruedocks and Kristy came back to see the cub play three more times. More and more, Compleet was becoming the star of the team and the solid favorite of the fans.

Connecting with the Bear

Communication is very important; our thoughts need to get out to others. The bear could communicate in different ways only with Ronny. When Compleet left the farm to join the Tenn Nine, it was as if he left his voice behind. Something had to be done; someone on the team had to learn to relay Compleet's questions and comments. Whenever Clyde talked to the cub about team strategy or when the third base coach gave the cub a sign or someone tried to help him with his game, no one was sure he understood. Often Compleet wanted to tell Spitz or another teammate something, but could use only gestures, which failed as often as they succeeded.

Spitz was not enthused with the idea of learning something new. But he told Clyde he would volunteer to study sign language so he could act as translator.

He contacted Ronny, who said he would mail Spitz the books he had used. Within a week, three books on signing arrived at the ball park. Spitz got to work immediately studying this new, very different, language. He found it hard trying to learn a language all at once. A young child learns to speak a language over the space of years. Spitz didn't have time to go slow. During every free moment he looked in one or more of the books so he could review some signs he had learned or try to learn new ones. A few signs were easy, such as bedtime, first, write, and listen, but so many were complicated, and the number of signs was depressing! There were hundreds and hundreds—actually over a thousand—representing words, concepts, letters, and numbers.

It was hard going; Spitz was far from being a scholar. On his cell phone he often called Ronny so the youngster could explain some feature of signing. Ronny told Spitz that when he was learning ASL[3] he sometimes found it better to make up an easy sign than use the one pictured in a book. He would send Spitz his list, which included the word and the appropriate hand, finger, and arm movements.

Spitz liked this idea and made up some signs of his own, most of them using mimicry, to teach the bear. He kept at it, and in time memorized many of the most useful signs in the books, together with substitute signs given him by Ronny. The result certainly wasn't ASL, and it wasn't exactly PSE.[4] It could best be described as SRPSE, Spitz and Ronny's Pidgin Sign English. It was a good compromise because it kept English language word order, word order deaf people "talking" to other deaf people don't use.

One evening after supper, when Spitz thought he had learned enough to be literate in signing, he told Compleet—who knew he was studying signing—to sign to him. The cub was so happy that finally he could "talk" to someone on the team. He kept signing to Spitz late into the night. But a lot of what the cub signed was misunderstood or not recognized by Spitz. It was hard for him to understand the bear's paw and arm (that is, leg) movements. They weren't like the pictures in the books, a fact Ronny had discovered earlier. But as you know, dear reader, practice makes perfect, or at least progress. Spitz learned to read most of the cub's signing, and Compleet was able to learn the made-up signs that Spitz had invented.

During the home stand there were a number of no-game days, which meant Compleet could stay overnight on the farm. One of the Bruedocks had to pick him up at the ball park. It was an inconvenience to pick him up, drive back to the farm, then later drive him back to Tomtowne and return home. But the family didn't complain. They enjoyed seeing the bear in his old haunts on the farm, and they knew they were indebted to him. All but a small part of the cub's pay checks were used to pay Clint's medical bills.

Since the Bruedocks knew the cub and Spitz had become good friends, they suggested the cub bring his teammate along on visits. Spitz said yes to the bear's proposal and volunteered to drive. On the farm, Spitz slept in the farmhouse. The cub liked to sleep out-of-doors. On a clear night, he would look with satisfaction at the moon and clusters of stars. The wind in his face always felt refreshing. He found a deep peace in staring into the friendly night or glancing at the soft lights in the farmhouse.

Near the end of the home stand, a major problem surfaced. Cubs learn good hygiene from their moms by watching and copying their habits. But bears don't think bad breath is a problem. To humans, halitosis, that is, bad breath, is a repulsive condition that people should try to correct. Spitz never seemed to mind the cub's breath, or if he did, he never told anyone. But the rest of the team would back away when Compleet came close. Sometimes in the clubhouse, the cub's foul breath made the players want to throw up.

At first, the players said nothing because the cub was playing so well, and they didn't want to change his mood. But when it became evident Compleet had gained a lot of confidence and could handle a rebuke, they thought someone should say something to Spitz. The team drew straws, and the second baseman Dusty (Plain) pulled out the shortest one. He promptly told Spitz how much the team hated bear breath.

Spitz said he would talk to the bear. When he did, the cub signed he would do what Spitz wanted, especially since he aimed to stay on the good side of the team. He agreed to a regimen of brushing and gargling. At first, he tried eating the toothpaste; it was mint and tasted good. When Spitz told him eating toothpaste was a no-no, the bear was disappointed. Spitz told him to squirt the toothpaste onto the brush, then put the brush next to his teeth, and rub back and forth. But the bear couldn't learn to hold the toothbrush, keep the toothpaste from falling off, and put the brush in his mouth at the same time. So Spitz told him to munch on the toothpaste, like he was eating something, and after a minute spit it out and gargle with Listerine. Compleet had never gargled before, and although he had become a skilled ballplayer, alas, he couldn't learn how to gargle very well. He always swallowed some of the Listerine, which made him choke. But the regimen worked well enough; the players took time to individually thank Spitz.

As long as he was teaching the bear good hygiene, Spitz decided to talk to him about bathing. In the wild, bears bathe by wading in a river, stream, lake, or pond. As a member of the Tenn Nine, Compleet had access to the showers his teammates used—at home and on the road—but he preferred to jump into water. A nearby stream or lake was often hard to find. And if there was one, when the cub splashed around in it, he usually scared away bathers or disturbed fishermen.

So Spitz told the bear he had to learn how to take a shower. He turned the water on for the cub and adjusted the hot and cold, but the bear didn't like the spray. So Spitz bought a big galvanized tub to put under the shower. When it was filled to overflowing, he would turn off the faucet and tell the cub to dunk himself. Spitz never gave the bear soap because he didn't think Compleet could handle a bar, but he did give the bear a rub down after each shower.

Trophies and a
White Christmas

With Compleet smelling almost like a rose, his team-mates became friendlier than they had been and didn't hesitate to get close to him and talk face-to-face. This made the bear happier, and his play showed it. He already was leading the team in batting. Now he took aim at adding to his RBI total, extra base hits, runs scored, and his on-base percentage. He took more chances trying to steal and trying to stretch singles into doubles and doubles into triples. As a real team player, he was often content to try to draw a walk. "With no one on base, it's as good as a single, no difference," Spitz kept reminding him. With a runner on third, he was happy to make an out, say, on a fly to left or right field if it brought in a run.

His teammates were aware of the cub's enthusiasm and dedi-cation, and soon everyone on the team had better numbers. Two trades bolstered the pitching. By mid-August the team was in a battle with the Chalkmon Cruisers for first place in the North Division. By Labor Day they were five games up on the Cruisers and won their division easily.

In the playoffs in late September, the Tenn Nine was matched against the Jompane Journeymen who had won the South Division. The teams split the first four games, but the Tenn Nine won the next two to take the series and the title. It was the Tomtowne team's first ever championship in the Down Home League. The fans voted Compleet the MVP of the series, and the league named him Rookie of the Year. In separate ceremonies, the cub received a small trophy.

There was a big parade down the main street of Tomtowne.

Heading the parade were the high school band and majorettes, followed by the players and coaches, and the mayor and council. Afterward, almost everyone went to the free eat-in at the ball park. The cub didn't get a chance to eat much because just about every fan at the eat-in wanted his autograph. Using an ink pad, Compleet made a big paw print in place of his name on the scorecards and autograph books shoved in front of him.

The next day, the bear got Spitz to drive him to the farm so he could show off his trophies to the Bruedocks. He offered the Rookie of the Year trophy to Ronny and the MVP trophy to Clint. Ronny put his on top of the bookcase in his room. Clint placed his on the wood mantel in the living room. At gatherings at the house, most guests were anxious to get a close look at the trophies. Even those that didn't follow baseball knew about the local sports hero who had become a household name in Tennessee and indeed much of the South.

The Tenn Nine owners regarded Compleet as the catch of the season. They were more than pleased with the big jump in attendance—both at home and away—that had occurred after the bear joined the team. With the cub as a draw in center in the coming season, they expected the Tenn Nine to set attendance records. By unanimous vote, the owners agreed to extend the cub's contract through the following year with a big increase in salary.

Back Home Again

With Compleet back on the farm until spring training, Clint decided to make some changes. Compleet's cage didn't seem appropriate for a bear of his standing. So Clint contracted with an outfit in Memphis to build a boulder house. It would stand near the flower garden and not far from the farmhouse. Clint could not really afford to hire outside help, but since he owed the cub so much he determined to have the house built and borrow to pay for materials and construction. The house was of huge rocks that fit together in such ways that allowed hollow spaces for rooms. There were different levels and flat surfaces for resting and eating, steep walls for climbing, and a horizontal roof so the bear could sleep out under the stars in good weather.

Ronny saw the boulder house under construction and wanted to do something special to complement it. He got some of his buddies on the high school baseball team to work with him for three weeks during the times they were not needed for farm chores. With the aid of a backhoe borrowed from the Bruedocks' nearest neighbor, Ronny and his friends were able to dig out a fair-sized pond near the boulder house so Compleet could wade in it to keep cool. They lined the rim with sized, colorful rocks. At a later date, Ronny planned to stock the pond with fish so the bear could have a snack whenever he wanted.

When the house and the pond were finished, there was a small ceremony attended by the cub, the Bruedocks, Kristy, the high school ballplayers who had helped to dig out and line the pond, their families, and the neighbors who had written letters of recommendation to the shelter. Afterward there was a party with a big cake, which had on it Compleet's name, the bear's silhouette, and a long message, "To our own Compleet, the best ballplayer in the state of Tennessee." For the cub there was also a special dish prepared by Ginny and Clara of honey, nuts, berries, greens, and salmon. It looked so good some of the ballplayers asked their moms to get the recipe from Ginny or Clara. Everyone got a piece of the cub's big cake.

The Bear's First Christmas

Compleet had never celebrated Christmas. In his first years on the farm, the snows had come early to the western part of the state, and the bear had sacked out for the winter in his lair, weeks before Christmas Day.

Bears don't belong to an organized religion. You might say they are nature worshippers. To them, the out-of-doors is like a great cathedral, and every day, in their own way, they celebrate the beauty of the world around them. But the cub didn't want to hurt the feelings of the family, who were very religious minded; he went with them to church services every Sunday between

Thanksgiving and Christmas Day. He sat with Ronny in the rear of the church so his presence wouldn't scare any of the young ones in the congregation.

Two weeks before Christmas, he helped Ronny chop down a good-sized pine in the woods near the stream and haul it to the farmhouse. The whole family helped trim the tree, which was placed in a large tub of coal in one corner of the living room between two windows. The bear was given the honor of putting a shiny star on top of the pine. While climbing a ladder to hang the star, he almost fell into the tree but luckily regained his balance and put the star in place. It was a little crooked and had a dent from the bear's holding it too tightly, but no one said anything.

On Christmas Day everyone gathered in the living room early in the morning. Ronny lit the big log in the fireplace, and the family and Compleet opened their gifts. Ginny gave the cub sweaters. At the last ball game she had attended in Tomtowne, she noticed the knitted sweater she had made for the bear was soiled and coming unraveled at places. Running the bases is very hard on knitted garments. So she knitted him not one, but a half dozen sweaters, all different colors, with the Tenn Nine logo on the front and Compleet's name on the back. The cub had grown some in the months since he had first put on her sweater, and Ginny allowed for his bigger size. All six were a perfect fit, and the bear's face glowed.

"Six might last you all next season," she said. "And if they don't, I'll knit you more. I'm so pleased you want to wear my sweaters. I'm glad I could do something for you and the team."

Clara bought him more baseball caps and read a poem she had written for him.

A bear with flair is our dear friend Compleet!
When the critics swarm and turn on the heat,
He answers loud with his oversized bat,
And charms the fans with a tip of his hat.

For the cub's house, Clint got the bear four large straw mats and some rubber non-skid mats, some huge scratching posts, and five framed prints of the bear. They showed him posing with his teammates, running the bases, and playing the outfield. Ronny gave the cub three new baseballs and a new, state-of-the-art, maple Radial bat and said he hoped the two could get in some good practices if the weather didn't turn too nasty.

Compleet knew he was supposed to give gifts in return. But he didn't know much about shopping and was afraid if he mingled with shoppers who didn't recognize him, he would start a stampede. So weeks before Christmas, he got Ronny to ask Ginny to make a list of all Clint's unpaid medical and rehab bills. Ronny made Ginny promise not to tell Clint about the list. With Ronny's help, Compleet had "talked" to the rep of a company in Nashville about putting the cub's picture on caps, jackets, T-shirts, bathing suits, pajamas, and other wear. As his agent, Ronny sealed the deal and signed for the bear. Clint signed also in case someone questioned the signature of a minor. No one else knew about the clothing contract except Spitz. The cub intended to use the advance money the company gave him, together with savings from his salary, to pay off Clint's outstanding bills. It would be his Christmas gift to Clint and Ginny.

When all the gifts had been exchanged, the bear gave Clint an envelope and motioned him and Ginny to look at its contents. Inside were receipts for all the bills Clint had owed. Each was marked "Paid in Full." Clint and Ginny stared at the receipts for a long time and hugged each other. Ginny started to cry, and they both hugged the cub.

Compleet told Ronny, who relayed the message to Clara, he would save money when the season started so he could buy her a better car. Hers seemed to be in the repair shop more than in the driveway. And he told Ronny he would help pay his college tuition. Now that he had taken care of the medical bills, Ronny wouldn't have to give up going to a good college. The youngster already had his eye on a top college and had told Compleet if he were accepted he wanted to take such subjects as soil conservation, dairy science, farm management, animal husbandry, and genetic engineering.

Both Clara and Ronny said they had no right to Compleet's money. They loved him as a friend and wanted him to keep his money to buy what he needed. The cub said he would save in order to help them just the same, that his needs were minimal, and that a friend helps a friend.

The subject was dropped. The talk turned to thoughts of what next year would bring. Everyone agreed it would be an especially good year. Compleet was making a name as the first bear to play professional baseball, and he was the reason Tomtowne had become a top tourist attraction during the ball season. Clint's hands had healed better than expected; the two operations and rehab had done the trick. Clint and Ginny didn't have to worry about unpaid medical bills. And Compleet had a house and pond. He told Ronny he was so lucky. He was sure he was the only bear in the whole state of Tennessee that owned a furnished house and a pond next to it. Ronny agreed.

Kristy paid a visit in the afternoon and gave Compleet a gift certificate to use at a nearby drive-in. She said they had good hamburgers and ice cream. And she suggested he try their chiliburgers, which were the best in the county.

Later that week, Spitz showed up. Compleet and Ronny had invited him to spend some time on the farm. Spitz's Christmas gifts to the cub were an autographed picture of Spitz in his younger days, framed and ready to hang, and some good quality bowls. Compleet had given up eating off the floor or grass months ago. After all, he was being civilized by Spitz. At the season's end, the cub had left behind some bowls in the baggage room of the clubhouse. On the farm, Ginny had given him some used bowls. One had a crack in it, so he was happy to get new bowls. He still used his paws to eat. He thought he would look silly if he tried to use a spoon, fork, or knife.

These were quiet, restful, happy days. Spitz, Clara, Ronny, Kristy, and Compleet often took walks along the stream and hikes through the woods. The air was usually very cold, which prompted everyone but Compleet to wear heavy clothes. The cub wore only the minimum: one of Ginny's new, knitted sweaters and one of Clara's Christmas caps. With his thick fur, he felt quite comfortable, even when a cold burst of wind hit his face and ran along his spine.

One day when the five were on a hike in the woods, it began to snow. It was the first real snow of the winter. It came down so fast they had to take shelter under some tall bushes. It was a half hour before the snow let up. They hurried back to the farm. When they got near the farmhouse, the sun came out and lit up the flakes of snow on the buildings and the ground and the tree trunks and evergreen needles. The whole world seemed covered in soft white. The bear was excited and in awe. It was like a great hand had reached down from the clouds and painted everything it touched. But the next moment Compleet felt a deep sadness; the scene reminded him of the northwest Jersey woods and his mom and sister. He hadn't thought of his own family for a long time.

When the group got back to the farmhouse, the cub was overcome with a sudden drowsiness. "Hey kid," said Spitz, "we understand. It's 'bout time for you to leave us and hibernate, ain't it?"

I guess it is.

The cub thought how comfy he would be in his new boulder house. His long sleep would give him time to dream of the farm, the animals, and the people he loved most, the Bruedocks, and Spitz. He thought he might even include some of his Tenn Nine teammates in his dreams.

Hibernation and Nightmares

During hibernation, bears are restless; they kick and turn over and sometimes wake up. They often dream, and Compleet was no different. Once he thought he was awakened by a loud noise and saw blurry faces in the shadows near him. Often he would roll about and kick at some imaginary foe. At times he was sure he heard the roar of the crowd and the crack of a bat.

He had nightmares of the car accident. He saw the glare of headlights, heard people talking excitedly, saw someone with blood on his chest and face, and his mom lying by the side of the road and not moving. She was alone. All the people were around the man with blood on his chest and face.

He turned around, looking for his twin sister. He wondered if she had spooked and run off into the woods. He wanted to call out but was afraid people would hear him. He decided to go to his mom. His mom would know what to do. She always had helped him in the past when there was danger. She had taken care of him every day of his life. She wouldn't fail now. He started to crawl toward her. He would wake her, and the two would escape into the woods and look for his sister. Everything would work out, but first he had to get to his mom. She was in the exact spot he had first seen her. He asked himself, *Why doesn't she move? Can she be asleep?*

Then tall, heavy men in uniform came toward him, handled him roughly, muzzled him, and pushed him into a closed space that had no light. He was there for a long time and had the sensation he was moving, even though he was crouched down and motionless. Often he was thrown against this side or that side of something strong and smooth that gave a deep sound as he struck it. And the darkness never left him.

When the doors opened, a light shone in his face. He was pulled out of the closed space, and many hands pinned him down. Someone felt over his body and said something. The voice was gentle. He was placed in a large, chain-link cage, and his muzzle was removed. He was left with water and food. The night was ablaze with stars, but he was so sad and felt so alone he moaned in a high-pitched voice and never looked up into the sky. He thought of his mom lying by the road. Where was she now? A deep cold came over him. He had no mom to keep him warm; no mom to play with or lick his hair and face; no mom to touch and nuzzle up to. And his sister, did she get away?

Again and again during the long months of sleep, Compleet dreamed this dream. And every time it was as vivid and detailed and filled with horror as the first time.

Year Two with
the Tenn Nine

"Hey, kid," said Spitz in a loud voice, "are you gonna sleep forever? The team's already in spring trainin'. Clyde said it's time I wake you up. How about it, lazy bones? You gettin' up or do I have to drag you outta this place?"

Compleet recognized Spitz's voice. The bear slowly roused himself. He blinked, yawned, stretched, scratched himself, shook his head, and stretched again. When you are asleep for a couple of months, it's not easy to wake up.

A little wobbly on his legs, the bear went outside. The sky was clear, and the sun was bright. The air was mild on this particular morning.

"Time to go, kid," said Spitz. "How long before you can get your things together?"

I...I don't know. Let me get some food in me. I'm so hungry I could eat a whole deer. Compleet thought of Autumn. *I mean, I could eat a whole moose and, for dessert, a bushel of acorns.*

Ginny prepared a big breakfast for the bear. While he ate, Spitz told him tidbits about some of the players.

"Tad and Pedro left the team and started a business together. Vern finally married, and Eric got engaged. Dusty's put on a lotta weight; you'd hardly recognize him! It seems like he's in the weight room most of the time tryin' to get the fat off."

Spitz took a deep breath; his voice grew serious. "Clyde told me he's expectin' big things from you. Everyone on the team is sure we'll repeat as league champs. And I think it's a good bet you'll be elected captain."

Captain! thought Compleet. *That means I'll be the leader. Me leading the team!*

From a shopping bag, Spitz took out a canvas duffel bag he had bought the day before. "Here, I got you a present to put your things in." He bent down and playfully pushed the bag into Compleet's chest. The bear grabbed it and examined it carefully.

Thanks, Spitz. I certainly can make use of it.

Compleet opened the drawstring (with help from Spitz) and put inside Ginny's six new sweaters, Clara's new baseball caps and her poem, and two of Clint's straw mats. The rest of the few things he owned he left in the boulder house. He couldn't lock the front door; there was no key and no door. Compleet didn't mind. He thought, *Would anyone want to rob a house that a bear lived in?*

Clara was at work, and Ronny was at school, but Ginny and Clint took time to see the bear and Spitz off. Ginny gave Spitz a ham and cheese sandwich, and the bear two chiliburgers to eat on the ride to Tomtowne. Chiliburgers were now Compleet's favorite snack; he had Kristy to thank for that.

When the bear and Spitz got to Tomtowne, they immediately headed to the ball park. Spring training took place at the ball park when the weather was good, and at the high school gym when the weather was lousy. Most of the Tenn Nine players were hitting balls or catching flies. A few were in a corner of the outfield, stretching and doing other exercises. When Compleet and Spitz came onto the field, they all took special notice of the bear.

"Man, oh man," exclaimed Dusty. "That ain't no cub no more!"

And he was right. Since the team had last seen Compleet in September, he had grown bigger and put on muscle. True, he had lost a lot of weight from his long sleep, but that only made his new muscles stand out. He now had an air about him, a look of confidence and authority.

"Hey, kid," said Clyde as he gave the bear a light punch in the side, "maybe I shouldn't call you kid anymore." He looked Compleet up and down and shook his head in wonder.

"He's still kid to me," said Spitz. "I'll bet he ain't even five yet!"[5]

The practice went well for the bear. He was surprised how steady his throws were from center field to the bases and how far he could throw the ball. He felt a new strength in his legs as he patrolled center and ran the bases. At bat, he hit four balls over the left field fence.

Clyde was watching the bear intently. "Yes, sir," he said to a reporter standing next to him. "I know we're gonna repeat."

Spitz as Instructor

In the days ahead, there were sweaty workouts, and important instructions and criticisms from the coaches. Compleet was a good listener and learned quickly. He was not at the top of his game yet, but his improvement was duly noted by coaches, the players, and reporters. Spitz especially was aware of the bear's progress. As an unofficial coach, he talked to the bear often about the mechanics of the game. But he hadn't said much about analyzing. He figured now was the time to talk about it.

Spitz wasn't that skilled a player, but he had stayed in the game longer than some by making a practice of looking carefully at the players on the other teams and their skills, the best pitches the starters and relievers threw, which fielders had good arms and were accurate, which players had speed on the bases, which infielders played their position best, and so on. Players all take notice of the opposition, but few make a science of it. Spitz did, and he didn't write things down. He preferred to store observations in his mind. His memory was phenomenal. He could remember almost to the day when such and such pitcher had struck him out on a nasty slider. He could remember what inning he had bunted safely on a third baseman that played him too deep.

One evening after he and the bear had eaten and cleaned up he said, "Kid, I wanna tell you 'bout analyzin'. . . . This baseball we play is a five-star sport." He took a big chew of tobacco before he continued. "And analyzin' is one of them stars. The other four are the skill, the experience, the fun and energy, and the mind game. The skill you can teach only to a certain point. After that, it's God-given. Either you're that good or you ain't.

"The experience comes with time and playin'. You can't rush it. You gotta go through hundreds of games until you feel at ease at the plate and in the field, until you know pretty much what's gonna happen next and how to meet it. The fun should come natural. I mean, if you can't get a kick out of playin', then you should hang up your glove. If you're havin' fun, you're relaxed and can play your best and get excited and have all that energy. You can't win for your team unless you're excited and energized. You got to be emotionally full but in control.

"The mind game, I told you how important it is. That was way back; remember, kid?"

When Compleet nodded, Spitz continued. "Now we gotta look at the last star, the analyzin'. I know you been doin' it kinda automatic. Let's put it into words." Spitz paused for a few seconds and took a deep breath. "Take the pitcher. You gotta learn to think like the pitcher you're facin' and get ahead of him. If the guy on the mound tries to throw hard fastballs past you in key situations, you gotta anticipate the fastball so you can get good wood on it. If he throws splitters that drop sharply and pick up dirt, you gotta stay away from 'em. If he's often wild, you gotta be patient and try to squeeze out a walk. You gotta learn how to hit the breakin' ball a good percent of the time, how to guess when the change-up's comin'."

Spitz spit tobacco at a nearby spittoon. It hit the inside of the metal pot, which gave a bell-like ring. He often said his spitting made him a better ballplayer, but he never explained how. "And the fielders—always know where the seven men in front of you are standin'. Forget about where the pitcher is; he's gotta be right on the mound. But the other guys—is the center fielder playin' too deep, the left fielder out of position? Is there a big gap between first and second? Is the third baseman guardin' the line? You gotta see all this right away. You pick it up in the on-deck circle. If the batter in front of you gets on base, you look 'round and see how the fielders adjust to the new situation. And you adjust your thinkin'. Always thinkin', kid; you gotta be always thinkin'."

Compleet trusted Spitz totally and believed his words rang true. The bear was already a better all-around ballplayer than Spitz, but when it came to analyzing, he knew Spitz could teach him a lot.

"Look how good analyzin' has kept me in the game," Spitz continued. "I'm a turtle on the bases, my swing is slow, and the power's not there anymore. But I play a good game of small ball, and I watch the pitcher's every move. I like to share what I know, especially with the kids on the team. Kids like you that listen when I say somethin' important. Kids that need a kind word at times or maybe a punch in the arm so they'll get up to speed. I tell 'em, 'This is a T-E-A-M sport, no room for hotdogs. The player don't ever win or lose; the *team* wins or loses! You're supposed to work with the other guys to get the wins. That's your job, period.'" Spitz stopped for a few seconds, then he said wistfully, "I sure would like to try managin' someday. But I don't think that day'll come."

The bear signed, *I know you'd be good at it, Spitz. You always give the best advice. As long as you're around, I can only get better. Just don't up and retire on me.*

"No chance of that. I'm stayin' in the game as long as any club can use a thirty-something who's been over the hill longer then he'd like to admit." Spitz's voice turned sad. "Long ago I gave up thinkin' I could ever make it to Big Ball. But Double-A ball ain't so bad. You play by the same rules as In-The-Sea Association. The money's not too good, and sometimes the players almost outnumber the fans. But it's still baseball, and that's all that counts."

Fine Start, Then Problems

The season opened at home for the Tenn Nine; the stadium was sold out. Bunting was everywhere. Ushers and vendors sported new green-and-white uniforms. There was a new scoreboard in left, larger than the old one. A fresh coat of paint covered much of the stadium. A new banner flew above the entrance: "Tomtowne Tenn Nine—Champions of the Down Home League, 1999." The fans, like the players and the front office, were looking for a repeat. The crowd was vocal and in high spirits.

Of course, the Bruedocks and Kristy were at the game. Spitz talked to them briefly during batting practice. And Compleet pointed with pride to his new sweater and new hat, which stood out from the uniforms—all regulation—of the rest of the team.

The Tenn Nine was playing the Haggenside Hornets. Both pitchers started strong, but in the fifth, Motsie Mangrove, the Tenn Nine pitcher, tired, and the Hornets scored four runs. In the seventh, Compleet poked a single between first and second. He stole second, then third, and came home on a double by Vern. Spitz brought Vern home with a bloop single. The manager of the Hornets sent in a relief pitcher who got out the side.

Still behind by two runs in the bottom of the ninth, Eric led off with a single, and Dusty drew a walk. Up came the bear, and the stadium rocked! The shouts of the fans echoed across the outfield. *If only I can get hold of one and send it deep*, thought Compleet. The relief pitcher he was facing had a nasty splitter. He already had struck out four with it. Compleet remembered what Spitz had said and stayed away from it. The bear ran the count to three and two.

He may try to cross me up and throw a fastball, he thought. Then he reconsidered. *No, he's got to throw a splitter; it's his best pitch. Now, if only I can reach it before it breaks too low.*

The pitcher spit, got the sign, brushed it off, got another sign, then wound up and hurled the ball toward the plate. Compleet saw it start to drop; yes, it was a splitter! He stepped up in the box, went down for the ball, and made contact before it had dropped too far. He got good wood on it; it went high up into the night sky and over the right field fence. The crowd let out a deafening roar, and fireworks of every color lit up the stadium. The new score was posted, and the words "We're number one" flashed across the top of the board. Eric and Dusty crossed home plate before Compleet. When the bear put his two front paws on home, the team mobbed him and pounded his backside.

Ballplayers all relish come-from-behind wins, especially in the bottom of the ninth. The memory dug deep. Long after this night, Compleet would count the team's come-from-behind win on opening day as one of the high points of his baseball career.

I t was a grand start to the season for the Tenn Nine, and for the first three weeks the team was in first place in the North Division. Then everything started to go downhill. The pitching went bad after Motsie developed elbow trouble, lefthander Juan Aragoone started to feel pain in his lower back, and righty Beau Hummle got called up to Triple-A. Joey Ghurtz, with a long history of injuries, complained again about his recurring knee problem. The relief pitchers struggled. Most of the hitters got in a slump and stayed there. The infielders committed too many errors, and the outfielders made a habit of misjudging fly balls or overthrowing a base or failing to hit the cutoff man.

The one bright spot in the lineup was Compleet. Through this dismal time, the bear's play changed little. But he couldn't carry the team, and the Tenn Nine slipped from first to fourth in the standings. Clyde tried everything: extra batting practice, a new coach to handle the bullpen, pregame meetings, a revamped lineup, strict curfews, extra days off, no days off. Nothing worked.

Talk in the Café

It was on a ride to Mullersburg, one of those long bus rides between towns that the team hated, that some kind of magic occurred. The bus broke down outside Grainstone, and the team had to wait in a café for three hours while a garage mechanic in town worked on the bus's rear axle. The team filled up on snacks and played music on the jukebox but still had a lot of time to kill. It was midmorning, and there were few people in the restaurant besides the team. Everyone was relaxed. It was good to get off the bus. Some of the players started to talk, personal stuff.

Vern really liked married life, but his young wife complained that he was away from home too much. Eric was having second thoughts about his engagement. Motsie told about the time he was playing A-ball, and the team bus got caught in a late spring snowstorm. "We took cover in a schoolhouse. When the teachers heard ballplayers were in the building, two of them asked us to talk to the students. Of course we said we'd be happy to. After the students were herded into the gym, the principal made some brief remarks, and our manager introduced us. Each told a short baseball story that was his favorite. This was insider stuff, and the kids ate it up!

"By then, the storm had passed. At the suggestion of the principal, the students were led outside, three of the janitors shoveled the snow off a large area, and the gym teacher and an assistant brought out some balls, gloves, and bats. We held a clinic and gave pointers to the kids on their batting and fielding. When we started to board our bus, the youngsters all lined up along the fence. They waved and shouted at us to come back soon."

Motsie said it was one of the most satisfying days on the road he'd ever experienced. Then the talk turned to ball games on the road. No married player said he liked long road trips away from his wife and kids. Some said they called home every day to keep in touch or cheer up the Mrs. or maybe check up on her. Dusty asked if that was fair. "If you don't trust your wife, your marriage is in trouble." Juan said he stopped calling home because his wife was always complaining about the kids or the neighbors or work needed on the house. She got him so upset it started to affect his game. That's when he stopped calling. Did he do right?

Spitz said he did right. Juan's work, that is, the game, came first. It put bread on the table. But he should try harder to include her in his work. Did he urge her to come to the home games? Did they have a relative nearby that could watch the kids? If not, could they afford babysitters? Did his wife keep a scrapbook of his best games? Did he tell her how much he missed her when the team was on the road?

"There's no gettin' 'round it," Spitz said. "Ballplayers have special problems to deal with. It's hard on both us and the families. It helps a lot if you think of the good side." Spitz's face was aglow. "Think of the hypnotic sounds of the game, the crack of the bat, the yellin' crowd. The cheers puff up your spirits and put the icing on a good day. Think how satisfied you feel when you throw out a runner, stretch a single into a double, steal second off a catcher with a good arm, or make a slidin' catch in the field. When things go right, it's a fun game. You can't beat it. And I'll be here with you guys long as management keeps givin' me a paycheck. You can retire, and you still got your families to look after and be close to. I got only baseball. It's my whole life."

No one said anything for a long time. All the players liked Spitz, and they greatly admired him. He was rough looking with that chew of tobacco bulging out his cheeks, and his always needing a shave. Sometimes he would steam up when a player made a dumb mistake. And if he made the mistake, he would berate himself. He was truthful, and yes, he had a soft side. If anyone ever needed cash to meet some emergency or needed someone who would show interest and listen, Spitz was the man to see.

The team knew his great love for baseball, and many of them had a twinge of regret he had only the game to love. There was a rumor he had been engaged a long time ago, and the girl had broken the engagement when she found out he drank a lot. None of the players had ever seen him take a drop, so they were sure the story was false.

There was more talk and then the bus came to pick them up.

Back on Top

Those three hours in the restaurant did something for the team. It brought them closer together. Players had talked about their personal lives, about problems at home and on the road. This wasn't the bench small talk that goes on during the game. This was heart talk; this was talk that mattered. No one said it, but many thought it. *Hey, guys, if we stick together and help each other, we can deal with our problems. And we can enjoy the game the way Spitz enjoys it.*

When the team took the field in Mullersburg, the mood of the players was relaxed and very friendly. A great gloom that had centered over them and followed them these weeks had suddenly lifted. Spring was here, the buds were opening, color was transforming the landscape, and most days the sun was warm.

Against the Mullersburg Majors, the Tenn Nine scored two runs in the first inning and three more in the second. Juan Aragoone was on the mound. "How's the back, Juan boy?" asked Dusty before the game.

"It's better. I've been goin' to a chiropractor, and trainer Mushie's been stretchin' the muscles and usin' cold compresses."

Juan pitched his best game of the season, giving up only one run and four hits in eight innings. Clyde brought in a relief pitcher in the ninth, not because he was needed but to give him some work. He retired the side—1, 2, 3. The Tenn Nine won the game 9–1, and swept the Majors in four.

It was the start of a tremendous turnaround. It seemed like almost everyone pulled out of his slump at the same time. Some pitchers went the distance. The bullpen got its confidence back and began to chalk up the saves. Players ran the bases with abandon; sluggers smacked home runs in clutch situations. The defense tightened. Compleet led the charge. His average went up seventeen points. He stole home three times. His play in center field was spectacular. When the team returned to Tomtowne, it was in second place and only two games out of first. A week into the home stand, the Tenn Nine was back in first.

The Future in Jeopardy

Sometimes events are going our way, and we think our good fortune will go on and on. But change is always in the wind. At any moment, life can throw us a curve. And sometimes that twist in fortune spells D-I-S-A-S-T-E-R.

It was two hours before game time when Spitz got a call in the clubhouse from Ronny. Earlier in the day, there had been a fire on the farm during a lightning storm. "The big barn burned down to its foundation," said Ronny in a weak voice. "I was waiting for the school bus and saw trails of smoke coming from the direction of the farm. I raced back in time to help Gran'pa and Gran'ma and three neighbors get all the animals out. But equipment was lost. And bales of straw and stacks of hay burned to ashes. We couldn't save the toolshed or the machine shed. Luckily, the tobacco barn and corn crib and granary were spared."

"What about the farmhouse and the kid's boulder house?" asked Spitz.

"Some sparks from the barn drifted over to the farmhouse but not enough to start a real fire. The fire truck used its ladder to wet down the roof and the outside. When the truck's water ran out, it got water from the stream. Compleet's house is okay. It's hard to burn down boulders." Ronny tried to laugh.

"Everyone here is exhausted. Ma was at work. I called her, but by the time she could get home, the barn was ablaze and nothing could be done. It took us almost two hours to round up all the barn animals. Our wild guys spooked. We still haven't located Autumn, Andy, and Coty. And the small ones are probably hiding in the brush or in the woods. Well, I thought Compleet and you should know what happened."

"Yeah, I'm glad you called," said Spitz, "but very sorry 'bout the fire. We had some rain earlier, but nothin' like you guys. No lightnin' that I recall. Yeah, I'll tell the kid, and I'm sure he'll wanna get down to the farm as soon as he can. I'll drive him, of course. Sorry again 'bout your loss."

"Yes, you think about these things from time to time. And you're sure when a disaster like this happens, you can handle it. But…" His voice trailed off.

"I know, son, it must have been hard on you, on everyone."

"I…I just stood there watching the barn in flames after we got the animals out. There was nothing I could do…nothing. Nothing anyone could do."

Spitz wasn't sure whether he should tell the bear right away what had happened or wait until the game was over. He changed his mind twice and finally decided Compleet should know immediately. He didn't like to keep secrets from anyone; it wasn't fair.

When Compleet heard the bad news, his face showed how troubled he was. *If only I had been there*, he thought, *I might have helped save some of the equipment. And I could have rounded up the wild animals.*

In his head, Compleet had all sorts of images of a barn in flames and animals caught inside frantically trying to get out of their stalls. He had never seen a big fire, but his instinct told him it must be something horrible. He felt so bad for his good friend Ronny and for Clint, Ginny, and Clara.

Spitz's account of the fire broke Compleet's concentration. The game seemed so small, so unimportant, stacked up against the story he had just heard. He went hitless and made an error in the field. The Tenn Nine lost 5–3.

A Look at Disaster

The next day the bear and Spitz left Tomtowne early in the morning. When they reached the farm, Compleet could hardly believe what he saw. There were ashes and deep tire marks everywhere. Charred wood covered the big barn's foundation; only fragments of the barn's huge, thick double doors remained. The smell of burnt wood was in the air. The tractor, seeder, rake, and rider mower had been scorched and were covered with ash. But the saddest sight was the huge gap where the barn had been. It was eerie, like some great giant had wrenched the barn off its foundation and thrown it beyond the trees and left nothing but silence.

Spitz parked by the farmhouse, and the four Bruedocks came out to greet him and Compleet. Ronny had gotten permission from the principal to skip classes. There were hugs to go around and a few tears. The bear signed to Ronny how badly he felt. Was there anything he could do?

"I don't know what's in the future. Gran'pa just got his hands back in passable shape and now this."

Everyone sat on the porch, and Ginny and Clara brought out some sandwiches and lemonade. Clint tried to sound upbeat, and Ginny said her daddy had survived a lightning fire when she was a little girl. Clara said she had some cash money she would give to her pa and ma.

"Thanks," said Clint, "but it wouldn't do much good. The big barn has to be rebuilt from the bottom up, equipment replaced. Everything's so expensive these days. I can get good secondhand machines, but they're not cheap any more."

"And there's no insurance money," Ginny said sadly. "You tell yourself you're saving dollars without a policy, and then Clint has his accident and now the fire."

Compleet's Plan

After more talk and commiseration, Spitz said he and the bear had to get back to Tomtowne for practice and the game. Neither could shake off what they had seen. Both went hitless, and the Tenn Nine lost for the second day in a row. After the game, Compleet cornered Spitz in a quiet place. He signed about the great destruction and the new burden it put on the Bruedocks, especially Clint and Ginny.

I've got to do something for them, Spitz.

"I know, kid, but even if the two of us put our savings together, it wouldn't be enough. Clint and Ginny will have to go into heavy debt to rebuild the barn and replace the equipment they lost. I don't see no other answer."

They're getting up in years, and their income is limited. I over-heard Vern and Beau talk about the problem of getting loans and the worry about meeting payments. I don't see that a loan makes sense.

"What then? Do you know any people with cash money? I mean anyone with a big pile of cash money?"

Compleet didn't answer right away. He was in deep thought. Then his face brightened. *Yeah, I know where there is big money!*

"Then you know somethin' I don't know."

You and I both know baseball owners are loaded. You can't buy a team or join a group that buys a team unless you have big bucks.

"You're right, but why would any of the Tenn Nine owners give you money or lend you money?"

I don't expect them to. But the guys upstairs might.

"Upstairs? What? You mean Big Ball?"

Exactly, and I got to get there. It's the only answer. I'll go for big money and maybe I can get a signing bonus. Then Clint and Ginny can start to rebuild, and in a short time the place will look like it did before the fire. They won't want to take anything from me. But I'll say something to Ronny, and together we'll talk them into accepting my help.

Spitz had heard an earful. He plopped down in the nearest chair. "Well, I'll be confounded! Compleet, I never knew you had that much gumption in you."

What's gumption?

"Gumption is being brazen enough to think you can just up and get into Big Ball."

I don't know what brazen means, but I know it won't be easy. I got to try.

Spitz ran his fingers through his hair and grabbed his chin. Then he spit out some tobacco juice and wiped his mouth. His eyes were thoughtful, and he hesitated as if trying to find the right words. "Kid, you can't just jump from Double-A ball to Big Ball!"

Why can't I?

"Because the system don't work like that. You go from Double-A to Triple-A, and then when you get experience at the higher level and you show promise, you get called up, usually near the end of the season, by the team that works with your team. And you get some playin' time. Unless you're really good, it's all iffy whether you stay. It depends a lot if the team needs someone that plays your position. Pitchers, especially relief pitchers, and catchers are most in demand. Sometimes it helps to be a lefty, which you ain't. Outfielders are a dime a dozen."

What does that mean?

"It means there are a lot of outfielders lookin' to make it to Big Ball. You may be up and down between Big Ball and Triple-A for years, and then you get too old and no one in Big Ball is interested in you anymore."

I know I might not make it, but I've got to try. I don't have time to play Triple-A ball. I need cash now, and that means I need to get to where the big money is.

"Kid, I wouldn't know who to see or what to say."

Let's talk to Ronny. He's smart, and he helped me get on the Tenn Nine team. Maybe he can bring me luck again. Will you help me?

"You know I will. But . . . "

But what?

"Nothin'. A bear tries to skip from Double-A up to Big Ball! I never heard of such a thing!" Then he gave a deep laugh. "Come to think of it, I never heard of a bear playin' ball till you came along. Kid, I'll do what I can, but that ain't much. I can stare down anyone, and I can spit tobacco juice in a fella's face at five paces. But I don't see how that can be of help."

Just stay by my side. I'll need plenty of support. That's all I ask.

Compleet's talk to Spitz seemed to solve a lot. Yes, it was a long shot to get to Big Ball immediately, but now he knew what he must do. The first thing was to talk to Ronny.

The next day was Sunday. Spitz and the bear drove down to the farm, but the family had already left for church. Compleet signed, *They're probably praying hard for the courage to hold on and get some answers.*

"Maybe we can help a little by cleanin' up," suggested Spitz.

The bear nodded, and soon the two were throwing charred wood on a pile, raking up debris, and searching what was left of the toolshed and the machine shed to see if anything could be salvaged. The animals in the big barn had been relocated to the tobacco barn. Spitz and the bear looked in and were glad they showed no signs of trauma. Near the berry patches, the two came upon Andy and Autumn. Spitz spoke to them as if they understood, promising that the farm would soon get back its normal look. Coty was the animal most disturbed by the fire. Spitz and the bear found him on the edge of the ball field pacing back and forth, back and forth. Spitz tried to calm him. Compleet, who was still Enemy Number One on the coyote's list, stayed at a distance.

Spitz looked at his watch and wondered why the family hadn't returned. "Maybe there was a special meetin' after church, or the family got into a long conversation with some of the neighbors." He and the bear, with a game on tap, decided to drive back to Tomtowne. They could talk to Ronny at another time. In the farmhouse, Spitz left a short note on the kitchen table.

Early Monday afternoon during a workout at the ball park, Compleet got Spitz to call the farm. Ginny answered the phone. Spitz said, "I'm sorry the kid and me missed seein' you and the family yesterday."

"We read your note," answered Ginny. "All of us appreciate the cleaning up you and the cub did while we were at church."

Spitz said he wanted to get in touch with Ronny. No, it wasn't an emergency. Ginny said, "I'll call the school and leave a message to have him ring the clubhouse as soon as possible."

Ronny called a half hour later between classes. One of the players answered and got Spitz on the phone. "Ron, Compleet has something big in mind he wants to get your opinion on. Can you miss your first class and maybe second tomorrow? I can drive to the farm with the kid early in the morning. The talk shouldn't take long."

Ronny agreed to the arrangement. This made the bear feel good. He had started the wheels turning, and he would soon know whether or not his plan had a chance. In the game that night, he had two home runs, stole two bases, and drove in five runs. The Tenn Nine won 9–6.

Three in a Huddle

Early the next morning, Spitz and Compleet made the short trip to the farm. Ronny went out on the front porch to meet them. He and Spitz sat down on comfortable chairs, and Compleet stood nearby. Ginny brought them bacon strips, eggs, grits, toast, and coffee. Then she returned to the kitchen. Clint was repairing a section of fence one of the wild ones had damaged. Clara was at work.

"Compleet has this far-out idea," said Spitz, taking a big strip of bacon in hand and turning to look at Ronny. "This idea he can leave the Tenn Nine team, skip Triple-A, and play for a team in Big Ball."

Ronny's eyes bulged and his jaw dropped. Spitz continued. "He says he must do it now because your grandpa and grandma can't afford a loan and need cash money badly. He thought you'd know how to go 'bout it since you helped him get on the Tomtowne team. He says he considers himself part of the family, and if his plan works, he can get big money to get the farm back to the way it was."

Ronny smiled at the bear and said, "I know your offer is from the heart, but they won't take any more money from you. I can help some. I'm not going to start college after I graduate. One of my classmates said he can get me a job in the supermarket in Tomtowne. And a farmer down the road said he might be able to use me part-time, maybe full-time. Kristy and I planned to get engaged in college. That will have to wait too. I talked it over with her, of course. She understands and even offered to give me some of her savings to help Gran'pa and Gran'ma. I said no; she might need the money herself later on or when we get married."

That's not good, Ronny, you having to change your life around, especially when I might be able to get enough money to help all of you. If I'm as good as the sports reporters say I am, maybe I can get to Big Ball now. That's where the money is and that's what I'm after.

"Compleet, you already have a team and a salary. Don't give it up for a shot at the moon. Besides, I don't know enough to talk to big-time owners and savvy lawyers."

You got me on the Tenn Nine team.

"I know, but the Tomtowne team isn't Big Ball. That's a huge step up."

You don't think I'm good enough to play in Big Ball?

"I didn't say that. Yes, I think you could play at the higher level but not now. You need more experience."

I don't have time; I told Spitz that. Your grandpa and grandma don't have time. We've got to—I've got to—do something now, not later, not next year.

"Compleet!" Ronny gave a sigh, and his voice trailed off.

"Watch the kid!" joked Spitz. "He can get 'round a person better then I can, or you!"

"Has Your Royal Highness picked a team he wants to play with?" asked Ronny with a smile.

Tomtowne is a farm team of the Cuspin Chum, right? So I thought the Chum.

Ronny didn't answer immediately. He looked out at the charred ruins of the big barn. Then he stood up, looked at the bear, smiled, and said, "Okay, I'll see if I can do something. I owe it to the family. I'll get in touch with Clyde. He won't like hearing this, and the owners won't like it either. Everyone—Clyde, players, owners, townsfolk—expects you to help win another championship."

The team is solid. It can win without me.

"Maybe yes," said Spitz, "and maybe no." Spitz leaned over and gave the bear a light punch in the leg. "If you leave the team, I won't have anyone to look after. I'll be lost!" Compleet looked at him but made no reply.

Ronny at the Wheel

Ronny had schoolwork and farm work to attend to. It was two days before he had time to call Clyde and two more days before the two could schedule a meeting.

Clyde's office in the clubhouse was small and untidy, and the air smelled of sweat. Ronny felt uncomfortable. The meeting started badly. Clyde looked with disbelief when Ronny said the bear wanted to leave the team and get a tryout with the Cuspin Chum.

"Who does he think he is? The Chum never even hinted they wanted to bring the bear up for a trial. He's staying here! We need him to help us win the championship again."

Clyde looked up at the light fixture overhead as if he needed time to think. "Is it the money? He got a big raise in his new contract. Well, maybe I can help get him a little more. And if we repeat as champs, I don't see why he can't ask for bonus money."

Ronny explained that Compleet needed much more than the Tenn Nine could offer. It wasn't the team. He told Clyde the bear liked playing for Tomtowne; he liked the players and idolized Spitz and said management had treated him fairly.

"What then?" asked Clyde. "What does a bear need a lot of money for and why now?"

Ronny told about the loss of the barn and farm machinery. Yes, Clyde had heard about the fire, and he told Ronny he was sorry about the great damage it caused. Ronny said his grandpa and grandma didn't have money to replace what was lost.

"They're too old to take out a big loan and keep up the payments. My ma doesn't make enough to help. I'm not starting college as I had planned. I'm getting a job instead, but I don't expect the pay will be good. If Compleet can get a big contract with the Chum ... " He didn't finish the sentence; he just stared at Clyde.

Clyde looked down at the papers scattered on his desk. "I don't know what to say. I know what the owners will say ... no."

"Maybe I can talk to them," said Ronny, "and explain what I explained to you."

"No, it's best I try. I'll call you when I get an answer."

Ronny had left the clubhouse when Clyde, in despair, threw up his hands and looked at the lamp on his desk. He muttered, "Just when I thought the team had straightened itself out. I was sure we would breeze through the rest of the schedule and into the playoffs, now this!"

It was three days before Clyde got in touch with Ronny. "I just got out of a meeting with the owners. As I expected, they said no. They said Compleet is under contract, and they expect him to honor it."

Ronny agreed the bear shouldn't try to break his contract. "There must be a way. I can't give up, not yet."

"We don't always get what we want. Usually no means just that. Sorry, kid."

Ronny was down but not out. He was stubborn just like his ma. In the phone book, he looked under the W's for Wathersmythe. There was only one Wathersmythe listed, Joseph Wathersmythe. "That must be him!" said Ronny out loud. "Now if only he'll talk to me."

The next day after classes, he walked from the school to Wathersmythe's house. It was mid-afternoon. There was no car in the driveway. *Maybe he's at his job*, he thought. He assumed Wathersmythe did something besides own a major share of the Tenn Nine team. Ronny thought he should give Wathersmythe a chance to finish work, have a good meal, and relax a bit. It was important he talk to him when he was in a good mood.

So Ronny set out to kill three or four hours. He bought some snacks and a newspaper and two magazines. He read almost every article in the paper and the most interesting articles in the mags. Then he walked the streets of Tomtowne.

Talk with Wathersmythe

At seven o'clock, he decided to knock on Wathersmythe's door. An attractive, middle-aged woman answered. "Yes?" she asked in a measured, pleasant voice.

Ronny introduced himself and asked if she was Mrs. Wathersmythe. When she said yes, he asked if he might talk to her husband. She invited him in, disappeared into a room, and in a minute or two, Joe Wathersmythe came out. He walked over to Ronny, extended his hand, and said, "Well, the last time we sat down together it was about a contract. You've gotten a bit taller and added some muscle." Ronny smiled. "I guess you came here to talk about Compleet."

"Yes, sir, I have. I hope you'll give me a few minutes of your time. The bear needs someone to go to bat for him, and I probably know him better than anyone else. I'd like to present his case."

Wathersmythe knew it had taken courage for the teen to approach him after the owners had made it clear they expected the bear to stay with the Tenn Nine. Wathersmythe liked people with spirit. Earlier, at the negotiations, he had thought Ronny sincere, polite, and friendly, all traits he admired.

He invited Ronny into his study. It was a large room with high ceilings and a stone fireplace. Shelves of books were on one side of the room and two large windows on the opposite side. An expensive-looking oriental rug was in the center of the floor. A large oak desk was near the windows; there was a chair near the desk. Ronny sat in it, and Wathersmythe sat behind the desk.

For the next fifteen minutes, Ronny told Wathersmythe about the fire and its damage and how Compleet had taken it on his shoulders to help the Bruedocks get back on their feet. He told how the bear needed to sign a large contract with a Big Ball team and how bad he felt about trying to leave the Tenn Nine. He had great respect for the players and was very fond of Spitz McOystre.

"Yes," interrupted Wathersmythe, "Spitz is a fine person and a good ballplayer in the clutch."

"Compleet might not be able to do what he wants," continued Ronny. "But he's asking permission from the owners, really from you, Mr. Wathersmythe, as the principal owner, to try."

Wathersmythe's mind started to wander. He thought of himself when he was Ronny's age, how he had left school and talked a locksmith into giving him a job. How he had learned the business and in time opened a store of his own. How he had gone wholesale, branched out, and become rich enough to end up as the principal owner of the Tenn Nine. The youngster needed help, and Joe Wathersmythe was in a position to help him, just as someone with a heart had helped him so long ago.

"Son, I like what you said. It makes sense. Maybe the club can repeat as champs without the bear. And if Compleet does leave, we can expect a top replacement from the Chum. We might get other compensation for losing such a standout."

T he front door closed behind Ronny. He stood still for a minute and took a deep breath. Then he put a piece of gum in his mouth. There was a light breeze; the air smelled sweet. The stars were out in big numbers, and there was a three-quarter moon. From the streetlights came a soft glow, which put Ronny in a thoughtful mood.

"I wonder what Ma would have thought," he said to himself. "I think I talked a man more than twice my age into giving a bear a chance to break into Big Ball."

Clara would have told him that stubborn, mixed with honey, often wins.

Big Ball in His Future

A week passed. Ronny had told the bear about the meeting with the owner. Compleet was sure Wathersmythe would grant Ronnie's request. He knew Ronny was a persuasive talker.

Clyde thought Wathersmythe would hold firm and complained to the owner that the loss of Compleet might jeopardize the team's chances of repeating. Wathersmythe told Clyde he was too much of a pessimist. "Let's first see what happens. I've already talked to the Chum general manager, and he's sending scouts down here soon. If we lose Compleet, you can be sure, Clyde, we'll get a replacement that will help the team."

Midway through the second week of waiting, Clyde approached the bear in the locker room. It was about an hour before the team's last game of the home stand. "Come in my office." As soon as Compleet crossed the sill, Clyde closed the door and said in quiet tones, "Well, son, you got your wish. Two scouts for the Chum will be in the stands tonight to look you over. My advice: don't think too much about them. Just play your game, and you'll be fine."

After Compleet left the office, he immediately told Spitz what Clyde had said. Spitz answered, "This is your chance, kid, the chance I never had. I know you'll do good. You're twice the ballplayer I was at my best. I'll be rootin' for you, and I may even bunt you down to second or over to third." Spitz gave the bear a slap on the back and laughed.

The game was close, and Compleet did well. He had two hits and made no errors in the field. He doubled in the first but was stranded on third. In the fourth, he went from first to third on Dusty's single and scored on a squeeze play. In the sixth, he threw out the runner trying to advance to third on an out. The Tenn Nine won 5–4.

After the game, the two scouts, Robbie and Max, talked to Compleet. They liked his play and wanted to see more of him. They had already called the Chum general manager to get permission to accompany the team on its upcoming road trip. At Compleet's urging, Spitz called Ronny to tell him the good news. "The kid's not in Big Ball yet, but I'd say he's awful close."

During the next two weeks the bear played some of his best baseball. He struck out only four times, hit five home runs, seven doubles, and raised his average fourteen points. Four times he threw out runners trying to score from third on outs, twice in one game. His play in center field was flawless. Three of his catches could best be described as spectacular.

At the end of the trip, the scouts sent a glowing report to the front office. It wasn't many days before the principal owner, general manager, team manager, the two scouts, and a few other important baseball people in the Chum organization got together to discuss the report and how the bear might fit into the team's plans. Yes, the team needed a better fielder in center and one with more power at the plate. The scouts assured everyone that Compleet would be an upgrade in center and at the plate. After more discussion, the principal owner and the general manager made plans to schedule a tryout.

On Display

It was a hot, muggy day in July, the day after the All-Pro Slugfest. Since players in both leagues had the day off, it was a good time for Chum personnel to look at the bear. Luckily, the Tenn Nine had an open date. Spitz, Compleet, and four teammates flew from Memphis up to the Cuspin Heights Airport. Clyde had been asked to send four utility players along with the bear and Spitz to help out with batting and fielding. For all six it was a fun day in the big city, and for the utility players the journey had a special meaning. They had a chance to hit and field in a Big Ball park.

All the players had been to Cuspin before except Compleet. His eyes bugged out when he saw the skyscrapers and the developed riverfront, the crowds of people on the sidewalks and in the parks. And the never-ending traffic! He asked Spitz, *How do the people get from one side of the street to the other without getting hit?*

"When you live in a big city, you learn how to dodge cars. It's like in a game. Say the pitcher's erratic, and he throws one too close. You're able to dodge it, right? You learn it from so many brush backs."

Yeah, but a baseball isn't as dangerous as a car.

"Right, but the principle's the same. You move to the right or left or fall back to stay in one piece."

At the ball park, which was called Tailors Station, the six players met the general manager, John Boslerts, who introduced them to the principal owner, Fred Miltones, then a few more top people in the organization, and manager Sal Frogertee. Robbie and Max had also been invited to the tryout. They were standing near the third base bag and waved to the bear and Spitz.

"Welcome to the home of the Chum," said Sal. He was a burly man, about sixty years old, with pale blue eyes, a ruddy complexion, and a clear baritone voice. "The players call me Frog, which is all right so long as they smile when they say it. I'm not an easy-goin' guy, but I try to be fair. And I think of the team first, always the team first."

He turned to face Compleet. "You make the team, you ain't goin' to grandstand. You ain't goin' to hog the reporters. Not with me, or you're out of here before anyone learns how to spell your name."

Compleet was taken aback. Clyde had never come on that strong with him. He had given the bear time to adjust to the team and his surroundings and to improve as a player. Spitz saw the bear was upset. He went up to Frog and asked if he could talk to the kid alone. The manager nodded, and Spitz walked Compleet to a corner of the infield.

"Don't let him get under your skin, kid. The stakes are too high. Remember what I told you. Block out the bad stuff; concentrate on what's in front of you. All five of us are in your corner rootin' for you. You got the skill, the emotion. Show 'em!"

Spitz's few words hit home. During the next hour Compleet played relaxed and confident. He had good bat speed and regularly hit to the deepest parts of the park. In center beyond the brick wall was a waterfall cascading over rocks. It was a pretty sight but also a distraction. It took the bear a while to put it out of mind when hitting.

During short rest periods he sometimes sneaked a look at the blue waterfall, which reminded him of a time so long ago. He had flashbacks of walks with his mom and sister under a canopy of trees, of snuggling with his sister next to his mom's furry body on a patch of grass, of splashing in the cold lake at High Point and chasing fall leaves—blood reds, lemon oranges, sparkling yellows, spotted browns—to the water's edge on a blustery November day.

The bear dazzled when running the bases and covering balls hit to him in center. When he trapped the ball on a catch, his release was so fast it elicited gasps from some of the onlookers.

Ronny, it's because of Ronny I'm here, thought Compleet. *He taught me the game; he got a scout to come to the farm; he negotiated my contract; he got Wathersmythe to change his mind. I owe him more than I can give in return.*

Compleet laid down a perfect bunt. When one of the utility players overran it, the bear continued onto second. Two bases on a bunt! Everyone clapped.

In Negotiations

When the tryout was over, the utility players excused themselves and walked to a diner for something to eat and drink. Compleet and Spitz followed Miltones, Boslerts, Frogertee, and Robbie and Max to the general manager's office. In the waiting room Spitz sat down, and the bear crouched by the window. Fifteen minutes went by, then twenty. Finally someone opened the door to the office and motioned them to enter.

Fred Miltones was the first to speak. Turning to face the bear, he said, "Of course all of us have heard about you, Compleet. You have blazed new trails, an animal in baseball! Amazing! And you've been a great success! TV news reports your comings and goings, magazine and newspaper articles extol your skills in the field and at bat, and I understand you even have a line of clothing."

Miltones hesitated, searching for the right words. "But you understand, well, there are obstacles. Not from the commissioner's office. Last time I saw Dwight we got to talking about you. He said you have been a credit to your forebears and all omnivores, and it's logical to assume you will be the first to break the animal barrier in Big Ball when the right time comes."

Miltones wiped his brow and gulped some water from a glass on his desk. "Our organization is not sure the time is ripe. We ask ourselves, how will the fans and players take to a bear playing in Cuspin and in other cities in the association? Will there be protests and boycotts? Will there be demonstrations in the stands or by players on other teams? Baseball is a business. We don't want any ugliness. I mean, is now the right time to put a bear in a Chum uniform?"

Spitz answered, "Speakin' for myself, I think it is time. The kid's done fine in Tomtowne and other towns and cities the team's played in. We're champs of the Down Home League in large part 'cause of his play. The players think a lot of him."

"Yes, I'm sure they do, but the Tenn Nine team is a Double-A ball club. It's a big jump from Double-A to Big Ball."

"You've watched him play," said Spitz. "I know Robbie and Max think highly of him. He has all the skills to be a really good, I think a great, player."

"I agree he has the skills. But the pressure. Can he take the pressure? If fans turn on him because he's not, uh … not … "

"Not a human," said Spitz, sounding annoyed.

"Exactly, not human. My question is, can he take it?"

"Absolutely!" said Spitz in a firm voice. "When he joined the Tenn Nine, there were rough times in the beginnin'. Some ugly things were said by players and fans. But the kid didn't go to pieces. He let his bat and his play in the field do the talkin' for him. I took him under my wing and tried to give him confidence. I think I helped him some."

Say it, Spitz. You helped me a lot.

"What did the bear tell you?" asked Miltones.

"He said I helped him a lot."

Miltones looked out the window. "All of our people know the club needs an upgrade in center. The team isn't quite there yet; maybe a trade or acquisition is the answer. We're in third place but not that far out of first. There's time to make a run."

I don't want to seem bigheaded, but I'd like to think I could make a difference.

"He said he might be the player to make a difference."

Miltones was silent for a minute or two. He tapped his fingers on the desk and shuffled his feet. "What do you think, John?"

"Offer the bear a contract. I have a feeling he'll work out fine."

"Frogertee, where do you stand?"

"I'm with Mr. Boslerts. I saw the bear cover the outfield today, and I saw him swing the bat and run the bases. Yeah, I think he could play center fine; I could put him in the lineup in fifth spot, behind Ham. It might be a good fit."

"Done!" said Miltones in a loud voice. "Now if we can come to terms on salary. Spitz, have you and Compleet got together on salary?"

"Yes, sir, we have. The kid wants 20 million for the season. Since he'll get a lot less 'cause this is already July, he wants a 3 million signin' bonus." Spitz swallowed hard. It was difficult for him to rattle off such big numbers. When Compleet had told him what he wanted, Spitz warned that the Chum wouldn't go that high. But Compleet wouldn't back down.

Miltones said, "Those are pretty steep figures for someone that has played pro ball for part of only two seasons. I don't think the organization can afford to meet those numbers." Of course, the organization *could* afford it, but Miltones was playing a familiar game. Pretend you can't go that high, maintain a stolid face, and maybe the other side will back down.

"Why such big money?" asked Miltones. "Prices in Cuspin Heights are high but not that high!"

Spitz answered, "The bear was adopted by a farm family that lives not far from Tomtowne, and the family recently had a big fire. The big barn's gone and a lot of machinery destroyed. The kid wants to give most of the money to the owners, the Mr. and Mrs., who are gettin' up in years and are desperate for help."

"I see," said Miltones in a quiet voice.

"There's something else," said Spitz.

"Oh, what is that?"

"Compleet was taught how to play baseball by one of the family, a teenager named Ronny. He's sixteen now, and the bear would like to wear that number in his honor. That is, if it's available."

"Frogertee, does anyone on the team wear sixteen?"

"I can check later, but I'm pretty sure it's free."

And tell him there's one more subject to discuss.

Spitz hesitated. He thought he had covered everything. "Now what?" asked Miltones.

"He said there's somethin' else to discuss."

"What's that?"

Tell him it's no deal without you. Tell him you'd be a good addition to the team as a utility player. Tell him you play small ball with the best of them. Mr. Miltones should ask the scouts what they think of you.

Spitz didn't know what to do. Compleet was asking to include him in the deal. He knew he wasn't on the agenda. If by some miracle he was signed along with the kid, he had doubts he could make it with the Chum, not at his age. His speech faltered, and he looked confused.

"What's going on?" asked Miltones, a little annoyed. "Are you two keeping secrets from me?"

"No, sir," replied Spitz. "It's just that he wants you to hire me too. He says you should ask Robbie and Max if I'd be useful to the team." He added, "I didn't know nothin' about this, Mr. Miltones."

Spitz stared at the bear, as if he wanted him to take back what he had just signed. Miltones was an old hand at reading faces. He saw Spitz was uncomfortable and uncertain and was looking for an out. "Maybe you two should talk over a few things. In the meantime, I'll speak with John and Frogertee and get some thoughts from Robbie and Max."

"Thanks, Mr. Miltones," said Spitz, and he quickly led Compleet out of the room and into a corner off a passageway.

"Kid, have you lost it? Miltones was ready to offer you a contract, and you blew it! The Chum ain't interested in me; it's you they want. I know what you're tryin' to do and don't think I don't appreciate it. But it won't work. Don't jeopardize your future because of me; think of yourself. I'll never get into Big Ball. My time has come and gone. It's okay, really."

I am thinking of myself. I need someone like you to sign to, someone I can trust. You haven't a bad bone in your body, and you'd make a top-notch utility player. Everyone on the Tenn Nine knows it, Clyde knows it, and Wathersmythe knows it. Robbie and Max must have been impressed with your play. Sure, their job was to watch me, but you played in every game I did. They must have noticed how few times you strike out, how often you advance the runner, how well you play your position, how much the other players respect you and look up to you.

"Kid, you almost have me believin' I'm that good." Spitz allowed a big smile to light up his face.

Who on the Chum knows sign language? I'm sure no one. Who wants to room with a bear? Who knows how a bear thinks and behaves? You, Spitz, you do.

"It's too big a gamble. Listen to me! If they say they're only willin' to negotiate with you, agree and take their best offer. It won't be the end for us. We can still be good friends. I'll stay in touch, I promise."

No! My way's the best. Look, it's July. The playoffs are only a few months away. The Chum people don't have time to train someone to replace you. I tell you, Spitz, they'll have to take you.

The bear twisted his mouth into something like a smile. *Besides, you're a better bargain than I am. They can get you cheap!*

Spitz let out a loud laugh and hit the wall next to him with both hands.

When they walked back to the general manager's office, the mood was light. The bear looked at Spitz as if to say, *A done deal. Mr. Miltones wants us. I see it in his eyes.*

Can the kid be right? Spitz asked himself. *This week, me in a Chum uniform? Nah, it's not possible!*

Miltones spoke first to Compleet. "Your salary figures are high for a player with only limited experience as a pro. But if we want to be a contender for the Bronze this fall, we have to make a move." Miltones paused. "So we'll agree to your salary and bonus figures."

The bear nodded and stared at Spitz. Boslerts allowed himself a wide smile, and Frogertee looked pleased.

Turning to look at Spitz, Miltones said, "John thinks you might do some good for the team. On the other hand, Frogertee says we don't need another utility guy. Robbie and Max spoke well of you—steady player, real professional, patient at the plate, dependable in the field. And so ..."

With a grin Miltones repeated his last words. "And so, welcome to the team, Spitz. If we can agree on salary, you'll soon be in rust-red pinstripes with your friend."

Part Three:
Ups and Downs
of Stardom

New Ball Club, New Town

Compleet and Spitz had little time to congratulate each other. The first game after the All-Pro Slugfest was the day after the tryout. Miltones wanted his new Chum in uniform and ready to play. He told them, "We play the Balflint Batfish. Be at the ball park on time!"

Of course, the first thing Spitz did was make a call to the farm to tell them that both the bear and he had signed a contract with the Chum. All the family beamed from ear to ear when they heard the news. When Spitz mentioned Compleet's salary, he heard gasps on the other end of the line. Ronny could hardly contain himself. After all, he had taught the bear the game and had watched him develop into a top pro. Now Compleet would realize every ballplayer's dream: To play in Big Ball! "My protégé!" he said to himself. "I'm so proud of him; great skill, unflinching determination, and sweat—that's a formula for success!"

It seemed to the bear and Spitz that part of one day just wasn't enough time to get everything done that needed to get done before their first game. Lodging was a big problem, and it was already past noon. Earlier, the Tomtowne utility players had taken a cab to the airport to get a flight back down to Memphis. The two were on their own.

On North River Boulevard, Spitz sought the advice of a taxi driver. The three drove along the river and around some of the area to the west. They stopped at a few hotels, and Spitz made inquiries. After talking it over, he and the bear decided to take up residence at a small, European-style hotel near the Hill Fire Station, an architectural gem reminiscent of a time when cities thought even functional public buildings should show style and class. The hotel was the Three C's, which had a big sign in the lobby: "We are all about high class, low cost, and deep comfort." Spitz and Compleet chose it because it was small, in a good neighborhood, attractive and clean, and the management promised to safeguard their privacy from the likes of reporters, photographers, baseball fanatics, and curiosity seekers. The hotel also promised them use of a private stairway so they could get to their room unobserved and not have to share an elevator with guests who might feel uneasy standing next to a four-legged, thick-furred creature.

Compleet and Spitz inspected their room and then left the hotel. Spitz had no dress clothes with him, only the Tenn Nine uniform he had worn during the bear's tryout and a sport shirt and scruffy pair of slacks. Compleet was wearing Ginny's knit and Clara's cap. That was all. But then he never wore more than Ginny's knit and Clara's cap!

Spitz thought there was still time to do some heavy shopping before the stores closed. Off they went to North River Boulevard to an area known as the Beautiful Boutiques on the Boulevard. Spitz didn't have much cash on him, but he wasn't afraid to run up the total on his credit card. He was a member of a Big Ball team now! His clothes should fit his new importance. Of course, his salary didn't come close to the bear's, but Miltones had offered him a figure a lot higher than the Tenn Nine was paying him. He accepted the offer almost as soon as the words had escaped the owner's lips.

Compleet was impressed with the fine styles and pretty colors of the clothes. But he bought nothing. His shiny hair and thick fur were all he needed, and he liked to show them off. *Why should I want to hide anything?* he thought. So while he just looked at the merchandise and tried to keep out of the way of buyers and salespeople, Spitz was busy buying two of this and three of that. He made sure all his selections were of good quality. They visited seven shops until Spitz had bought as much casual wear, dress wear, and sports wear he and the bear could carry. And in a drugstore, he bought an alarm clock, writing paper and pen, and toilet articles.

The two struggled to carry all the boxes and bags back to the hotel, dropping some with almost every step. Spitz finally admitted defeat and hailed a cab that took them the short distance to the hotel. More packages fell when the bear and Spitz got out of the taxi and when they entered the lobby. A bellhop came to their rescue and put most of the packages on a luggage carrier for easy transport.

Neither of the two fell asleep until after two o'clock in the morning. There was so much to discuss, so much to dream. Their first game as a Chum was only hours away! Would they do well? Would team members accept them immediately? What would they think about Compleet, a bear that had received a lot of press, almost all of it good? Would they be jealous? The papers spelled out the bear's salary and signing bonus. His salary was more than most on the team had signed for, and few had been offered a signing bonus. Would they resent his big bucks?

The alarm was set for 7:00 a.m., but Spitz and Compleet were up before six. They ate breakfast in the café off the lobby. By now the bear had assumed fairly good manners. He ate his meal off a tray and kept his face rather clean while eating. At Spitz's instruction, the waiter poured water into a large, heavy bowl, which allowed the bear to lap up the water without knocking over the bowl. At meal's end, Spitz wiped the bear's snout and paws with a table napkin and left a tip for the waiter.

Leaving the hotel, the two took a morning walk over to River Boulevard. It was cool with a strong wind blowing out of the northwest. Compleet felt like loping but didn't want to leave Spitz behind. Spitz knew the bear's need for exercise and walked at a fast pace. They covered a lot of ground, getting as far east as the Pioneers' Village and Museum in High Rock Park and as far south as the Museum of Long Ago. Of course, the bear was noticed, but no one hailed him or asked for his autograph. A few local photographers followed and took a lot of pictures, but they were polite enough to stay at some distance.

Big Game for the Newcomers

The clubhouse at Tailors Station was far superior to the clubhouse in Tomtowne. It was bigger, cleaner, and newer. Spitz picked up his uniform soon after the two entered the clubhouse. By coincidence the uniform had the number thirty-eight on it, which was his age. He and the bear were assigned lockers next to each other. A trainer gave each a rub down, asked questions about their general health and baseball-related aches and pains, and then wrote everything down in a small, beat-up notebook. Later, most of the Chum took time to introduce themselves and cracked a joke or wished them luck. The players used their nicknames; none gave his last name. *Maybe it's an initiation kind of thing*, thought the bear. He heard Ham, Drum Drum, P.U., Jimbo, French Fry, Gee Gee, Payday, Santa, and Muffy, and minutes later had trouble matching names and faces. Spitz had the same problem.

Compleet looked glum and hesitant. Spitz noticed it and thought he should try to pump up the kid. "Remember Tomtowne?" asked Spitz when he and the bear were alone. "The beginnin' is always a little hard. But events have a way of workin' out. The names and routine will come soon enough. Each new day, each new week, things will get a lot easier. In two months you'll think you've been a Chum for years, guaranteed!"

During pregame batting practice Spitz and the bear took time to take in the majesty of a Big Ball park. Tailors Station was one of the oldest parks in the association. Some of the red brick wall that went around the outfield was original. There were mosaics and small, fancy stone carvings at different locations in the stands. Brass railings marked off the most expensive seats. Old, solid, highly polished wood was in the press boxes and broadcast booths. All this gave the impression the stadium was meant to last forever.

The huge waterfall was a fairly new addition and the prettiest section of the park. Above the waterfall was a large metal cutout of a fisherman, his boat, and Chum jumping up in the air about the boat. Flags and pennants flew from either side of the cutout. A large rectangular scoreboard topped by pennants was above the bleachers in left. Beyond right field and the bleachers was a parking area for VIPs, then North River Boulevard, the park, and the river. Of course, Compleet couldn't see over the bleachers in right, but he could hear the motor traffic on River Boulevard and the boat traffic on the Muddy Muck.

The bear was already thinking big. *I wonder if anyone has ever hit the cutout over the waterfall or hit a ball over the right field wall and bleachers, past the boulevard, and into the river.*

True to his word, Frogertee had inserted the bear in the lineup behind Ham. When the announcer went through the starting lineup and mentioned Compleet's name, the bear's fur stood up along his backside. *My name is going out over the PA system at historic Tailors Station!*

When he took the field in the top of the first, he got oohs and aahs from many of the spectators near him seated to the right and left of the waterfall. The bear felt the friendliness of the crowd. There was expectation in the air. Fans were anxious to find out whether a real bear on the field, at bat, and in the dugout could become a leader and take the team to a pennant.

Earlier in the day, the Cuspin papers had splashed Spitz and Compleet's pictures and Down Home stats over the front page. The *Illustrious Illustrator*'s headline read, "The Chum Land a Whopper!" And in the subheading, "Team Acquires a Bear to Play Center." The *Riverside Reader* printed, "Can a Bear Find Happiness in The City by the Bluff?" The subheading read, "Chum Put Out the Welcome Mat." The *Gazette Guide* wrote, "Get the Bear Facts," with the subheading, "Read On and Dream!" The subheading referred to Compleet's stats. They were impressive!

In the outfield the bear was sandwiched between Ham in left and French Fry in right. *Between two foods!* he thought. He gave a happy grunt and something like a smile lit up his face. The Chum were his team now. *Spitz was right*, he thought. *Things will fall into place, and routine will take over and wipe away uncertainty.* He wanted to be friends with everybody and was hoping the team had that closeness, that special feeling for one another the Tenn Nine had developed after the bus breakdown at Grainstone.

In his first at bat, Compleet flied out to deep right near the flagpole. He walked his second time up and singled his third trip to the plate. In his final at bat, he grounded out to third. Spitz pinch-hit for the pitcher and managed a soft single over the first baseman to lead off the seventh. Two outs later, he scored the Chum's third run on a triple by Jimbo.

The game was decided in the top of the eighth. The Chum were ahead 3–2, but the Batfish got two singles and a walk after two were out. Bases loaded. A single would put Balflint ahead. The Batfish's Gunsten Gonzalez, "Killer Kong," their power hitter, was at the plate. The first two pitches were balls. Killer knew the pitcher had to get the next one over. The pitch was a fastball belt high and a little to the outside. Killer reached out for it and connected!

The ball hurtled toward deep right center. Compleet squinted as he tried to pick up the ball as it came out of the infield. When he saw it, he raced at full speed to his left; he was in the chase he so loved! French Fry was after the ball too. Since it was his first game with the bear, he didn't know how the bear played balls hit between two fielders. Did the bear think it was his ball or would he back off at the last minute? Compleet couldn't yell out, "I got it!" French Fry caught a glimpse of the bear's legs churning, saw that mass of fur and muscle, and decided to pull up and let the bear go for it.

The ball had almost reached the turf when Compleet got to it. Because it was low, he couldn't trap it on his chest. He reached out with his right front paw, somehow got his claws out of the way, and gripped the ball. He hit the ground with such force the fans near him later swore the ground shook. The bear rolled over and thrust his leg and paw in the air to show the ump the ball hadn't hit the ground. The stadium erupted in cheers and shouts of "Bear, bear, bear, bear." There was no further scoring, and the Chum won 3–2. It was a game Compleet and Spitz would replay in their minds many times.

T hird place is good if you think that's the best you can do. The Chum players knew better. With a few breaks, batters getting a hot hand, and some of the pitchers getting in a groove, the team could move into first place in the Coral Division. Fulerbay and Balflint were the two teams in front of the Chum. There would be three more games with the Batfish. The Chum would see the Fulerbay Flagfish at the end of the home stand.

Seeing the City

It was a long home stand, and Spitz and the bear decided to see as much of The City by the Bluff as the Chum schedule allowed. Compleet was warming up to big city life. It was all so exciting: the hurrying crowds, the bumper-to-bumper traffic, the tall buildings, the museums, and the riverfront.

On their first free day since joining the Chum, the bear and Spitz decided to walk to the top of the bluff, the high area of rock and soil that was a landmark on this section of the Muddy Muck River. From a small observation deck on the bluff, the two watched the river traffic far below. They saw many pleasure craft and barges, and a paddle wheeler (for the tourists). The last outshown the other boats in size and elegance and had a steam whistle with a sound that echoed up and down the water. The bear looked with unblinking eyes. He had never seen a river from this height. The view was mesmerizing!

The river is so long and wide and so interesting, he signed to Spitz. *I never climbed a tree that gave me a view like this.*

"I read that the bluff we're on is the highest land around here."

I'd like to climb the tallest tree. I bet the view would be even better than this.

"Then you'll have to climb one of them real tall trees in California.[6] We'll be playin' in California sometime soon."

If we see the tallest tree there, will you climb with me?

"Uh ... I'd rather stay on the ground and be a cheerleader."

While they were walking, a man approached them and said

to Compleet, "Excuse me. My son, he's twelve, thinks the world of you, Mr. Bear. Would you please sign a page in his book? He and I, and my wife, saw you in your first game. He's standing over there." The man pointed to a skinny boy with a smooth, handsome face and curly locks. "He's shy."

Of course Compleet obliged. He reached down to the ground and rubbed his right paw across a patch of mud. His paw was so big his print filled up most of the page. Others nearby saw what the bear had done and walked toward him for a signature. Compleet put his paw print on every piece of paper shoved in front of him. It took him almost a half hour before everyone who had wanted a signature got it. Spitz waited patiently a few feet to one side.

"Hey, you're gettin' to be famous already. Soon you'll be better known then the mayor of Cuspin or the governor."

It seemed to be in the cards. The bear was fast becoming a legend. His spectacular catch in the top of the eighth against the Batfish had been discussed again and again on talk radio and TV. Both radio and TV wanted to interview him, but he declined. Spitz would have to accompany him. Compleet thought this would be too much of an intrusion on Spitz's free time, and his own. And, being shy, the bear wanted to stay out of the public eye as much as possible.

One morning the two took a boat ride south on the Muddy Muck. They hired a boat, not wanting to take a tour and be stared at by others. Compleet put one of his paws over the side of the boat into the water. It was cool and reminded him of the lake waters at High Point. He and Spitz marveled at the beauty of the skyline. A number of American cities have pretty skylines, but perhaps none have the symmetry and beauty of the Cuspin Heights riverfront. The buildings all looked so clean, and the different colors of glass, metal, and masonry stood out against the cloudless blue sky.

The bear signed to Spitz, *Now I understand where most of the people in Cuspin live—in those huge buildings. They go down to the street to work in the city during the day and go up in the buildings to their homes after work. Don't they feel really hemmed in, living on top of one another?*

"I guess they do at times," said Spitz. "But floors and walls and doors give them their privacy."

Another favorite activity of the bear and Spitz during their free time was taking long walks in the river parks. Along the river from one end of Cuspin to the other were neatly groomed parks and walking paths. Compleet kept off the paths, preferring to feel the green grass underfoot rather than cinder or dirt. The parks had flowers, trees, shrubs, and statues to enjoy. Although not woods, the parks offered the bear a respite from the noise and bustle of the city.

Spitz and the bear often visited Michel's Park, which was south of High Rock Park. It featured about thirty busts and full-length marble or bronze statues of famous Americans, especially those from the watershed of the Muddy Muck. The bear was drawn to the statue of Abraham Lincoln by the noted American sculptor A. Cinllon. Compleet had trouble explaining to Spitz why he liked the statue.

Maybe it's in the face, something in the eyes, he signed to Spitz one morning during an early walk.

Spitz had been only a so-so student, but he had always done well in history. He had read a lot about famous men and women. "Interestin' you should mention the eyes," answered Spitz. "Lincoln was our saddest president, our most introspective president, and also one of our greatest presidents."

What does introspective mean?

"It's when you think a lot about why you think as you do and act as you do. Lincoln—his friends called him Abe—had a lot on his mind. His marriage wasn't always happy; his wife was a society lady. Abe had worked hard all his life and disliked the fancy life. Their third son, Willie, died before he had a chance to grow up.[7] And there was this awful war. The country broke into two for a time and fought each other. Thousands and thousands were killed and many more wounded. No, Abe was not a happy president, but he sure was a good one. He was smart and ambitious, and man could he write! There was the Gettysburg Address, the first and second inaugural address, the letter to Mrs. Bixby, and more.[8] Kids in school sometimes memorize parts of what he wrote because the writing is that good."

Spitz noticed the bear had a far-off look. "You okay, kid?"

Yeah, I was thinking about Willie and my sister. Neither one had a chance to grow up. Compleet turned his face toward Spitz; his eyes were red.

"You told me about your sister. Let's hope she's safe in some forest or with some family."

I wish I knew. The bear signed no more; the two walked on in silence. Even a bear sometimes needs to be with his private thoughts.

Spitz and Compleet couldn't see all they wanted to see in Cuspin Heights during that first home stand. That was okay. Even longtime residents of Cuspin often complained they had never seen this historic place or that well-known statue or been to all of the festivals that Cuspin celebrated every year. There would be other home stands and other opportunities.

Besides, it was baseball that was more important. It was necessary that both kept their minds on the game and the pennant race.

Solving a Ball Problem

At bat Compleet was doing well: getting hits, driving in runs, smashing home runs. But he struck out too many times. Often the third strike was a fastball he couldn't pick up in time. He thought, *It's my eyes. I didn't have trouble when I was with the Tenn Nine. But in Big Ball, a lot of pitchers can throw a fastball ninety-six miles per hour or more.*

In truth, the bear's eyesight wasn't bad. It's a myth that bears are all but blind. Maybe it got started because a bear's eyes are small in relation to its head and body.

Spitz noticed that Compleet seemed distracted and down in the mouth. "Hey, kid," he said one day, "perk up; we got a pennant to win." The bear tried to look happy. He wouldn't tell Spitz what was bothering him. No, this was a problem he would have to work out himself.

The bear found the answer when he wasn't looking for it. It was the top of the second inning during a game against the Prumfort Porgies. Compleet was in the dugout, and French Fry was at the plate. He fouled the third pitch, and it went on a line into the Chum dugout and lodged behind the water cooler. The players didn't watch the ball's flight; they were too busy trying to get out of the way. Santa stood up, laughed, and shouted, "I saw it and then I didn't. Where is it?"

Compleet immediately signed to Spitz, *Tell him to look behind the water cooler.*

"The kid says look behind the cooler."

Santa walked over to the cooler and pulled the ball free. He held it above his head and said with a grin, "Hey, he was right!"

Spitz asked, "How did you know it was back there?"

I smelled the ball.

Spitz laughed. "I forgot; bears have great smellers!"

And he was right! A bear's sense of smell is legendary. A bear can pick up a human scent hours after the person has disappeared. If the wind is right, he can smell a blueberry pie miles away sitting on a window ledge to cool or a dead possum on the side of the road around the bend or far-off rotting fruit in an orchard.

Of course, thought Compleet, *my nose is the answer to my problem! I should be able to smell a baseball coming toward the plate. It's got the pitcher's sweat from his pitching hand. The ball's got its own smell and the smell of ash or maple when the bat grazes the ball.*

The bear no longer had to worry. Not only could he see the ball with his eyes, but he could smell it with his nose! In the weeks ahead, this ability proved to be his secret weapon. See, smell, see, smell! No other ballplayer could pick up a blazing fastball coming toward the plate as quickly as the bear!

An Eye on First

The players and Frog were quick to notice that Compleet did not strike out as often as before. Often he was hitting the fastball for extra bases. As reward, he became the cleanup hitter (batting fourth) when Jimbo was moved from third spot to fifth. The bear's improved play began to rub off on the team. Some picked up their game, and the wins came more frequently. The team took three out of four from Fulerbay. At the end of the home stand, the Chum were in second place behind the Flagfish.

Ahead was a long road trip. Compleet and Spitz were understandably a little nervous but also excited. It would be a chance to see different ball parks, other cities. Would fans in other parks accept the bear as wholeheartedly as the Cuspin fans?

In Fitetoun, the fans rose to cheer Compleet the first time he loped out to center. In the bottom of the second, a helicopter appeared over the stadium and hovered near the foul line in left field. Surprised players and fans watched a female descend from a ladder attached to the copter. Jumping off near the ground, the woman raced toward center with a teddy bear to hand to Compleet. Before she got to him, two security guards cut her off, escorted her out of the stadium, and handed her over to two policemen on duty at the front entrance. The helicopter disappeared but was later spotted at the city's airport. The pilot was arrested. In court, he and the woman, who were friends and had planned the stunt, told the judge they meant no harm. They wanted to give the teddy bear to Compleet in a way that would draw notice. The judge was not amused. He charged both with being disorderly and a threat to public safety. Each was fined $2,500 and put on probation.

Compleet felt sorry for the woman; he hadn't been harmed or even insulted. He got Spitz to write her a note saying he was sorry he wasn't able to get her gift. At the end of the letter he put his paw print. After the young woman got the note, she got permission from the court to read its contents on Fitetoun sports radio and described in detail the bear's signature. With some prodding from the radio station, many Fitetoun fans decided to make good on the young woman's attempt. In the next three days, a total of 1,858 teddy bears were delivered to the bear at the Chum motel.

The incident got on the sports pages all across the country and on quite a few front pages. It got on radio, TV, and the Web. The Chum publicity people decided to play up the event. Every time the Cuspin Heights Chum went to a city to play a series, an attractive young woman with long hair and in bear dress started off the bottom of the first with the presentation of a teddy bear to Compleet in center field.

Compleet benefited from the increased publicity. Manufacturers all across the country wanted to sign him to big contracts to do all sorts of things. He got offers to have his face on cereal boxes, to praise this safari trip, or that fish product, this pet food, that hair shampoo, nail clippers, or knit garment. There was even an offer to appear as the lead in "Bear Bait," a film written with Compleet in mind.

The bear turned down these offers; they didn't interest him in the least. But he did sign (with a paw print, of course) a big contract with a merchandise company to allow it to put out a full line of Compleet stuffed animals, including teddy bears, and bobble-heads and action figures. Within three weeks, the first shipment of these items arrived at the ball parks the Chum would soon visit. Vendors in the stands now walked the aisles selling not only taco chips, hot dogs, popcorn, and soda, but bear items, items that often sold out before the seventh inning stretch.

Compleet didn't forget his first fans, as some do when they become famous. He got his sponsor to open a big plant in

Tomtowne to make some of the stuffed animals, bobbleheads, and action figures. This gave work to 330 women and men.

The Team That Plays Together...

By the time the Chum returned to Cuspin Heights, they were in first place, three games ahead of the Flagfish. The plane carrying the players, coaches, and other personnel landed at Cuspin Heights International Airport near midnight, and three thousand noisy, happy fans were there to greet them! In Batterspark and other hotbeds of Chum mania, all the talk was about the Chum and their surge into first. The possibility of a Neptune League pennant was real. And that meant a trip to the Bronze Series! The wait had been so long, with many near misses. Not since 1910 had a Chum team won the Bronze! It had been over sixty years since the Chum had been in the Bronze finals! Fans had watched with envy as first the Sardines, then two other teams, won a championship after a long, long wait. They asked, "Why not the Chum?"

Why not? On talk radio, a fan asked sadly, "Is there no justice? Have any fans been more patient, more forgiving?"

If the fans were hot for a pennant, the team was hotter. There was no big talk. No, that might put a jinx on the effort. It would take actions, not talk, to win a pennant. The mood in the clubhouse was upbeat, but the talk was still about the trivial. The constant joking relieved tensions. On the field, when the joking stopped and most talk ceased, each member of the Chum got down to business. They were playing a kid's game, but for them it was a business. Enjoy it if you can, but win, win, win. They hadn't been able to do that in recent years. Of course, none of the Chum players who had been in a Bronze Series was still in baseball to urge the present Chum on. The players had to get the winning spirit from deep inside.

E very team has leaders, those who play hard, encourage others to play hard, give good words of advice when asked, and come through when it counts. The Chum starting lineup was stacked with players that could take charge.

In the infield, third baseman San Diego Santana (Santa) was a leader. He had won Gold Gloves the past four seasons and rarely misplayed a ball hit his way. He was soft spoken and never bawled out another player. When a bad play happened, he would say something like, "That's okay; forget about it and look ahead to the next batter. Let's go! We can do this! Concentrate!" His reassuring words almost always worked. One bad play was followed by many good plays and maybe a spectacular play.

James Nicholas Gathorin (Jimbo) was the first baseman. He was a slugger and had won quite a few games these last few months with his big hits. At second was Jack Frumme (Drum Drum). He was a streak player. When he was hot, he was very, very hot. And when he was cold, he sent a chill over the whole team. At such times, Frog and the hitting coach took turns talking to him. Frog's approach was more hard-nosed. Sometimes it worked; sometimes it didn't. If it didn't, then the hitting coach took charge. His approach was analytical. He'd show Drum Drum a video of himself at the plate and say he should do such and such instead of such and such. "Look, see what you're doing wrong? Look at your swing and notice where your feet are!" The hitting coach's nickname was Jury since he would tell players if they were guilty of a bad swing or a bad stance or a bad read on certain pitches or if they were impetuous at the plate.

At shortstop was Gary Payoly (Payday), a kid of twenty-one. He had been a member of the team only two months. He had been groomed two seasons in Triple-A ball. Before he was called up, the Chum regular shortstop was hit in the knee by a hard liner. The team doctor examined the knee and ordered X-rays. When he saw them, he said the shortstop needed surgery and was probably finished for the year. The Chum general manager put in a phone call, and the next day Payday joined the team. It was Santa's job to talk to him often and see that he felt a part of the team and was confident he could handle his position. He kept telling the kid the team was behind him. Any time he had a question, he should ask. Anything that bothered him, he should bring up. "Don't keep trouble inside," Santa would say. It was his favorite expression.

Philip Unterfuss (P.U.), the catcher, was tall and burly, with immense biceps and a crooked nose, which he had broken years before in an auto accident. He looked tough and often talked tough, but off the field he was gentle as a soft breeze. It's as if he changed personalities the minute he walked into or out of the clubhouse. He was one of the most popular players on the team and often took charge when a game started to go bad.

In left field was Claude Hammer (Ham), another power hitter. He was perhaps the most athletic of the regular players and the team's poster boy. He was over six feet with muscles everywhere. His palms were callused, but the outside of his hands was smooth and pretty. He had curly dark hair, a wide smile, and a handsome face. He was twenty-six years old and had seven years of Big Ball experience. He had skipped Little Ball and broken into the Chum regular lineup the third month on the team. He had a good eye at the plate and was patient. In the field, he had a sure hand. Many of the teenage girls, and those in their twenties, who regularly attended games had a crush on him. He was polite and always answered a question put to him, but otherwise he didn't talk much. He loved country music. In the clubhouse he was always hooked up to the latest music download device, listening to this country star or that one.

The right fielder was Emile Jean Pierre Fri (French Fry). He was a graduate of Franklin Mars University in New York and decided to follow in the footsteps of another Franklin Mars man who, a long time ago, had become one of the great players of the sport. French Fry was always trying to give advice to anyone who would listen: how to get a hit off this pitcher or that one or play this hitter or that or how to play the changeable winds that came sweeping down from Canada. Whatever the subject— baseball, classic autos, money management, fly-casting—he had an opinion. And when the team wasn't hitting, he regularly came up with a new lineup card. Before the game he would hand it to the manager. Frog would take it in hand, look it over, screw up his face, and say, "Ahhhh!" then throw it in the trash. Later he would post a new lineup which would be the one French Fry had handed him. Time and again, French Fry said he wanted to be a Big Ball manager after his playing days were over. Almost everyone on the Chum thought he'd make a great one.

And in center, of course, was Compleet Bear, good in the field, good at bat, and on the bases. He was hardworking and reliable. You might say he had all the good qualities and skills of his teammates and no bad habits. Clint would have said, "That bear sure is complete!"

More Sightseeing

Between games, the bear and Spitz often used the time to see more of Cuspin Heights. They liked to ride the El (elevated train) and look into lit office buildings or down at people walking below them. They often walked the length of the parkland along the Muddy Muck and became so enamored with the muddy waters and the sounds of the river that they often went fifteen or twenty minutes just looking and listening, not uttering a sound.

One day, when they were in Muddy's Park, not far from Tailors Station, Compleet looked over the boulevard at the ball park, and then signed to Spitz, *Tailors Station is an odd name for a stadium. It sounds like the name of a railroad stop or a military outpost. I wonder who Tailors was.*

"You got it part right," answered Spitz. "I read about it not long ago in a sightseein' guide. Way back before the stadium was built, there was a railroad station on the site. It was one of two stops in Cuspin on the rail line that ran along the west bank of the Muddy Muck. As the story goes, a tailor—I forget his name—from one of 'em foreign countries in Europe set up shop in the station. He was a real craftsman and soon was makin' lots of money from travelers on the rail line and from his regular customers in town. Well, the word spread in Cuspin that this tailor was makin' money hand over fist, so two tailors in town closed their shops and moved their business to the station. You mighta thought in a rail station with three guys all in the same trade they'd go broke. But they were so good at their work that the three made an all right livin'. The official name of the rail stop was North Cuspin Station, but soon everybody was callin' it Tailors Station after the three tailors."

Spitz paused and watched a barge loaded with coal on its way downriver. He scratched an ear and continued. "When the rail line moved its track in Cuspin to a site farther west outside the town limits, the station was bought by some guy who tore it down and built a ball park. He gave it his name. I think it was called Suppie's Stadium. Then the guy got the Chum ball team to move here. The townsfolk liked havin' a Big Ball team in town, but they didn't like the name of the stadium and started callin' it Tailors Station. In time it became the official name. Outside the main entrance is a statue of the three tailors all workin' side by side at benches, which of course is not like it was since each had his own shop. You might of missed seein' the statue 'cause we always come and go by the side gate."

Most often, Spitz and the bear visited the south end of the city, which housed three fine museums and an aquarium and a zoo. Of the three museums, their favorite was the Museum of Long Ago. In a darkened large room, they saw a reconstructed market street and shops, as they may have appeared about AD 1350. There were mannequins, merchandise in barrels and on tables and shelves, and recorded sounds of shop chatter and street noises.

It must have been fun to shop in those days and watch skilled workers make their wares for the house and farm. And hear shopkeepers in a loud voice trying to get customers to buy their goods.

"Yep, I guess it woulda been all right to live back then, but only if I was one of them rich merchants or maybe a nobleman."

Compleet saw "AD 1350" in large print and pointed to it. *If that number is a year, it must have been a long time ago.*

"You bet, kid," said Spitz with a smile. "A long, long time ago."

In the Museum of Models they saw a miniature downtown Cuspin Heights.

Compleet signed, *Why would someone build a downtown in miniature when the real downtown already exists? I mean, the miniature is a fake. No one works or lives in those little buildings.*

"Some people like to see small things. It's kind of a special art."

In the Museum of Future Tocks Compleet was bored and restless. He didn't see the need for clocks.

Why do people have to be at this place at a certain time and that place at a certain time? Why not let them come and go as they please?

"Well," said Spitz, putting a wrinkle in his brow and trying to think of a good answer, "if that happened, not much work would get done, too many people without regulation. A few people can get by without clocks, perhaps, but with a lotta people it's different. They need organization and direction. You gotta schedule things when a lotta people are together, and that means you need clocks."

I think it would be better without them. You don't need clocks in the woods.

"You're right, kid, you don't need clocks or watches until you're ready to leave the woods and want to know if you can get home in time for supper, which is always put on the table at six o'clock."

It seemed that Compleet always had questions to ask. Spitz thought the questions were odd, but then, they were coming from a bear. A bear that loved playing at Tailors and most often found the city interesting, but a bear that often had trouble understanding why things were as they were.

He didn't understand why people found it necessary to move so fast early in the morning and late in the afternoon if they didn't enjoy it. He didn't understand why they lived in such little spaces and cooked their meat after it was dead. He didn't understand why they drove around in a closed car when they could walk with the wind and the sun in their face. He didn't understand why youngsters were sent to school when their moms could tell them everything they needed to know.

Spitz tried to answer all his questions and allay his worries. Sometimes he couldn't find the right words. Then he would say, "Kid, it's … it's just the way we humans do things."

Talk of the Town

If the city, its people, and its attractions sometimes puzzled Compleet, Tailors Station and the Chum did not. The bear could identify with the game of baseball. It had a rhythm he liked, and there were quiet moments; it wasn't all slam-bang. There were a lot of rules, and they gave the game a solid structure. That appealed to the bear since all animals like activities that repeat and are predictable.

There was the history of the game and its traditions, which were kept alive by the many books on the sport and by movies, old-time photos, baseball cards, and the stat sheets. So many statistics! The sport feasted on stats! There were stats about every player who was still active or had ever worn a baseball uniform. There were year stats and lifetime stats and stats for the postseason. There were stats for every position on the field, including special stats for relievers and pinch hitters. Every franchise had stat sheets about its own players. There were stats about the longest games—in time and innings—and the greatest attendance for a single game, for a series, for the season, and postseason. Compleet imagined there must be a stat sheet that listed nothing but the different kinds of stats!

Of course, the bear knew there was more to baseball than the stats. He loved the fans who cheered him and his teammates. He loved being around the players. But most of all, Compleet loved the game because he was playing well.

The bear was the talk of the town. In the clutch he was great at the plate, he made amazing catches in the field, and he ran the bases like no other had before him. During one stretch, he stole home safely five times in nine games.

But it was what happened during a day game in early August that grabbed the biggest headlines in the local papers and made for constant chatter on sports talk radio. Since the bear's first game at Tailors, Compleet had a special interest in the right field brick wall and the Muddy Muck beyond the boulevard, an interest in hitting a ball that far. In August, this urge of his became a primary goal. It was a challenge he could no longer ignore.

Of course the player to talk to was French Fry. But when Compleet got his attention one afternoon, Spitz wasn't there to translate the bear's signs. He was back at the hotel lying down with a sore knee and a headache. So Compleet tried mime. With any other player, it probably wouldn't have worked. But French Fry quickly figured out what the bear had on his mind. "Compleet, if it were early in the season, I'd tell you to forget about hitting a shot that far. The winds shoot down from Canada and frustrate even the best hitters. But this is August, and that means the jet stream sometimes takes a dip and comes up from the south. A jet stream can be fierce."

For a time, French Fry stopped talking, spit, then pulled out two sticks of gum and put them in his mouth. He was thinking. Then he said, "My advice is to pick an afternoon game when the weatherman is predicting strong winds, get a good look at the flags and pennants before you bat, and watch for a crosswind. It can be nasty and upset all your plans or it could give the ball a boost. If you can get a hard fastball belt high and get a real strong gust of wind at the same time and you connect … well, who knows."

Compleet wanted to know whether any player had hit the ball that far. "Yes, a few of the best sluggers have. Al "Long Ball" Rutherum of the Haddock was the most famous. Used to hit 'em that far on a regular basis. But he was real special. Usually it happens only once in a blue moon. You got to get everything in your favor."

After listening to French Fry, Compleet later took up the

matter with Spitz. "Sure, kid, I'll help. If we both try to gauge the wind and watch the flags and pennants, maybe you can get lucky. Drag bunts are my specialty, so I can't help you with the correct power swing."

You bunt for a single, and I'll bring you home with a smash into the Muddy Muck. Is it a deal?

"A deal, kid."

Compleet knew it was 362 feet from home plate to the right field wall, near the flagpole. He would need a real solid hit to clear the wall and get over the bleachers, the parking lot, the boulevard, and the beach. He realized the odds were against him. This goal of his became an obsession and a grand nuisance. He didn't sleep well and sometimes dreamed disturbing scenes: hundreds of baseballs falling on him and burying him alive, or a solid wood wall behind the bleachers in right that was so high it almost shut out the sun, or the right fielder using a ladder to catch one of the bear's hard-hit balls and the ump saying it was a fair catch.

Compleet picked at his food; sometimes he even ignored Spitz when his friend asked a question. Spitz understood. He knew how determined the bear could be. He knew Compleet wouldn't get back to his usual self until he did what he so desperately wanted to do.

And on this particular August afternoon, Compleet felt the fur stand up along his back. He had a hunch this might be the special day he had longed for. A bear's senses are much keener than a human's. Life itself might depend on a bear knowing what's hiding in the bushes or behind a tree, knowing whether that certain smell is friendly or not. The wind was in his nostrils, and it was stronger than he had ever felt it.

Spitz said, "The announcer on mornin' radio warned of high gusts that would last the afternoon." The bear didn't answer. He was in deep thought.

The Chum were playing the Horsatonic Herring, always a

strong team, month after month and year after year. The Herring pitcher had a fastball in the high nineties. *Perfect*, thought Compleet, *and he doesn't walk many*. The bear looked out to right field, then focused his attention on the pitcher. Payday was at the plate. Compleet studied the pitcher's wind up, his release, his follow-through.

"Strike!" yelled the umpire as he shot out his right arm.

"Come on, ump, inside, inside," said Payday with a scowl.

On the next pitch, he hit a weak grounder to second for the first out. Spitz was up. He had replaced French Fry, who had gotten permission to attend his sister's wedding. On the third pitch, Spitz laid down a beauty, a perfect textbook bunt that hugged the third base line. Spitz was slow running to first, but the pitcher overran the ball, and Spitz got to first base two steps before the ball. The scorer gave him a hit.

Ham was the next batter. He flied out to shallow center. Spitz was still on first. Compleet came to the plate. *What's this?* he thought. *It's happening just like I said, a bunt for a single, and then…* He shook his head. He didn't want to jinx himself; he needed to concentrate. The wind was blowing so hard he had to brace himself to keep from falling. His cap blew off three times before he took his first swing.

"Please, a fastball over the plate," said the bear to himself. The first pitch was a slider—wide. The second was a curve—inside. "Fastball, fastball," pleaded the bear. And it was!

Afterward, Compleet could remember in detail everything that happened next. He opened his nostrils wide and picked up the ball from the sweat, the cowhide, and the ash. The ball was coming at him just where he wanted it. He felt every muscle strain as he made contact. He started toward first; he looked up at the ball as it arched toward the wall and the bleachers. But would it have the distance to reach the river? Spitz was running and jumping up and down. When a gnat got in Compleet's eye, the bear was distracted for a few seconds. He picked up the ball as it sailed out of the stadium and disappeared. The big screen in right center field kept the ball in sight until it landed in the muddy waters. The roar of the crowd drowned out every noise on the field except Spitz's booming, excited voice. "You did it, kid! You're a part of Tailors history! You did it!"

Compleet's tape-measure blast was the margin of victory. The Chum won by the score of 4–3.

A Setup

Compleet had been top news since his first game as a Chum. Photographers and reporters always followed the bear and Spitz when they left the hotel. Of course, the two preferred to see the sights or take strolls or go to an eatery without people following them and asking questions or wanting them to pose for pictures. It got to be a game, how to lose the photographers and reporters! At first they tried disguises, but that rarely worked. It's hard to make a bear look like a human!

The two tried leaving the hotel by a back entrance, but the photographers and reporters got onto their scheme and started to station some of their group in the back of the hotel as well as in the front. Once, the two hopped onto the back of a delivery truck as it left the hotel and then hopped off when the truck stopped at a light four blocks away. Spitz laughed for days at their clever stunt.

Events took a different turn when Compleet hit his monster home run into the Muddy Muck. It brought a new kind of photographer to the hotel, the paparazzo![9] This was a photographer that most often worked alone, not for a particular newspaper or magazine. His aim was to get high-interest photos of his subject and sell them to the highest bidder. If the pictures were really good, he could get four figures for them, five figures if the photos made public some of the private life of a celebrity.

After the tape-measure home run, the paparazzi descended on Compleet like fleas on an alley dog. Everywhere the bear and Spitz went, the photographers followed—ten or twelve of them, sometimes more. When the two went for a walk, they followed a few steps behind, pleading for a picture or two. On one occasion, Spitz knocked two of them out and destroyed their cameras. Hauled into court, he had to pay a fine and replace the cameras. One time on the El, the photo jocks circled Compleet and begged him to pick a fight with a passenger. The bear, of course, declined. Spitz broke through the circle, picked one guy up and threw him the length of the car, and spit tobacco juice at the rest. They backed off. Hauled into court again, Spitz argued that the paparazzi were harassing the bear. They were upsetting both of them and affecting their play in the field and at bat. This time the judge sided with Spitz, lectured the paparazzi, and dismissed the charges.

The C Meeting House Restaurant was a favorite haunt of the bear and Spitz. Its walls were plastered with Chum memorabilia, the food was extra tasty and priced right, the atmosphere was friendly, and the talk was always upbeat. At noon one day, the two were having lunch. A photographer approached their table and tried to coax Compleet to eat off the floor or hold a glass of beer and pretend to drink. Spitz was steaming, but he didn't want to get into any more trouble with the law. He went outside, hailed a cop, and had the paparazzo arrested for harassment.

The next day, Compleet and Spitz hired a boat to take them out on the river. Sure enough, five paparazzi followed them in a larger boat and, trying to get some close-ups with their camcorders, rammed the smaller boat. Spitz was knocked into the water and shouted to the paparazzi with his mouth half full of river water. One of the photographers got a good shot; the next day, Spitz saw his picture in the *Riverside Reader*. The headline read, "This Chum Says, 'Come on in, the Water's Fine!'"

Then, all of a sudden, the paparazzi stopped following the two, and neither of them could figure it out. "They might think we're gonna bring a law suit against them," suggested Spitz, "and are lyin' low for a while."

In truth, the paparazzi had called a meeting to plan how to separate the bear and Spitz. "It's that pesky sidekick who's always around the bear," fumed a paparazzo. "The guy with the mean right, the one that spits tobacco juice!"

"You should know about the juice, Stunkie," said another. "You got it in the face that time on the El!"

"The two stick together like Abbott and Costello,"[10] said a third. "I mean, they're always in lockstep."

"I have an idea," said another. "Listen, come closer."

The others gathered round, listened, nodded, and smiled.

The Ruse

Spitz and Compleet had a day game, so their free time was limited to the morning. They decided to go running as soon as the sun came up and hoped they could evade the paparazzi. When they left the hotel, only three paparazzi saw them. They started to trot, and then Spitz let out a groan. "Oh no! I left my wallet back in the room. You go ahead, kid, and I'll catch up."

He turned around and headed back; Compleet kept going. The three paparazzi immediately sized up the situation. "It's our lucky day!" said Stunkie. "The big guy's not with the bear. Quick! Get a cab over here."

A paparazzo hailed a cab, got inside, and instructed the driver to pick up the other two confederates and catch up with Compleet. On the way, the cabbie picked up three more paparazzi, then stepped on the gas, and soon pulled up beside the bear.

"Hey, Bear," said Stunkie. "Get in. Your friend told us to take you to this place in Troefield near the river. He said he'd meet you there, and then you and him would jog back to the hotel."

Compleet stopped running. It didn't sound right. The two seldom jogged on the other side of the river and never took a taxi when they ran. *Then again*, he thought, *if Spitz said I should go by taxi, he must have had a reason.*

He squeezed into the cab, stepping on toes and bumping into arms and legs and expensive photo equipment. One paparazzo was up front, and five paparazzi and the bear were in the back, leaning all over one another and trying to get comfortable, which proved impossible.

Stunkie directed the cabbie to a bar and grill in a rundown section on the west side in Troefield. It was still very early in the morning, and the restaurant was dark. A "Closed" sign hung in the door window. Near the door was a large picture window, in the middle of which were the words, all in caps: CASEY'S BAR & GRILL. Some of the letters were worn and hard to read. Stunkie saw someone on the second floor standing at an open window. "Hey!" Stunkie shouted, taking a hundred-dollar bill out of his wallet and waving it. "Open up now and this hundred is yours. We got Compleet here, you know, the Chum center fielder! You might get your picture in the *Troefield Times & Telegraph*."

Compleet got agitated and shook his head back and forth furiously. Stunkie put his hand on the bear's shoulder. "It's okay, Bear. I just said that to get him down here. We're gonna wait in the restaurant until your friend gets here. Then you're free to leave. No pictures? Then we won't take pictures."

Compleet calmed down, although he wasn't sure the paparazzo was telling him the truth. Outside the entrance, the six paparazzi and the bear waited and waited.

Finally, a bald, heavyset man who needed a shave unlocked the front door, turned on the lights, and removed the "Closed" sign. Stunkie slipped him the hundred when Compleet was looking for a place to stand or lean against. Getting out a slip of paper and a pencil, Stunkie scribbled down an address and pushed the paper into the hand of a paparazzo standing by the door. Stunkie whispered, "Go to the address on the paper—it's only a couple blocks from here—and get hold of Matti. Got the name? M-a-t-t-i? Tell her she's wanted at Casey's. There's money in it for her, but only if she can get here pronto. Got that?"

The paparazzo nodded and went outside. Stunkie called to the bartender, "Hey, how about something for my friend here?" He turned to Compleet who was standing near the far end of the bar. "Bear, what'll you have? Soda, juice, water? Anything you want."

Compleet shook his head from side to side. He was very thirsty, but he didn't want a drink from any of these people. They weren't his friends; he wanted Spitz here now! He looked toward the door.

Stunkie saw him staring at the entrance, worry and anxiety written on his face. "He's comin', Bear," said Stunkie, trying to sound cheerful. "I promise, and Stunkie always keeps his promises. Your friend probably had trouble gettin' a cab. Yeah, that's it." He asked the bartender for a bottle of Coca-Cola. "Here, Bear, have a coke. And when you finish it, your friend will open the front door and say hello. In no time you and him will be outta here."

Stunkie pushed the bottle of coke down the bar, even though he knew the bear couldn't drink from a bottle. "This won't do," he said, pretending to be surprised. He got a deep dish from the bartender, retrieved the coke, and, when Compleet wasn't looking, poured the coke and half the contents of a small packet into the dish. He told the bear to drink up.

Compleet wanted to leave. The air was getting stale, and oh, how he wanted Spitz to walk through that front door! *Maybe*, he thought, *if I drink the coke it will happen like he says, and Spitz will open the door.*

Dear reader, how many times have you believed something you knew deep down was wrong, but you went on believing it simply because you wanted to? Well, the bear reasoned just that way. So he took a drink. It didn't taste like coke, but he kept on drinking. He began to feel dizzy and weak in the legs and got down on the floor and rolled over.

"Now that ain't very friendly," said Stunkie. "And lookie here who's coming through the door. It's someone who wants very much to meet you." Compleet looked up, hoping to see Spitz. Instead he saw an ill-defined outline of a woman. Her face had a carnival look with its heavy rouge and painted lips. Her dark brown hair was streaked and frizzy, as if brushed with little care. It was Matti Gimcrack, who had been in bed when she got the message from Stunkie's gofer and had hurriedly dressed and smeared on makeup. Beneath the heavy makeup was a face with good lines. It was evident that a few years back she had been quite attractive. She was short, about five feet two, and too thin for her height. She was in high heels to give the impression she was taller. She had a soft, quizzical look.

"What's up, Stunkie? It better be good. I like to stay in bed this early."

"Babe, this is good; this here is Compleet, the champ of the Chum. I thought we'd get a few pictures. There's a hundred in it for you if you smile pretty."

"Sure, why not. But ... I gotta lie on the floor?"

"No, no." Stunkie and two of the paparazzi somehow got the bear into a chair and pulled it close to the bar. The two kept Compleet from falling over, and Stunkie got Matti to sit on a stool next to Compleet.

"Get up close to the bear, Matti," said Stunkie.

"Do I have to? I don't like bears!"

"He won't bite; he's almost out. And smile, babe, smile! Act like you're having a good time."

"With a bear? You gotta be kiddin'!"

Through all this, Compleet's mind was in a fog, and his body seemed detached. He couldn't concentrate and could hardly keep his eyes open. He felt like throwing up, and he had trouble breathing.

The paparazzi got their photo gear ready. "Smile, everybody," said Stunkie. "Smile and think of money and driving a sporty, fire-engine-red Aston Martin loaded with extras up and down River Boulevard."

The flashbulbs went off and blinded Compleet for a few seconds. *What's going on?* he thought. *Where am I? Has the game started?* He didn't know the answer to any of the questions. He looked at a shadow in front of him. Was it Spitz? The shadow moved away.

"It ain't right somehow," said Stunkie, thinking out loud. "We need more action." He faced the bartender and said, "Get some dames here, and I'll give you a fifty for each one."

The big bartender didn't need any urging. "This guy's a real money machine," he said to himself. In no time at all, he was making a phone call. While he was waiting for someone to answer, he said to Stunkie, "I know three gals who room together five or six doors down the street. They like to waitress when they can get work. I'm sure they'll come if..."

He interrupted himself and talked into the phone. "Who's

this, Dolly?…Hey, we want to take pictures here at Casey's with some gals in it to add interest. You and Debbie and Lolly come over quick, and you each get cash and a free breakfast. Okay?…Try not to take too long."

When the women showed up, sleepy-eyed but smiling, Stunkie told them to form a line in the middle of the room. "You too, Matti. I want you gals to high kick to music to give the scene some sparkle, like we was all havin' a jolly time."

"C'mon, I ain't no Rockette," replied Matti.

"Rockette—that's what I mean," said Stunkie. "Like them dolls in Radio City, the ones that get in a long line."

"How does he dream up this stuff?" asked Matti under her breath. She put her arm around Dolly Dampling's waist, and Dolly did the same with Debbie Drumsticke, who did the same with Lolly Lental.

"So where's the music? We gotta make up our own?" asked Debbie.

"Naw," said Stunkie, "hold on a minute." He walked over to a jukebox that looked like it had seen better days, put some quarters in it, and soon loud music with a fast beat filled the room.

Stunkie turned Compleet's chair so the bear was facing the four women. He raised Compleet's head. "Look up at the dames; they're real pretty, and they're dancing just for you. Can you smile, Bear? Uh, I guess not. Just try to look happy."

At first the four women looked silly on the dance floor. They couldn't coordinate their kicks and hold on to one another at the same time. "Those girls in Radio City make it look so easy," said Lolly, breathing heavily. "How do they do it?"

Dolly looked at herself in the big mirror behind the bar and started to laugh. She looked awkward and thought it was funny. That broke the ice! All four laughed, relaxed, and started to look like…well, not Rockettes, but passable line dancers.

"Get your shots, boys," said Stunkie. "They're smilin'." Compleet was slumped in his chair with glazed eyes and a blank expression. His head swayed from side to side.

The flashbulbs popped. Some paparazzi stood on the bar

to get a bird's view of the bear. Some concentrated on the four women in the middle of the room doing their high kicks and laughing all the while. Some shot into the big mirror.

When the paparazzi thought they had enough pictures from every angle, they quickly scurried to the door, hoping they could sell their best pictures before too many hours had passed. Stunkie was the last to leave.

As he walked toward the door, Matti stepped in front of him and asked, "Hey, big man, where's my dough?"

Stunkie pulled a fifty out of his pocket and pressed it into her hand. She stepped back, put her hands on her hips, and said, "I'm smilin' pretty, and I don't see no hundred. You're short!"

Stunkie slowly took out his wallet, got a fifty, and held it up in front of her. "So take me to the cleaners!" he said.

Matti took the bill out of his hand and said, "Right! And how much you gonna get for me posin' near that smelly creature? A thousand bucks, I bet!"

"More than that, babe," said Stunkie, laughing as he went out the door.

A Muddled Picture

When Spitz retrieved his wallet and left the hotel, he headed for the boulevard. He figured he would soon get a glimpse of the bear. But he saw few people and no bear. "The kid must be sprintin'," he said to himself. After about ten minutes of fast jogging, he realized something was not right. "He'd never get that far ahead of me."

Spitz asked two street cleaners and four early-morning walkers if they had seen a bear jogging. None had, and Spitz decided it best to return to the hotel and wait. When no bear showed up after a half hour, he got worried and called the police. When the officer on duty heard that the missing bear was the Chum star center fielder, he put out an APB.[11] "He was last seen jogging near the Hill Fire Station, heading east."

About an hour later, two Troefield police spotted the bear lying near the curb outside Casey's Bar & Grill. The bear looked dazed; his eyes were glassy. He gave a deep, pitiful moan. The two policemen got out of their car, put Compleet in the back seat, and went into Casey's for questioning.

Everyone inside seemed surprised when told a bear had been outside the restaurant. "Are you sure it's a bear?" Matti asked playfully of one of the officers. "Need new glasses? We may have some rough ones livin' this end of town, but, scout's honor, none of 'em look like they come from the jungle!"

"Somebody here is not telling the truth," replied the officer. No one would say anything further, so the two policemen took down everyone's name, address, phone number, and driver's license and left.

They turned the bear over to their Cuspin counterparts, who then turned Compleet over to Spitz in the lobby of the Three C's Hotel. The police told him what they had learned, which wasn't much. With the help of a bellhop, Spitz got the bear up to the room and onto a bed and called Frogertee at Tailors. He told him to take the bear out of the lineup for the afternoon game. "He's got some kind of virus, I think. The doc ain't sure. He has a fever of 105, and he's been throwin' up every fifteen minutes. He can't even stand up." Only the last sentence was true.

Before Spitz left for pregame warmup, he asked Helen Achts to look in on the bear every half hour or so. Helen was one of the desk clerks and told Spitz she'd be happy to help out. And if she were busy at the desk, she would send a bellhop to the room. A woman in her midthirties, attractive, small-boned, blonde, she was always cheerful, courteous, and helpful to the guests and residents at the hotel. She and Spitz had become good friends and enjoyed short talks about baseball. She was a great fan of the Chum, read everything in the city papers about Compleet and the other stars on the team (Spitz was rarely mentioned), and often went to games at Tailors. She usually sat in the bleachers near the waterfall. When she was on duty in the lobby, she always had her cat Mai Tai with her. Most often the cat was dozing in a small basket on the floor at one end of the desk. Strangely, the cat took a liking to Compleet and would rub up against one of the bear's legs whenever Spitz and the bear stopped at the desk.

When Spitz got to the clubhouse at Tailors, some of the Chum players were reading a special edition of the *Troefield Times & Telegraph*. It was all about Compleet, together with pictures of him and the four women. Santa handed the paper to Spitz, who stared at the pictures and the headline, which read, "Compleet Paints the Town." Spitz skimmed the article, which was filled with clichés, generalities, and supposings. He looked again at the pictures and said, "What a mess!" then slumped down on the bench in front of his locker.

Payday hurried up to him and said, "Frog wants to see you right now, and he's steaming! Better have a good story."

Spitz walked into Frog's office and said, "The paper... I can't tell you what happened. I don't think the kid knows either."

Players had lied to Frog before, and he was certain Spitz was lying now. He glared at him, pounded his desk, and threw a notebook on the floor. "What kind of an organization do you think we're runnin' around here? First you tell me he's got a high fever and now this... this scandal plastered all over the papers!"

Spitz started to say something, but Frog pointed his finger at him and shouted, "Don't you dare say a word! You listen to me and listen good! In the papers it looks like your friend is drunk. And what are those women in front of him doin'? Dancin' the cancan?"

Frog was so worked up he had to stop and take a few deep breaths and wipe the sweat from his forehead. Getting control of his emotions, he said, almost in a whisper, "Now, I want you to sit down at this desk and write out everything you saw and anything else you know." His voice rose again. "It better be more than good! And don't hold anything back!"

He shoved some sheets of paper in Spitz's face and threw a pen on the desk. "And another thing; you ain't playin' today! I don't care if we're in the sixteenth inning and nobody's left to sub but you. I'll forfeit first!" With that remark he stormed out of the office and slammed the door.

Spitz wrote down all he knew, but it filled only half a page.

He put the paper in the center of Frog's desk and quickly left the office. He didn't want to run into the general manager or another bigwig who might stop to chew him out. He walked past a half dozen players who were staring at him. "What's with the bear? Is it true?" asked P.U. Spitz shrugged but said nothing and returned to the hotel.

In the lobby he met Helen, who told him the bear was awake but groggy. "Have you seen the papers?" she asked and pointed to newspapers strung out on one corner of the front desk. "It appears like all the Cuspin papers are going after your friend."

Spitz shuffled through the papers with an eye for pictures and headlines. In the *Gazette Guide* the headline read, "What Would Momma Bear Say?" In the *Riverside Reader*, the headline, which was beneath a half-page photo, read, "Bear Relaxes Between Games." The *Illustrious Illustrator* decided to use some alliteration: "Big Bad Bear Enjoys Himself on Troefield's West Side."

"They're tryin' to crucify the kid!" moaned Spitz. "Somethin's rotten! I gotta get to the bottom of this."

He tucked the three papers under his arm and went up to his room. The bear was lying on the floor and groaning. "Kid, are we in trouble! Frog caught me in a big lie tryin' to cover for you. I probably feel as bad as you do. Wanna tell me what happened?"

With difficulty, Compleet raised his head. Every part of his body ached. His face was drawn. Slowly he signed to Spitz, *I don't remember it all. I kind of remember Matti, but she was more like a shadow than a real person. And Stunkie, and that's about all.*

"Wait, you lost me. Who are Stunkie and Matti? And how did you wind up outside a bar and grill in Troefield?"

I got in a cab with guys with big cameras, and Stunkie, he was the one giving orders, told the cabbie to go to Casey's Bar and Grill in Troefield.

"But why did you get in a cab with people you didn't know? Couldn't you tell it was a hoax?"

Stunkie said you told him you would meet me at Casey's, and then we'd jog back to the hotel. It didn't seem like anything you'd say, but, well, I got in the cab anyway.

"I never talked to no Stunkie."

I'm not surprised. I wasn't thinking right. I made a mess of everything!

"It's okay, kid," said Spitz in a quiet voice. He ran his hand over the top of the bear's head. "It's my fault. I should never have left you alone!"

The bear continued, *Inside, I must have passed out. That was after I drank a coke from a dish. Stunkie said you'd walk through the door if I took a drink. So I did. It didn't taste like coke. It was bitter but I drank it. I don't remember anything else until I woke up here on the bed, and Helen was wiping my face with a cold cloth and asking me how I felt.*

Spitz showed the front page of the *Riverside Reader* to the bear. "This is why we're in big trouble! You recognize any of the women?"

This one, signed Compleet, pointing to one of the four. *I think it's Matti but I'm not sure. I don't know the other three.* The bear turned away from Spitz and faced the wall. He started to groan again.

Not only did Spitz feel sorry for his friend, he felt angry. "Don't worry, kid, I'll find them sons of Satan if I have to knock on every door in Troefield and Cuspin!"

That evening, Spitz and Compleet stayed in their room and watched the coverage of the bear's escapade on TV. Spitz didn't dare leave the bear, who was sick in the stomach and threw up every hour or so. The bear was depressed. Spitz kept telling him, "You get well, kid, and I'll take care of business in the morning."

Separating Fact
from Fiction

"Stunkie and Matti, Stunkie and Matti," Spitz kept repeating to himself. He was sitting in a police car on the way to the west side of Troefield. He had called the Troefield police and said he had a lead on the bear story. The same officers who had found the bear had volunteered to take him to Casey's.

Inside were four couples eating breakfast. The bartender was washing glasses, but the bar was closed. One of the policemen said to the bartender, "There's more to the story of the bear than what got in the papers. What do you know about Matti and Stunkie?"

The bartender looked up, nodded, and said, "Naw, the names don't ring a bell."

"Well, you better know something! We'll find out one way or another. You withhold evidence and you'll find yourself before a judge!"

The bartender was silent for a spell. He put down a glass and said, "Come to think of it, there was a Stunkie in here. He was one of them guys, what are they called? Papa-paparootsi? They were all shootin' pictures."

"Then he's a photographer?"

"Yeah, that's it."

"How did the bear get drunk? You can't serve animals."

"Hey, who said the bear was drunk? I didn't see anyone outta line."

"And the female? The one called Matti?"

"Matti, naw, I don't know no dame called Matti."

"You recognize the other females in the pictures?"

"Naw."

The bartender started to wash glasses again.

Since the police could get no other information, they walked toward the door. Spitz followed. One of the officers turned around and said, "We'll be back, so stay in the area."

S pitz got a bus on the West Side back to the hotel. He needed time to think. He was certain the bartender knew more than he had told the officer.

Helen was on duty at the front desk and told Spitz that Compleet was still under the weather, but at least he wasn't throwing up. "A Mr. Boslerts called shortly after you left. He said he would call back."

As Spitz opened the door to the room, the phone rang. It was John Boslerts. He wanted to know how Compleet was doing, and he wanted to know if the story in the papers was true. Spitz said the bear was a lot better than yesterday and swore the story wasn't true but said he couldn't prove it yet. "Well, you better find out something right soon. The commissioner is on our neck and has threatened to suspend Compleet for thirty days." Spitz told Boslerts he would call him if he learned anything new.

Second Time Around

Spitz knew he had to go back to the West Side again. He might get lucky and learn something that would help his friend. Up early the next morning, he had a hurried breakfast. The bear was still asleep. Spitz asked Helen to make sure someone checked on the kid periodically, and then he hailed a cab.

When he walked into Casey's, he wasted little time in getting the bartender aside. "My name's Spitz McOystre. I play ball with the bear at Tailors Station. I was here yesterday with the two cops. I know things didn't happen the way the papers wrote it; the kid's clean. He'd never take a drink. Help me, and I give my word I won't tell a soul you told me anythin'. And this is for you." Spitz held a hundred dollar bill in his hand. Playing for the Chum, even as a reserve, he had money enough to hand out a hundred on the spot.

The bartender kept looking at Spitz, but for a long while he said nothing. Then he took the hundred and said, "I told about Stunkie because he was actin' high and mighty, and I don't like those kind. He comes in here now and then, but he ain't one of us; he ain't from the West Side."

The bartender looked around the room, then he led Spitz to a corner where there were no customers. He spoke in whispers. "Matti, sure I know her. She's one of them office temps. You know, temporaries that fill in for someone who's sick or on vacation. She comes in here regular when she ain't workin'. Matti's a good dame. You might get her to tell you what happened."

The bartender extended his hand to Spitz. "Name's Wilmont, but my friends call me Willie." The two shook hands. Willie put a hand on Spitz's shoulder and turned him toward the booths against the wall opposite the bar. "See the two women talkin'? One's Matti, the other's Dolly. Tell Dolly I'd like to ask her somethin'. You and Matti need to be alone."

Spitz walked over to the booth. He recognized the two women from the photos in the papers. He introduced himself and told Dolly that Willie wanted to see her.

When she had left, Matti gave Spitz a friendly look and said, "Sit down. What's up, hon? Want a piece of my chicken tenders? Casey's are the best on the West Side. It's his seasoning makes it special."

"No thanks. I wanted to talk to you about the bear."

"Oh, that creature! You his trainer or somethin'?"

"Naw, we play baseball together at Tailors Station."

"Well, I'm a Trout fan myself. They say all the fancy, moneyed dudes go to Tailors. The hard-workin' good guys come to the West Side to watch the Trout."

"Ma'am, I need your help. If the truth don't come out about what happened here, the bear's gonna be suspended. You wouldn't want that to happen, would you?"

"What do I care what happens to a bear. I don't speak up for animals. I got enough trouble keepin' myself above water."

"I don't believe that. Willie said some nice things about you. He said you were a good dame."

"Hah! He can be a charmer, he can!"

Matti looked at Spitz a long time; then she asked, "So what's in it for me if I talk?"

"I can't give you nothin' now. People would find out, and they'd say you spoke up for the bear on account of the money. But I promise I'll help you later with spendin' money if you need any."

"Well, well, all that but nothin' up front. It sounds phony to me. I look after myself. I don't expect flowers and jewels."

"I'll fill your arms with flowers if you'll help me. You and me know the bear didn't take a drink or want to be around women. It's a frame. And I think you know who's to blame—Stunkie."

"Stunkie? Well, if you know Stunkie, go talk to him. He's a big shot, thinks he is anyway!"

"Somehow he don't seem like the kind would own up to the truth."

"Look, hon," said Matti, "I ain't got nothin' against you. But Stunkie would beat my brains out if I spilled."

"I promise he won't. If he lays a hand on you, I'll beat him raw."

Matti grinned, "I think you would!" She sat quiet for a time, then she said, "No, it's too risky. Why should I stick out my neck for a bear? He couldn't even say thank you."

"No. But he'd give you a big hug, and he'd be eternally grateful."

"That's just what I need, a bear hug! No, and I mean no! That's final!"

"Please, ma'am."

Matti cut off a piece of chicken tenders and looked at Dolly and Willie at the bar. She gulped down her food; then she spoke in a loud voice, "The conference is over. Come back, Dolly."

Spitz returned to the hotel and immediately went up to the room. Compleet was feeling much better and was eating a dish of berries and pine nuts that Helen had got from the kitchen.

"I see Helen's been here."

Yeah, she's a good friend, Spitz.

"Well, we're gonna need all the friends we can get. I come from Casey's and talked to Matti, but she won't budge. I don't know if I should try to find Stunkie."

He can't be trusted. He'd just lie to you.

"Then we have no case."

Compleet was downcast. *I don't care about me. But I didn't want Clint and Ginny and Clara and Ronny to think the story is true. Spitz, I really miss them.*

"Me too, kid."

A Turn of Mind and Heart

After Spitz had left Casey's, Matti talked to Dolly awhile and then went into the street. She walked to no place in particular; she just wanted to give herself some time to think. She pictured Spitz. *Guy's got a rough face, a good face, strong and dependable. I like that. I could go for that man.*

She shifted her thoughts to Compleet. *The bear! How did a bear get on the Chum team? He should be dancin' around in the circus or layin' on a rock in the zoo. Stunkie made mincemeat of him. Stunkie... blaaaah! How repulsive!*

She thought again of Spitz. *That face! I wanna dream about that guy! Wonder if he's got a girl. He's right; the bear done nothin' wrong. That slippery Stunkie! Wish I'd never known him.* She walked on and on, not thinking much anymore, just listening to traffic, the honking and the engine noises, and the *tap tap* made by the shoes of pedestrians.

When Matti woke up the next morning, she lay in bed the longest time. She thought about her conversation with Spitz. She compared him to some of the men she had met over the years. She said to herself, "Guy's got looks could tame any gal!" She thought of Stunkie. *What a no-good, arrogant weasel! Whoever made room for him on this good earth?* She thought of Compleet. *The bear got a raw deal. The worst is he can't even talk and tell what happened and point a finger. He should go back to the jungle and be with his own kind.*

Whether it was the wrong done to the bear that influenced Matti or the good effect Spitz had on her or her great dislike of Stunkie, who can tell? Suddenly, she sat up in bed and said out loud, "I'll do it, and if I get in trouble, that's okay too."

She dressed quickly, drank a cup of coffee, ate a bagel, and left her flat. She took a bus going east, got off in the business district, and walked to the building that housed the *Troefield Times & Telegraph*. Inside at the front desk, she said to a clerk, "I got a story to tell, and it's big, so get someone out here before I change my mind."

The clerk gave her a friendly look and asked, "What is the story about?"

"It's about the bear. It was a frame, and I was there right in the middle."

The clerk knew immediately what she was talking about; all Troefield and Cuspin were talking about the *scandale celebre*.[12] On second look, the clerk recognized her from her pictures with the bear. "Wait here and don't move! I'll get someone to talk to you."

She was ushered into a small room and joined by two reporters, a photographer, and an editor. She talked into a recorder and was interrupted every now and then to clarify or to elaborate. When she was done, the photographer took her picture—after she had put on new makeup and fixed her hair. The editor shook her hand and told her she had courage and had done the right thing. He went over to his desk, opened a drawer, pulled out an envelope, and took out three one-hundred-dollar bills and gave them to her.

She looked at the bills and smiled. "Thanks, hon, this will help. It's sometimes hard goin' when a girl's on her own."

Within an hour, a special edition of the *Troefield Times & Telegraph* was on the streets.

Baseball and Lovers

Spitz first heard the good news from Helen. She could have called the room, but she wanted to spread the glad tidings in person. Pounding on the door, she shouted, "Spitz, open up. Hurry, I got something very important to show you!" Spitz was lying in bed watching TV, and Compleet was curled up on a rug, half asleep.

"Wait," yelled Spitz, as he tumbled out of bed, tucked in his shirt, and smoothed his hair. When he opened the door, Helen shoved a newspaper in his face.

"Look!" she said. "The pictures were a fake! A guy called Stunkie Fonkules set up the whole thing! One of the four women confessed!"

Spitz looked at the banner headline: "Rockette Clears Bear, Says Photos Were Rigged!" He skimmed the lead article, and then he read part of it to Compleet. All three were ready to burst. They formed a small circle; Spitz shouted, "Whoopee!" Helen sang out, "I say amen!" and Compleet grunted in agreement.

It wasn't long before the news covered the city of Cuspin Heights. John Boslerts phoned to tell Spitz he was glad for the bear. He asked if he knew why Matti had decided to talk. Spitz said he wasn't sure; maybe she felt guilty knowing the bear was framed.

Frog was apologetic when he called. "I ... I always knew the bear was, uh, was innocent. But, well, you know a manager's got to be careful. I can't have wild headlines about my players embarrassin' the club." Spitz didn't think Frog meant all that he said, but the manager couldn't dampen his sunny spirit. Compleet was in the clear!

When Fred Miltones phoned, he said he would make sure

Stunkie and his cohorts were arrested, put before a judge, and reprimanded and fined. "Suit up for tonight's game. All's forgiven. It was just one big messy business. I read what you wrote for Frogertee. I know this unfortunate series of events occurred only because you had to go back for your wallet."

"Yes, sir, Mr. Miltones, and it won't happen again. I won't never let the kid out of my sight. Or if I can't be by his side, I'll get someone I can trust to sub for me."

"I'm sure I can count on that. One final comment: I just got off the phone with Dwight Hofenpfeiffer. Seems he had written a letter to Compleet, telling him of his thirty-day suspension. He was about to mail it when he heard the breaking news on the radio. He said the first thing he did was tear up the letter."

"I'm glad he did. I'll tell the kid all you said. We'll be at the ball park early; you can bank on it."

Later, before the two left the hotel to go to Tailors, they got a call from the Bruedocks. Ronny was on the line and told Spitz he was glad Compleet was in the clear. "I was right. I told you in our earlier conversation one of the women might come forward. I know the bear, and I knew in my heart he would never act like that. On and off the field he has always set a good example for his fans.... Tell Compleet to give me a grunt." Ronny heard a soft grunt in the background and laughed.

Ronny put his mom on the phone. "Hi, Spitz. Tell Compleet I said hi. He'll have to learn how to hold a phone so we can talk to him. Tell the bear I'll send him some more caps. When we watch the games on TV, I'm so pleased to see Compleet wearing one of my caps. Both of you take care. Here's Ma."

"Hello. The woman who spoke up was a good person. I'll send more knitted sweaters. I have four done and will knit a few more. Stay healthy, you two. We love getting your phone calls. And keep writing letters, Spitz. We always enjoy reading them. Here's Clint."

"Spitz, how are you and Compleet? The neighbors keep telling me how happy they are that the bear has become the star player on the Chum. One of them said jokingly I should be an animal trainer! Of course it was our grandson who taught Compleet. Keep well and God bless. Here's Ronny again."

"If the team gets in the Bronze Series—and I know they will— maybe some of us will drive up to Cuspin for a game. Kristy would like to see a Big Ball game. She's never seen one. More on that later. Love to all. Bye."

Return to Baseball

The Chum were playing the Gallsun Goldeye, a team that was in first place in the Saltwater Division. The players greeted Spitz and Compleet when they entered the clubhouse; the talk was upbeat and warm. The team was as glad as management that the so-called *scandale celebre* was over. It had been a distraction, and, more importantly, it had kept Compleet's bat out of the lineup. When the team came onto the field for warm-up, there was scattered talk in the stands from the early arrivals, and almost all of it favored the bear.

Spitz was hardly ever in the starting lineup. When he did make an appearance, it was usually in the late innings to rest a player or add good defense. This night he started at third because Frog wanted to make amends. He had been hard on Spitz in his office and didn't want him to bear a grudge. Frog knew a player with a chip on his shoulder often performed badly and could spread discontent. He didn't know that Spitz had long since forgotten the incident. He thought Frog had a right to be mad; he had lied in his effort to protect the bear.

When the team trotted out of the dugout in the top of the first, the bear and Spitz were the last two players onto the field. A great cheer greeted them; the fans were all standing. Some held homemade signs high above their heads and waved them back and forth, competing for attention. One read, "The truth triumphs! Back to business, we got a pennant to win!" Another said, "We knew you were innocent, Compleet-ly!" A third read, "We care, we care! We need the bear!" Spitz read some of the signs to the bear before they took up their positions. Compleet felt reassured—the fans were behind him, and he was together again with the team.

The game was close. In the bottom of the eighth, Compleet led off with a single to center, but Jimbo popped up to the third baseman, and P.U. struck out. The bear was still on first. Spitz came to the plate and beat out a bunt for a single when the third baseman slipped while reaching for the ball. The next batter was Drum Drum. On the third pitch, he ripped a single to right center, and Compleet scored with a hard roll into home. He hit the catcher so hard the ball popped out of his mitt. The Chum won 3–2.

It was almost a must win for Cuspin. The team had lost ground to the second-place Batfish during Spitz and Compleet's absence. The win got the players back on track. The fans felt good about the team again. God was in his heaven; all was right in the world of baseball.

During the next three weeks, the club played with confidence and came away with one victory after another. They won or tied every series, including a sweep of the Flagfish in Fulerbay, and held a comfortable lead over the Batfish and the third place Flounder. Only a big letdown would keep the team out of the playoffs.

A Threesome

Spitz and the bear crossed the Muddy Muck to the west side of Troefield. In a florist shop, Spitz bought two large bouquets, and in Casey's Bar and Grill Willie gave him Matti's address. When Matti answered the knock on the door, she was amazed to see the two.

"What's wrong? Is the bear in trouble again?"

"No," said Spitz. "Here, take these," and he handed her the bouquets. "We wanted to thank you for clearin' the kid's name."

Compleet signed, *Without your help I would have missed a month of baseball. I can't thank you enough.* Spitz translated.

"It wasn't much. I help bears all the time." She laughed.

She invited them into her flat. It was small and clean, but the slipcovers were faded and the furniture looked secondhand. The living room had only one window that looked out on an airshaft.

"As you see, this place ain't much, but it does me service."

"Remember, I told you if you need money I'll help out."

"I'm all right, at least now. I haven't worked in two weeks, but sometimes I have a job that lasts a month or more. I'm an office temporary."

"Yes, Willie told me."

Matti and Spitz talked for a while, and at times Compleet interrupted to comment. On Spitz's suggestion, the three went for a walk along the river, and Spitz treated the two to a meal at a restaurant near the Trout stadium.

Honey B.

It had been a long season, and the aches and pains and tension were a constant bother. Between games the players tried to relax as best they could. Compleet's favorite place to unbend was at Backlore Haven Zoo, which was a short distance from the museum complex.

The bear and Spitz had discovered the zoo during an early sightseeing jaunt. As a large mammal, Compleet felt a special closeness to the big, more complex animals at Backlore. It bothered him that he was on the outside of the screens, bars, moats, and fences, free to move about and then leave the zoo.

He thought a lot about whether zoos were good or bad for the animals, big and small. His feelings were mixed. True, the zoos kept the animals safe and healthy, but the price was high. Their freedom was forfeited. The restriction of animals to a particular space was sometimes permanent. Often the space was small. If they were moved, most often it was to a similar space. Only when Compleet saw animals in some of the wide enclosures at Backlore did he believe they felt some degree of freedom. Most troubling were the times he saw the listless faces, or when he saw animals pacing back and forth, sometimes for hours. He noticed the big cats especially were impatient and high-strung, as if they would give anything to bound across open grass or join in the chase or leap from big branch to big branch.

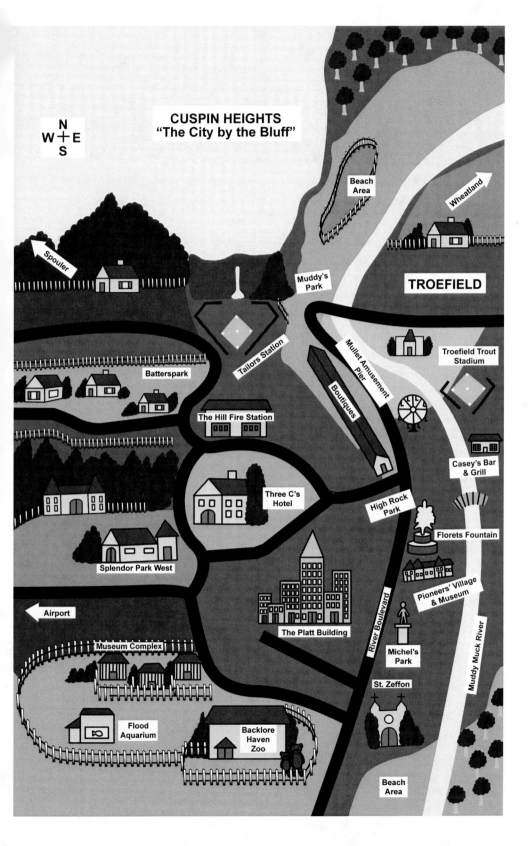

If only I had the money, he signed to Spitz one afternoon, *to put these animals in a great expanse so they would feel there was no boundary. Of course, it would be just a feeling, not a fact. There would have to be fences or other barriers. All freedom has limits. But to allow animals to see different landscapes continually and never have to look through bars! That would be my dream.*

"Play for the Chum a few more years, kid, and maybe you can. With your salary and other income you might be able to buy out the whole zoo population at Backlore!"

There was a particular reason Compleet liked to frequent Backlore Haven Zoo. That reason was a young bear Compleet was attracted to the first time he saw her. She was small, with a good shape, a pretty coat of hair, dark brown with some black, and the most appealing face. But Compleet figured out right away she didn't understand what Spitz or any other human was saying. To teach her signing was out of the question; she was just an ordinary bear. But Compleet observed she was gentle, pleasant, athletic, alert, playful, and warmhearted. Those traits mattered a lot to him.

On entering the zoo, the bear always insisted he and Spitz head first to the Island Sanctuary, where the black bears hung out. At first Compleet wasn't sure the female noticed him, but on his third visit the sow[13] ambled over to him, getting as close as she could. She sniffed, drawing in his musky smell, and stared at him. She grunted and shook her head playfully.

He was smitten—those kind, observant, dark eyes, that pretty face, her expression, that figure! He grunted softly and pretended he was nuzzling her. He made a clicking sound with his tongue and sniffed the air.

After that first get-together, Compleet visited the Island Sanctuary as often as his baseball schedule allowed. Each visit brought the two bears closer together. They couldn't rub up against each other or touch noses or walk together, but they could communicate their feelings with their eyes, an expression, and body language. And they could talk bear talk—as a grunt, click, deep purr, or huff—which could mean, depending on the sound and circumstance, "Glad you're here," "I missed you," "Stay longer," "I'm scared."

On one visit to the Island Sanctuary, Compleet signed to Spitz, *About names … I have a name and you have a name and so do other humans. It's a nice custom, and I'd like to give the sow a name. Do you have any ideas?*

Spitz put his hand to his brow and thought for a while. "Let's see. Bear Fect… Bear Beauty… Bea Bear… Luv B… Rare Bear. Any of those names appeal to you?"

They're all nice names, but no, none hits the spot.

"Well, she certainly is a honey of a bear. How about Honey Bear?"

I like that name, but maybe Honey B. is better. Then the B can stand for bear and bee.

"How are you gonna tell Honey B. she has a name?"

I can't. But if you say the name to her often enough, she'll catch on maybe. And you and I will know her name. She knows I love her; that's the important thing.

Planning an Outing

Compleet was always a little upset when he visited Honey B. because the two couldn't get next to each other. Backlore, like other zoos, insisted on an ironclad separation between humans and the larger, unpredictable animals. *There must be a way*, he thought. *Maybe she would enjoy seeing me play at Tailors? I'd see her in the stands during the game. Maybe the two of us and Spitz could go out to eat afterward before we took her back to the zoo.*

He asked Spitz what he thought of the idea. "I don't know, kid; it's a new idea, I'll say that. But there are problems. I mean, it's not a simple thing to take a bear to a Chum game. You can't just walk out of the zoo with her, get into a taxi, go to Tailors, and sit her down in the grandstand. People will notice; people will talk. You gotta get permission from Boslerts and Miltones. You'll have to talk it over with Frog, tell the team what you plan to do, and maybe get the green light from Commissioner Hofenpfeiffer. Of course, whoever runs the zoo will have to agree to it. In short, it will take a heck of a lotta work."

She's worth it, Spitz. You got to help me.

"Sure, kid, you know I'm always on your side. But don't be too disappointed if it don't work out."

So Spitz contacted all the necessary people. Frog didn't like the idea; he thought it would interfere with the bear's concentration. The commissioner thought it might set a bad precedent. The president of Backlore Zoo at first said no; there were too many obstacles to overcome. But he finally relented when assured Honey B. would be watched over by a special security team at the ball park. Boslerts couldn't make up his mind whether it was a good move or not. Miltones was the most enthusiastic. He thought it would be a good photo op, and the event would become part of the storied history of Tailors. At length he convinced the other naysayers.

Spitz took one final precaution. He and Compleet got Helen's attention one morning at the hotel, shortly before Honey B'.s introduction to baseball. Spitz asked if she had heard that the bear's girlfriend would be at Tailors to see him play. She said yes; she had heard on sports radio which game the sow would attend and had made plans to be there. She was anxious to see Compleet's new love.

Miltones had leaked the date to the newspapers in order to boost ticket sales. His ploy worked. This was a love match all Cuspin wanted to know more about. Rumors were widespread. Some thought she was just as smart as Compleet and could understand English and could sign. Some were told she had played softball a while back, had badly injured her knee, and had been sent to Backlore Haven Zoo for rehab. Some swore they had seen two bears all lovey-dovey in High Rock Park. One teen magazine said Compleet would propose to the sow during the seventh inning stretch.

Spitz asked Helen if she would mind sitting next to the sow. "It would make the kid feel better if he knew you were watchin' her. If you have a ticket for the bleachers, I'm sure I can get the front office to change it."

"I'd be happy to sit next to her and help out. But there may be a problem. I like to take Mai Tai with me to the games. I call him my good luck piece. Of course, I have to sneak him past the gate and security, but I've become pretty good at that, you know, wrapped in a light jacket carried under my arm or hidden in a tote among junk."

"Hey, that means Honey B. won't be the only animal in the stands at the game!" Spitz joked, "But we won't tell!"

"Thanks! Mai Tai has taken a liking to Compleet; perhaps he'll also warm up to Honey B."

"I think it will work out," said Spitz.

"I hope so."

Crime and Punishment

H oney B. was nervous from the time she, Compleet, and Spitz left the zoo and got into a cab. This was so new to her, on the outside and in motion! It was a noisy and fast-moving, unsettling world, and there were no corners to hide in! There were no other bears to commiserate with except Compleet. She gave a chuffing sound through her nose every now and then. It was the sound a steam engine makes when it leaves the station: choo-choo-choo-choo. It meant the sow was anxious and stressed out. She pressed against Compleet as hard as she could. He liked that and started to purr. It was a deep, soothing sound that meant there was no need to be alarmed. He would make sure no harm came to her. He grunted and rubbed his face against hers.

Getting out of the taxi at Tailors, they were met by special security. Unfamiliar people in uniform made the sow chuff again. Compleet got in front of her to block out security. Spitz and Compleet waited to enter the clubhouse until Helen showed up. When she did, she saw that the bear was upset and talked softly to her. Mai Tai peeked out from the jacket under Helen's left arm and gave a meow that was quiet and nonthreatening. None of security heard it. "He likes you, Honey B.," said Helen in a reassuring voice.

Helen and the sow had seats in the grandstand in the second row, a little beyond the Chum dugout, near the rolled up tarp. Helen left the bear's seat up so Honey B. could stand in front, and Helen continued to talk to her to try to get her to relax. During batting practice, the bear grunted when she saw Compleet and kept her eyes on him. When he disappeared into the dugout, she got anxious again. When he came onto the field in the top of the first, she quieted down.

In the bottom of the first, Compleet got a double, driving in two runs. A huge, long yell filled the park. Honey B. had never heard so many voices in unison. The volume made her jittery, and she leaned up against Helen and let out a high-pitched moan. The next batter was Jimbo. He doubled to deep left center, and Compleet easily rounded third and crossed the plate. Honey B., still moaning, followed his every step.

Compleet heard her moan and knew she was frightened. In the dugout, he signed to Spitz, *This was a mistake bringing her here, too many people, too much noise. And she doesn't understand the game. What can we do?*

"Not much now, kid. Just keep an eye on her."

Compleet tried to play his position and watch the sow at the same time. In the third inning he let a ball to left center get away from him, and a run scored. In the sixth he dropped a fly but recovered in time to get the runner trying to take an extra base on the miscue.

Then came the bottom of the seventh. The score was five all, and Compleet was at bat with a runner on first and one out. As he ambled to the plate on all fours, he looked over at the sow and noticed two men seated two rows behind the sow and Helen. They were arguing and raising their voices.

The first pitch was a strike. Compleet didn't watch it cross the plate. He was thinking only of his Honey and the mess he had made of the day.

The argument heated up and soon the men were trading punches. Honey B. had been up close against Helen since the first inning. She saw the men fighting, heard their loud talk, and let out chuffs and a long moan. This was a new threat to her safety.

The men began to wrestle, and one of them was knocked over the seat in front of him and landed in the row above the sow. He struggled to his feet and in the process put his hand on the railing in front of him. His hand grazed the bear's back. The sow's ears went back, and her mouth opened wide to show white, sharp teeth. The bear let out a deep, guttural moan that frightened many of the fans near her. It was a cry for help.

Mai Tai stuck his head out from under Helen's jacket and let out a long guttural sound that Siamese cats make when they are very disturbed. It's a sound that seems to come from a voice in another world. It wasn't aimed at Honey B.; it was meant for the man who was frightening the sow.

Compleet had heard the cry for help and could concentrate on nothing else. "Strike two," yelled the umpire as he shot out his arm. The bear turned toward the stands and let the bat fall from his paws, all in one motion. He dropped to all fours, lowered his head, and let out a frightening roar that sounded like it came from a lion. Everyone in the stadium heard it. Like his ancestors for millenniums before him, he was prepared to attack to protect his own. He was the male, and Honey B. was his mate. No one dare harm her; it was part of an unwritten law of the wild. Females were protected by the males; young ones were protected by the moms.

He was a terror to behold with his deep, guttural sounds, hair and fur on end across his back, sharp teeth showing, ears back, mouth full of saliva, and claws extended to dig into flesh. Without thought he charged toward the stands. As he went by the dugout, a figure leaped over the railing and raced after him. It was Spitz! He had been watching the drama build. Afraid events might get out of hand, he had moved to the top of the dugout after strike one. He had jumped over the railing after strike two and in seconds saw the bear streak by him. Spitz knew he had to stop him. He never moved so fast in his life! He was surprised he could still react so quickly. He and the bear got to the first row of the stands at the same time.

Mai Tai was almost as upset as Honey B. He was upset because she was upset. When he saw Compleet reach the stands, he gained courage and decided to help his friend protect the sow. With that unearthly sound, he leaped out of the jacket that hid him from the crowd and jumped at the brawler's face, leaving deep scratches in each cheek and drawing a lot of blood. At the same time, Compleet climbed past Honey B. and reached for the brawler. But Spitz was at his side and put his arms around Compleet's neck and squeezed, temporarily preventing him from jumping on the man's chest. Helen stood up, lunged at Compleet, and grabbed the bear's right front paw and held on for dear life. She was almost swept off her feet by the bear's forward motion.

"No, kid!" shouted Spitz. "Lay a paw on him, and you'll never play another game! Me neither! Let security handle it!"

Special security and police had already pushed past patrons toward the men. With strong arms they prevented the one nearest the sow from moving. "My face! My face!" the young man screamed. "Look what that monster done to my face!" He was holding his cheeks. His hands, as well as his face, were covered with blood. Flashbulbs went off right, left, high up in the stands, on field level, from the bleachers, everywhere! Network cameras caught every moment of the high drama!

The umpires quickly took control of events. The bear was declared out for leaving the box, and he and Spitz were ejected from the game for climbing into the seats. Compleet's teammates had rushed out of the dugout to side with the bear and help establish order. The plate umpire told them to get back in the dugout immediately.

The police handcuffed the two men and all but dragged them out of the ball park while hisses and threats from Chum fans filled their ears. Helen grabbed Mai Tai, hid him in her jacket again, and left the stadium. Compleet and Spitz escorted Honey B. into the team's dugout and through the tunnel and locker room. They met Helen and her cat in the front of the stadium by the statue of the three tailors. Spitz hailed a cab, which took him, Compleet, Helen, Mai Tai, and the sow to the zoo. She was going back to the familiar, back to safety. In the cab the sow was shaking and moaning. Compleet put his head next to hers and grunted softly. He thought, *This was supposed to be fun for both of us. I botched it! It hurts me when I see you sad and afraid. I'll make it up to you, I will.*

As to the play on the field, the fracas so upset the Chum it took them out of the game. The team didn't score after Spitz and

Compleet were ejected. Their opponent, the Horsatonic Herring, scored six runs in the eighth and won the game 11–5.

National News!

The newspapers had a field day. This was national news. Talk about high drama. Talk about the weird and unexpected. Talk about a story that couldn't miss. In their rush to print a sensational story, the newspapers got some of their facts wrong. But their headlines certainly got the attention of readers. Every paper accused Compleet of mauling the brawler.

Of course, dear reader, you and I know the bear didn't harm anyone. Unfortunately for Compleet, the network cameras filmed from angles that left out the cat, almost. The bear and Spitz were right in front of the brawler, and Helen was to one side. Only the small, skinny tail of Mai Tai showed up on one film. It was easy to jump to the conclusion the bear was the culprit. His front paws were only inches from the brawler's face. His claws were extended, hatred written on his face. The brawler's shirt was wet with the bear's saliva.

The fans near the scene had a better view, of course, but afraid of being injured, they scrambled to get away. In the confusion, no fan had time to take a good look at what was going on between the brawler, the sow, and Compleet.

The morning after the melee, Spitz and Compleet went before a judge who set a hearing two days hence. When the two returned to the hotel, reporters and photographers mobbed them in the lobby. They were forced to fight their way to the private stairway they always used. The photographers and reporters tried to follow them up the stairs but were kept back by three policemen who had been assigned duty at the Three C's. Spitz and Compleet stayed in their room the rest of the morning, hoping the hoopla would die down if they kept out of sight.

But this story was too explosive. In the early afternoon, the mayor of Cuspin Heights, with three of his staff and a large police escort, showed up to find out the facts. In his room Spitz told the mayor he thought a cat had scratched the brawler. He was vague about where the cat had come from. "A cat!" exclaimed the mayor. Turning to face the bear, he added, "Thank the stars it wasn't you, Compleet! We need your bat for the playoffs."

A little later Boslerts, Miltones, and the Chum's top lawyer showed up at the hotel. They wanted to talk to Spitz and Compleet and then plan strategy. This hearing was a serious matter. If the bear's case were botched, Compleet would go on trial and probably miss the playoffs. Helen was a key. Would she inform on her cat to save the bear? Would Spitz tell all?

Miltones said, "I have it on good authority Judge Lance McCrewl will preside. He's a tough egg! Does anyone know if he follows baseball?" No one did. "Has anyone seen him at a Chum game?" No one had.

Judge McCrewl, the Decider!

Although it was only a preliminary hearing, the courtroom was packed. Many stood against the back wall and in the side aisles. Reporters from as far away as Japan and South Korea were on hand. Of course Frog, Miltones, and Boslerts were there, and P.U., the player representative. Spitz and the Chum's top lawyer sat at a long table. Compleet stood nearby. The two men—one was Dan Cuff and the other was Marvin Smytes—were at a second long table with their lawyer. The face of Smytes was heavily bandaged. Often he held his hands to his face and let out a long, low moan, as if he were in great pain.

When Judge McCrewl entered and sat down, he looked at Cuff, Smytes, Spitz, and Compleet for the longest time. The judge's face had deep lines and little color. Word was he could be a terror but that he tried to be fair.

According to state law, both sides were entitled to counsel, but the judge, not the lawyers, had the right to cross-examine witnesses. First to give testimony were the special security guards, then the police who had handcuffed both men and taken them to the hospital and then to the precinct station. Next, Smytes spoke. He was convinced—he would have sworn on a Bible—that Compleet scratched his face. Wasn't the bear right before his eyes, slobbering and looking like he'd kill his own mother? Who else could have mauled him? Smytes had never liked bears and thought zoos were a waste of money. "Let the animals out and fend for themselves," he once said.

"Why were you and Mr. Cuff fighting?" asked the judge. "That's what got the sow all riled up."

"I'd like to answer that, Your Honor," said Cuff. "I'm afraid we got a little hot under the collar. Marvin, that is, Mr. Smytes, wanted me to lend him money to spend on his girl. I said I was low on cash. Then I said something I shouldn't have. I said if she was a good date she wouldn't want to go to so many expensive places. That made him mad, and soon we were throwin' punches."

When Compleet's turn came, the bear moved on all fours to the front of the long table. Spitz got up from his seat and explained to the judge he would speak on behalf of the bear and also relay to his honor the messages the bear signed. Judge McCrewl understood and gave Spitz a nod.

Mostly, Spitz's message was that the bear was trying only to protect the sow.

"What was a bear doing in the stands?" asked McCrewl.

"The kid, that is, the bear, thought Honey B., that is, the sow, would enjoy the game," answered Spitz.

"Does the sow know baseball?"

"No, Your Honor."

"Then why was she in the stands? This whole outburst happened only because the sow left the zoo!"

"Yes, Your Honor," said Spitz in a quiet, dutiful voice.

It's my fault, Your Honor. I'm to blame. I talked Spitz into making arrangements to take Honey B. to Tailors. Spitz relayed the message.

"What about Mr. Smytes's face?" the judge asked. "Did you do that, Mr. Bear?"

Spitz answered, "I can clear that up, Your Honor. No, he didn't. I caught him as he was about to attack Mr. Smytes and held him back. Helen Achts, who was with Honey B., also grabbed the bear. The bear was steamin', and I think he was justified. When the sow let out that awful moan after Mr. Smytes got too close, the kid, I mean Compleet, thought the sow was in danger. The kid was only tryin' to protect the sow. We'd protect our women folk, too, wouldn't we, Judge, if somethin' like that happened?"

"Don't bring me into this," said the judge, a little annoyed. "Then who did the scratching?" McCrewl looked over his glasses and scowled.

"Well, Mai Tai," answered Spitz in a polite voice.

"And who or what is Mai Tai?" asked the judge, his voice rising.

"Your Honor," said Spitz, "Mai Tai is a cat. It's Helen Achts's cat. Mai Tai attacked Mr. Smytes because the cat was helpin' his friend Compleet. I guess security never saw the cat because, well, you know how cats are. He was in hidin' under some seats. The scene was awful confused."

"I think we're all confused!" said McCrewl in a loud voice. "No one mentioned a cat before. Why was a cat at the game? And don't tell me the cat likes baseball!"

"No, sir, at least I don't know if he does or not. But Miss Achts likes to take him with her to the games. She sneaks him in. And the bear and I thought if she sat next to Honey B., she could make the sow feel at home. That didn't work out at all. The whole idea was a disaster! But the cat did the scratchin'. Its tail is in one news clip. That's all you can see, the tail, because the bear and me took up so much space."

The judge sat quietly in his seat and took out a handkerchief and wiped his brow. Then he said in a quiet voice, "A cat and two bears in a melee! What were the security guards doing all this time? I find it hard to believe they didn't see the cat."

"Well, sir," said Spitz, "things happenin' so fast, the guards couldn't stop the scratchin'. And they never saw the cat because it was so quick. You know, a quick scratch and then it went into hidin'. But as you already heard, the guards and police got hold of Mr. Smytes and Mr. Cuff fast enough, and the police took them out of the stadium before the fans could get their hands on them. And I hope Your Honor don't mind my correctin' you, but only one bear was in the melee. Honey B. is a real lady. The sow was just scared and kept next to Miss Achts."

The Chum's lawyer looked at Spitz and whispered, "Son, never tell a judge he's wrong. If he says you should jump in the lake, do so immediately."

Judge McCrewl had heard enough to understand what had taken place at Tailors. Now he wanted to see hard evidence. He looked at a photo that showed a tiny tail sticking out near Compleet and Spitz. After looking for a moment at the bear's tail, McCrewl knew the tail in the picture couldn't possibly be the bear's. Next, he examined photos of Smytes that were taken at the hospital. The scratches were red and deep and thin. One look at the bear's claws told McCrewl the bear would have inflicted much greater wounds.

"If we could only get the cat here," said the judge, "maybe we could end this bizarre story."

Helen Achts stood up in the back of the courtroom, gave her name, and said she had Mai Tai with her. "May I approach the bench, Your Honor?" When the judge nodded, she walked toward the front of the room and asked, "Do you want to examine him?"

"Yes, put him here." The judge pointed to the top of his desk.

Helen put the cat in front of the judge. McCrewl gave him a pat and said, "So you're the fella that did the nasty business." The cat just stood there looking at the judge. Then he lay down and began to play with a pencil within his reach. The judge grinned and said, "Just like my two kittens."

"He likes cats. That's a good sign," whispered the Chum's lawyer to Spitz and Compleet.

The judge was silent for a long time. Then he said, "I find no probable cause for this case to go to trial." He hesitated. "Under legislation recently passed I have the authority to set fines and allot minor punishments when necessary. Normally I wouldn't rule immediately, but because of the need for a prompt decision,

I declare a recess of three hours. At the end of that time, we will reconvene and I'll present my findings."

"No probable cause, legislation recently passed, fines, minor punishments," repeated Spitz to the Chum's lawyer. "What does it mean? Are we in the clear or not?"

"Be patient. Be thankful you two have been spared a trial. We'll have to sweat out the next few hours. Pray that we get lucky."

When the judge returned to the bench, he spoke to Cuff, Smytes, Spitz, Compleet, and Achts in order. "Mr. Cuff, I fine you three thousand dollars for being disorderly and part of a scenario that might have ended in tragedy. The court places you on probation for two years.

"Mr. Smytes, I fine you ten thousand dollars for being disorderly and causing a near riot, and I sentence you to thirty days in jail. You also must serve two years' probation. To your benefit, a great tragedy was avoided due to the quick thinking of Mr. McOystre and Miss Achts. Because security was lax, I order the Chum organization to pay any medical bills you have incurred and may incur in the future to treat and properly heal the wounds to your face."

McCrewl paused for a moment and drank some water from a glass on his desk. Then he continued, "If a cat can get into Tailors Station and cause so much damage, then security at the stadium needs an overhaul." He picked out Miltones sitting in the second row and stared at him. Miltones quickly nodded.

"Mr. McOystre, I congratulate you on preventing Mr. Bear from laying his hands, uh, I mean paws, on Mr. Smytes and inflicting heavy wounds. Mr. Bear might even have killed Mr. Smytes. I hope you realize now how foolish it was to take a bear out of a zoo and put her in a stadium and expect nothing out of the ordinary would occur."

"Yes, Your Honor, I do. It was a bad idea!"

"Mr. Bear, uh, would you mind if I called you Compleet? Mr. Bear just doesn't sound right."

Your Honor, Compleet is fine. Spitz relayed the message.

"Compleet, I understand your desire to protect the sow. But climbing into the stands with the intent to harm a spectator was a wrongful act. I hope you realize what Mr. McOystre did for you. He saved your career in baseball."

I am grateful to my dear friend for holding me back. Spitz translated.

"I fine you thirty thousand dollars for being disorderly with intent to harm. I hope the commissioner of baseball suspends you for *x* number of games as an example of what ballplayers must not do: Go into the stands during a game. And I order you to serve thirty days house arrest—"

Spitz interrupted, "Beg your pardon, Judge, but the bear lives in a hotel."

"Be quiet, Mr. McOystre, and let me finish. To serve thirty days house, or hotel, arrest, said time to be served starting five days after the last game of the Topwater Bronze." The judge looked at Compleet and Spitz; then he stared at Miltones. "I assume the bear will be busy in the Bronze Series hitting home runs."

Compleet, Spitz, Helen, Miltones, Boslerts, Frog, P.U., and everyone else in the courtroom that was a Chum supporter gave a sigh that reverberated across the room. The judge was a Chum fan! McCrewl heard the collective sigh but ignored it.

"And finally, Miss Achts, I order you to pay Mr. Smytes five thousand dollars in penalty for injuries to said victim and an additional five thousand dollars for pain and suffering. In the future, Miss Achts, I hope you will leave your cat at home when you attend games at Tailors Station."

Part Four:
Reach for the Bronze
and Conclusion

The Tedious Wait

O utside the courtroom, Spitz couldn't thank Helen enough for coming to the bear's rescue. And Compleet signed his gratitude and gave her a big bear hug, almost crushing Mai Tai inside her jacket. The cat was surprised and bruised. It peeked out of the jacket and meowed. Compleet leaned down and put his head next to the cat. Mai Tai purred.

Miltones, Boslerts, and Frog joined the three (or four, if you count Mai Tai). Miltones told Helen not to worry about the fines; the Chum organization would reimburse her. He said, "My only concern now is Hofenpfeiffer. I'm sure he'll impose a fine and a suspension. But how many days will he keep Compleet out of the lineup?"

T he commissioner wanted to act quickly. What happened at Tailors was nasty business, and it had gotten national coverage. He didn't want Congress to intervene, and he didn't want the fans to stay away because they were afraid a melee might happen again at Tailors or a stadium hosting the Chum.

At the same time, he had to think of the playoffs. The Chum were a tremendous draw around the league because of the bear. Compleet had to be reprimanded, fined, and suspended, but the suspension had to be short. It was too near October and the play-offs. With Compleet in the playoffs, fan interest would surge, and the big corporations would gladly pay top dollar to place ads on TV, radio, the Web, billboards, and in magazines and newspapers. Toys, computer games, board games, and clothing were on the drawing boards of companies waiting to learn the bear's fate.

Hofenpfeiffer met with the bear and Spitz and heard their side of the brawl. And he talked to Miltones, Boslerts, Frog, and Helen by phone. It was unusual for a commissioner to talk to a spectator in a matter such as this. But her involvement in the scuffle was critical, and Hofenpfeiffer wanted to get the story right.

Within a few hours of hearing what everyone had to say, the commissioner made his decision. Before making an official announcement to the press, he called Spitz at the hotel to give him the news. He had decided to fine Compleet fifty thousand dollars for charging into the stands with intent to inflict bodily harm on a spectator and to suspend him for ten games. The commissioner said he would officially commend Spitz for keeping the bear from injuring Mr. Smytes.

The commissioner then notified Miltones, who called Boslerts, who told Frog, who informed P.U. Spitz got in touch with Helen, and then he texted a message to Ronny. "Bear fined and suspended for only ten games. He'll make the playoffs! Tell everyone."

Good news always leaks out. Before Hofenpfeiffer got a chance to make his official announcement, special editions of all the local newspapers were on the streets of Cuspin Heights with the details of his ruling. Within an hour, every paper had been snatched up. Smiles and happy talk followed. Chum fans breathed a sigh of relief. The team could function without Compleet for eight days and ten games. Why only eight days? On the schedule were two doubleheaders, day-night games, to make up for two rained out games back in April.

Time to Sort Things Out

Boslerts and Frog got together and decided to take Spitz off the roster for the eight days so he could keep an eye on the bear. Compleet was a hot commodity. Since he was somewhat naïve, he had to be protected—no more exposes, no more melees!

Spitz was pleased with the assignment, and Compleet was glad someone would be with him until he returned to the lineup.

The two thought it best to stay out of the public eye and spent most of their hours in the hotel, often in their room. Sometimes, to breathe fresh air and see other than four walls, they went for a stroll between two and five a.m., when most neighborhoods were quiet and mostly deserted.

With so much time at their disposal, they did a lot of talking about the farm and the Bruedocks, about the chances of the Chum in the playoffs. Cuspin fans had such high expectations for the team. Would the players disappoint? They wondered how long they would stay with the Chum. Three years? Five years? Every ballplayer has a life beyond baseball. What would it be like for Spitz and Compleet?

The bear especially was worried about his future. How would he get along in a world of people? Would he be able to settle down with Honey B. and raise a family? After the horror of her visit to Tailors, would she still want to be with him? If so, would the two go back to Compleet's first home in New Jersey near High Point? Can someone ever go back?

Spitz's Past

One night halfway through his suspension, the bear was stretched out on a park bench, and Spitz was sitting nearby. They had been walking for an hour and decided to take a break. The moon was only a small crescent. A cold wind was blowing out of the northwest. Spitz had on a warm jacket. Compleet felt refreshed as the wind rippled the hair and fur on his backside.

The bear raised himself slightly and signed, *I never asked where you got the name Spitz. I don't know anyone else called Spitz.*

"I was baptized Spencer but growin' up hardly anyone called me that. I come from Arnville, on the Susquehanna in PA. It was a rough mill town back then. There's no more mills now since the steel industry went bad, but once there was a half dozen or more. My daddy—his name was Elmer, but everyone called him Dutch—said, 'Son, you gotta learn how to protect yourself if you wanna survive'. So he taught me how to get the most outta my fists."

Spitz got out a chaw of tobacco and put it in his mouth. He continued, "There was this real pal of mine. He was older then me and hard as hickory. He was always pickin' a fight with someone. I noticed every time he got ready to fight, he'd spit on the ground. It was like the bell for the fight to begin. And durin' the fight and at the end of the fight he'd spit some more. Since I really admired my pal 'cause he was a good friend, and 'cause he hardly never lost a fight, I started to do the same thing. The kids on my block and in school started to call me Spitz. Along the way, I changed to spittin' tobacco; the name stuck. I took boxin' lessons for a time, startin' when I was seventeen. I enjoyed it and became pretty good. In fact, I thought I was good enough to make pro if I got more experience."

Spitz pulled the zipper up to the top of his jacket. The wind was stronger now and colder. He looked up at the night sky and the thin moon and said, "This next is kinda secret. It's no one's business but mine, but we're best of friends, so I'll tell it. This pal of mine started to drink heavy, and of course I followed in his trail. We got into trouble sometimes 'cause of the drinkin'. Nothin' real serious, but we got in a lotta fights, got fined sometimes, and twice spent a couple of days in the town jail. Well, my pal moved away; I gave up boxin' and took up baseball. I continued to drink, and it cost me the only gal I ever loved. Her name was Julie. Just thinkin' 'bout her gives me goosebumps. We were plannin' on gettin' hitched, and then she found out I couldn't hold my liquor. I told her I'd quit, an' I did for a time, but it didn't last."

Spitz stopped talking and looked into the distance. Compleet wanted to sign to make him feel better but decided not to. Sometimes doing nothing is doing someone a favor. A few minutes later Spitz stood up and said, "Well, kid, shall we head back?"

They started to walk. The bear thought it would be all right to begin the conversation again. *I never saw you take a drink, so I figured the stories I heard from some of the Tenn Nine players were false.*

"After I lost Julie I started to drink hard. Soon the manager—I was playin' in some mountain town in Carolina—began to notice. He suspended me for two weeks. I got sober, came back, but started drinkin' again. This time he took me by the collar and said if he ever caught me with so much as a breath of alcohol, he'd run me out of baseball. Well, that scared the daylights outta me. I mean, with Julie gone, baseball was all I had left. So I stopped drinkin' on the spot and never took it up again."

That shows you can do something right if you want. I'm proud of what you did. And maybe it's not too late with Julie.

"It's always too late, kid. She's outta my life for good."

What makes you say that?

"I don't know. It's just … I'm unlucky that way. Let's leave it, okay?"

The Bronze in Sight

After the bear hit that monster home run into the Muddy Muck, he began to think about the high waterfall in center and the metal cutout above it. Could a ball be hit that high and that far? From time to time the question popped into his head.

For a while, the paparazzi imbroglio and the brawl at Tailors Station turned his mind from baseball. But during his ten-game suspension he had time to zero in on this new challenge.

One morning at breakfast, he signed to Spitz, *What do you think? Can I do it?*

"Do what, kid?"

Hit the top of the waterfall in center and maybe the fisherman or boat.

"You still got that on your mind? Forget it; it can't happen. You'd likely need a seventy-five-mile-an-hour wind behind you, an' we're almost to October. The winds in the fall and summer ain't the same."

Compleet looked dejected. *Then it can't be done? Ever?*

Spitz didn't answer right away. He smoothed down his hair on one side, and then took up a fork in his hand and pointed it at the bear. "You know, this is just supposin', but let's say you got a hurricane-like wind comin' up from the south, and you hit the ball to center, a little to the left. You hit it good, I mean real good. The crosswinds might help the south wind an' carry the ball up and bend it to the waterfall. It's an idea; I don't say it will work. But it's somethin' to consider."

You think there's a chance?

"I don't know, but if them conditions ever show up at Tailors, I'll sure give you a *carpe diem*."

What?

"A *carpe diem*. It's Latin. It means *seize the day*. You know, like do somethin' special, somethin' big."

I didn't know you could speak a foreign language.

"You mean Latin? Naw, I can't speak Latin. But we had a guy in the minors, Billum Ghraye, left fielder on team in this town in Texas, who knew these words. He couldn't speak Latin neither, but he learned them two words. Never told us where he picked 'em up or from who.

"So one time durin' a night game, he gets up to the railin' in front the dugout and shouts those words to our batter. Of course, the batter don't know what he's sayin', and the guys in the dugout are laughin' at this fool player at the railin'. But on the next pitch, the batter hits a home run!

"Well, after that, whenever a big moment came in a game and one of our guys was at the plate, all our team got to the railin' and started shoutin' *carpe diem!*"

Did it work?

"Sometimes it did and sometimes it didn't. But I don't think shoutin' *carpe diem* had nothin' to do with it."

Then why would you say it?

"So it don't mean nothin', but you never know."

Mother of All Home Runs

After this conversation, nothing was said about the waterfall until the first game after the bear's suspension. The team needed a win. They had lost three straight, each by one run. And Compleet and Spitz needed this game to get their rhythm back. The bear, of course, was in the starting lineup, but Spitz, as a utility player, began the game on the bench. It was a day game; the opponent was their long-time rival across the river, the Troefield Trout. Amat—his real name was Amo Amas—was on the mound for the Chum. He didn't have his good stuff and was taken out by Frog in the third. The Trout pitcher wasn't much better; he lasted four innings.

The game was a hitter's dream. After six innings, the score was tied eleven all. Compleet already had a home run, two doubles, a single, and seven RBIs. Spitz entered the game in the fifth at shortstop after Payday got hit in the forehead by a ball that took a bad hop. When he complained of double vision, Frog pulled him. Spitz hadn't played much at shortstop—with the Chum or any other team—but he handled cleanly two balls hit his way.

The reason for the big score was the wind: the kind that makes home runs out of deep, catchable fly balls, and doubles out of singles that skip hurriedly by outfielders. It was a wind that fattens a ballplayer's batting average.

It took all the players by surprise. The morning's weather forecast gave no hint of a gale wind. It was so strong the players were forced to lean into it to stay afoot. The bear thought back to his monster home run and the high wind.

Spitz and Compleet knew what the other was thinking: the waterfall and the metal cutout! Was this the day the bear would do what no other Chum player, or player on any visiting team, had done? Could this gale-force wind be the X-factor?

The Trout scored twice in the top of the seventh. In the bottom of the inning, French Fry led off with a single and Ham followed with a double. Compleet came to the plate. The fans let out a cheer that could be heard outside the stadium for twelve, fifteen blocks. All of a sudden, the gale-force winds increased. Caps, bandannas, paper cups, newspapers, scorecards, thunder sticks, and other items went flying about the field. The flag in far right, worn and faded, ripped on the post side. Pieces of metal from high up in the grandstand clanked as they fell in front of the seats in near left. The ump behind home plate stopped the game until the grounds crew could clear the ball field.

Compleet felt a surge of energy. He thought briefly of High Point and the strong winds that often played around him and his mom and sister. The wind, his recollection, the slate sun in a slate sky, and the loud cheers of the fans all seemed to come together, all seemed to urge him forward.

The first pitch was a ball, low and outside. From the dugout came a loud cry, "*Carpe diem*! Now, kid, now! The target's darin' you! Go!" The bear turned and his eyes met Spitz's. Shouting, with his hands on the rail at the top of the dugout, Spitz felt foolish. But it didn't matter; he was doing this for the kid. The second pitch was a strike; it caught the inside part of the plate. Compleet had watched it go by. He held up on the next two pitches, both balls. Again Spitz shouted, "*Carpe diem!*" Compleet heard the words, but he didn't turn his head. He was concentrating on the pitch.

Stay calm, breathe deep. The pitcher released the ball. The bear's nostrils widened, his ears went back, and his muscles bulged. The pitch was a hanging curve, a ball that should have dropped. At that moment, a huge gust of wind blew toward the outfield, and a crosswind ripped from left to right.

Compleet swung with all his considerable might. As Spitz would have said, he got it good, real good. The ball had height, it had speed, and it had distance. Everyone in the stands and the bleachers stood up. Some cheered, but many waited ... and waited. They sensed this might be a shot they could tell their kids and maybe their grandchildren about. They could say they were there at Tailors on this day of days.

The ball carried and carried, out to left center, over the wall, then it changed course, driven by the crosswind, and got on a line to the waterfall. The fans in the bleachers watched in disbelief and joy as the ball went flying by high over their heads. The ball seemed to have a life of its own! It lifted itself, as if it were climbing up the waterfall, and finally settled on a target: the metal fisherman in the cutout atop the waterfall!

Compleet had almost reached second when the ball found its target. The shouts of fans bounced around the stadium, filling every corner and passageway. The sound reached to the top of the grandstand, then floated out and spread in the open air. It seemed to magnify as it expanded beyond the stadium toward the river and in other directions. If ever Tailors had witnessed a cheer to end all cheers, this was it! All eyes now turned toward the bear as he touched home plate, high-fived Ham and French Fry, and retreated to the dugout. So determined were the fans to honor their hero, the bear had to come out of the dugout five times for shouts and words of praise.

How far had this monster shot traveled? Well, the distance on a line from home plate to the wall in center measured about 445 feet. Beyond the wall were the bleachers, the waterfall between, and the stoical fisherman forever casting for chum (and never getting a bite!). So how far? 500? 530? 562? It seemed like half the crowd was locked in a discussion on how far the ball had traveled. Frog told Compleet he would ask Miltones to get a surveyor to take an accurate measurement so the world would know.

The scoring wasn't over, but there were no more monster shots like the bear's. Compleet got another double before the game ended. The Chum won 19–16!

When the regular season ended, Cuspin was on a nine-game winning streak and sitting on top of the Coral Division. Fulerbay, in second place, was four games behind. Cuspin Heights was in the playoffs for the first time since 1970. Baseball fans on the west side of the Muddy Muck were ecstatic. With solid hitting, strong pitching, good relief, and airtight defense, most fans expected the team to win the Topwater Bronze. If ever a group of patient, optimistic fans deserved a reward, it was the Chum following.

Advancing in the Playoffs

In the first round of the playoffs, the Chum were matched against the Fitetoun Flounder. Cuspin Heights swept the series, although the margin of victory in each game was only one run. Before the next round for the Neptune League title, Frog called a closed-door meeting. Frog was considered one of the best managers in Big Ball even though his teams had never won the Topwater Bronze, never even been in the Bronze playoffs. He knew what Spitz called the mind game inside out. The players braced themselves for a five-star pep talk.

"Watch out, Spitz," whispered Santa with a grin, "Frog is probably going to call us on the carpet for sweeping the Flounder!"

"The Flounder were a good team," began Frog, "but not as good as our next opponent—Prumfort." Frog stopped talking to let his words sink in. He looked around the clubhouse as if he were searching for a particular player. Then he continued, "Of course, you men heard of Julius Caesar, the great warrior and politician of Rome. Well, I know something about this man."

Frog cleared his throat. "This Caesar said some famous words besides the *Et Brute* speech to Brute. He said, 'I came, I saw, I conquered it all'."[14]

"Just like that?" asked French Fry.

"Just like that," repeated Frog. "But before he conquered it all, he got the lay of the land, he figured out what armies he'd have to beat, and he worked out plans to bash each one."

Frog stopped again and looked at the ceiling. Then he peered at the faces directly in front of him. "Any you gentlemen know what I'm drivin' at?"

There was silence for a time. Then Jimbo said, "I guess you mean we have to do our homework: know how to play balls hit in their stadium, where to place our hits, know the best stuff their pitchers throw, and don't take anybody or anything for granted."

"Bingo!" shouted Frog. "You get the Kewpie doll. That's exactly what I mean. Don't let the Flounder win give you guys big heads. We gotta prepare and concentrate and not get ahead of ourselves. I want Prumfort, and that gets us into the Topwater Bronze finals. I wanna win now! I can't be sure there'll be another chance; I'm gettin' on in years."

"I'm with you, Frog," said P.U., standing up so the players could focus on him. "I'm tired of watching other teams win the Big One. Prumfort we gotta beat. We gotta be ready, know what's gonna happen before it comes. I want that ring for my wife and kids and me."

"P.U., you forgot to mention the new coat your wife wants out of this," joked Drum Drum.

"If I don't get a Bronze ring, don't any of you speak to me!" said Frog.

"We'll get you a Bronze ring," said Payday, "and one for each player. We want this title as much as you do."

Frog said, "That's what I wanted to hear. Now we're on the same page. Good luck…and pay attention to the team curfew."

The Prumfort Porgies, who had won the Flotsam Division, had the pitcher, Elroy Speedbal, with the most wins in the Neptune League—twenty-four—and the lowest ERA—2.12—among league starters. The Chum would most likely see him on the mound at least twice in the series: in game one and again in game four or five. The Porgies' lineup was strong, but none of the players could smack the ball as far as Compleet, Ham, and Jimbo, or field as well as Santa and Compleet.

The first game was at Tailors Station, and of course it was sold out, as was the series. This game was a chance to savor a win. You might say the fans were drooling at the mouth. This was their year, no question of it. They talked about it, they felt it, they dreamed about it.

Frog sent Frank Jammache, nickname Jammin, to the mound. He had won nineteen games in the regular season, and his ERA was a respectable 3.43. He was a master at keeping batters off balance with his arsenal of pitches. For the first five innings he was brilliant, allowing only two hits and three base runners. Speedbal had kept pace; after five innings it was still a scoreless ball game. But the Porgies scored three runs in their half of the sixth on two singles, a triple, and a sacrifice bunt down the first base line. Frog replaced Jammin with Greg Grumpet, nickname Gee Gee, who retired the side without further damage. Compleet got a single in the bottom of the sixth and a double in the ninth but was stranded both times. Final score: Porgies 3–0 over the Chum.

Cuspin won game two by the score of 3–2. All the Chum runs scored on singles. In game three at Prumfort, the Chum made three costly errors and lost 4–3. Frog called a meeting before game four.

Ham entered the locker room after the other players had filed in. When everyone was seated, he sat on top of the desk that the trainer sometimes used. "I asked Frog if we could meet without him. I said sometimes it works best if the players talk among themselves. He agreed." Ham stopped talking and looked around the room, trying to make eye contact with the players. He continued, "Three costly errors were the cause of our losin' last night. Now the Porgies have the edge. Well…what are we goin' to do about it? Where's our concentration? We all got to field better, hit better. We can't let the series get away from us. We need this next game." Ham was popular with the players. He always played hard, and he never complained. He was one of the first to show up at practice and usually the last to leave.

Santa stood up. "Ham's right. If we lose tonight, we'll be in a deep hole. If we play our best we won't lose, and that's what we have to do. Think 'Win' and go out and do your job."

As the players left the locker room, some gave Ham or Santa a tap on the back or arm. The players didn't say anything; they didn't have to. Ham and Santa had said it all.

The Chum made no errors in game four and three spectacular plays in the infield. Ham had a home run with two runners on, and Compleet had two RBIs. The Chum won 6–2.

With the series tied two games apiece, Jammin and Speedbal faced each other again in game five. The first half was a carbon copy of game one; neither team could score. In the top of the sixth, the Chum got to Speedbal, who began to tire. He was missing with his best pitches. The first two Chum waited out walks. After French Fry struck out, Ham lined a double to right and one run crossed the plate. There were runners on second and third, and one out.

Compleet came to bat. On the second pitch he hit the ball down the left field line. It was fair by inches, rolled to the corner, and popped out of the fielder's glove when he reached for it. Compleet, almost at second, saw the miscue and dug for third. He got to the bag the same time as the ball and rolled hard into the bag and the third baseman covering. The dust was so thick the third baseman lost the ball. Compleet got up and without a word or sign from the third base coach, immediately headed for home. He raced toward the plate like a freight train, two hundred and fifty-five pounds of bone, muscle, and fat, knocking over the catcher who was waiting for him with the ball. The catcher's feet went up in the air, the ball squirted out of his mitt, and the ump shouted, "Safe!"

Speedbal left in favor of a reliever. The Chum scored two more runs in the eighth. In the ninth, their top reliever, Bule Penn, replaced Jammin, who had told Frog of painful spasms in his pitching arm. Penn quickly got three outs, and the Chum won 6–0. Jammin had pitched one of the best games of his career. He had walked none, struck out eleven, and allowed only two hits.

When the Chum plane landed at Cuspin Heights International in the middle of the night, five thousand fans were there to greet the team. In the morning, Spitz got a call from Ronny. The family had watched the game on TV. They stood up and cheered when Compleet ran toward home in the sixth. Ronny said he jumped so high when the bear scored that he hit his head on a beam that angled from the ceiling. "Tell Compleet all of us expect the Chum to win the Bronze for themselves and the city. And for the Bruedocks!"

Game six was a day game. The stadium was overflowing, and it was rockin'! Amat was on the mound for the Chum, Dig Deeper for the Porgies. Amat was the winning pitcher in game two; the crowd expected a repeat performance. The Chum needed one more win to advance to the finals.

The Gallsun Goldeye had already defeated the Spouton Sardines of the Atlantis Division. They would represent the Triton League in the Bronze finals.

The Chum were confident. They had won two straight, one of them a shutout by Jammin and Penn. And they were playing at home before an adoring crowd.

Payday and Ham homered in the first, and P.U. and Santa doubled in the second. Dig Deeper lasted only an inning and a third. Meanwhile, Amat was in top form and didn't allow a run until the seventh. The Chum won easily 8–2.

Tailors Station erupted! Fireworks shot into the air in all directions. The stadium was bathed in sound and color. The cheers of the fans carried out to the Muddy Muck and the west side of Troefield and up and down the river. After the Chum players had collapsed in a massive heap at home plate, hugged one another, and high-fived, the team ran around the stadium in a victory lap. A chant started in the center field bleachers. "We want Gold!" It quickly spread to the rest of the stadium. The players ran another victory lap. Flashbulbs blinded. "We want Gold! We want Gold!"

Abee and Yodel

The players had a few days to rest before the first game with the Goldeye. Some of them began to think about Abee. His story had been on their minds lately. Why had the Chum been denied a championship for so many years? After Cuspin Heights had won its last world title, the team made six appearances in the Bronze finals and lost all six times, the last in 1933. Was it the fault of Abee and his owner?

Who was Abee and what was his story? Well, dear reader, there is more than one version. The one I like best goes something like this. The year was 1915. Although the population of Cuspin Heights was only thirty thousand, the city was home to a Big Ball team, the Chum. Near Tailors Station, in a small, well-kept house, lived a thirtysomething Swiss immigrant named Yodel Beisst. Yodel was a nickname given to him because he had won half a dozen contests in yodeling in his native town, Basle. Yodel loved animals and had a number of pets, one of which was an aardvark called Abee. Yodel chose the name because the aardvark is sometimes called ant bear, from its huge appetite for ants and its resemblance to a bear.

It seems Abee had discovered ants in the food bins at Tailors Station. Yodel kept his animals in a large, fenced yard, but one night Abee burrowed under a section of fence and wandered over to the stadium. Since the Chum were on the road, the place was dark. This suited Abee fine. In food bin after food bin, Abee used his long, sticky tongue to gorge himself on ants that were gorging themselves on food leftovers. Toward morning, Abee returned home and was careful to cover over the hole it had burrowed under the fence.

Abee repeated this pattern even after the Chum returned from their road trip. Of course, if there was a night game, it stayed in the yard. It didn't want to rub shoulders with fifty thousand fans.

Events seemed to be going Abee's way until the cleanup crew at Tailors became suspicious of the large mounds of food and other discards in and near the bins. They thought maybe some cats or dogs or squirrels or rats had been creating the mounds while digging for free food. Of course, no one suspected an aardvark. None of the crew knew what an aardvark was. Told about the mounds, the owner of the Chum, Vache Montvue, ordered one of the crew to make the rounds of the bins during the night in an effort to solve the mystery.

The first night on duty, the crewman fell asleep, and of course detected nothing unusual. But on the second night, the worker spotted Abee digging furiously in one of the bins and creating a huge mound behind him. He thought the creature looked something like a small kangaroo. The worker yelled for help and started to run away. In a dimly lit area, he fell down concrete stairs and broke an ankle. Abee, of course, heard the ruckus, immediately stopped digging, and promptly returned home.

When Montvue learned what had happened and heard a description of the animal, he knew it must have been some exotic pet at work. He sent some of the Chum staff into the neighborhood to make inquiries, and they soon learned of Yodel's aardvark. Summoned to the Chum front office, Yodel was confronted by Montvue, who demanded Yodel pay his worker's hospital and doctor bills and get rid of his mischievous pet.

Yodel refused. "I feed my pet; he never goes hungry. And my yard is fenced in. If I had known about Abee's trips to the stadium, I'd have done something about it." He looked at Montvue with watery eyes. "Sir, I'm a man of modest means, and you have millions. You should pay the bills. My pet wasn't responsible for your worker falling down stairs." Montvue shook his head and scowled. Beisst took a deep breath and continued, "I go to the Chum home games regular. And I cheer louder than anyone around me. Is this the reward I get for being a loyal fan?" He stamped his foot and said, "You're wrong! Under no circumstances will I ever get rid of my Abee!"

Within days, Yodel had to make a court appearance. The judge agreed with Montvue that Yodel should pay the hospital and doctor bills, but he said Yodel could keep his pet. In return, he had to promise to take measures to keep the aardvark away from Tailors Station. Yodel agreed but left the courthouse mad. The next day he placed a public notice in one of the local newspapers, telling the citizens of Cuspin Heights about his conversation with Montvue, and asking them to decide if he had been treated fairly. Shortly after the incident, Yodel moved out of the city and left no forwarding address.

Fast forward, dear reader, to the year 2000, a few days before the first game between the Chum and the Goldeye.

Spitz got the story of Abee from French Fry. The two joined a group of Chum players who thought it would be a kind gesture to invite members of the Beisst family to sit in box seats during home games with the Goldeye, at the Chum's expense. It might make Yodel's kin feel better and in some way help the Chum in the series. In the phone book, the Chum office staff found forty people in Cuspin named Beisst. And with help from Beisst families, the staff located married women whose maiden name was Beisst. Miltones had invitations printed and sent to every Beisst, or former Beisst, in the city. Sixty-two answered and said they planned to attend at least one game.

Out of the Past

It was the evening before the Chum's flight to Gallsun for game one. Compleet and Spitz were in their room at the hotel. A bellhop knocked on the door. When Spitz opened the door, the bellhop gave him a folded note with Spitz's name on it. Spitz thought the handwriting looked familiar but couldn't place it. The note read, "Meet me in the lobby, please! You won't regret it. It took me an hour to get up courage to write this note." There was no signature.

Spitz said, "This is strange."

The bear looked up at Spitz and waited for him to explain.

"Something tells me I should satisfy my curiosity. I'll be back soon, kid."

But Spitz didn't return for an hour and a half. When he came back, he apologized to the bear for staying out so long. He had a sparkle in his eyes, something Compleet had never seen before.

Where did you go? And why do you look so happy?

Spitz answered, "Who do you think was in the lobby waitin' for me, large as life, in all her loveliness?"

Julie!

"Right, kid! At first I didn't know what to say. But when she put her arms around me, I just melted and said all kinds of dumb things. We went for a walk, and she told me she got a divorce six months ago, so I hope I'm back in the picture."

Then she got married after you two broke up. Does she have any kids?

"Yeah, a boy, Charles. I think she said he's ten, and a girl, Carly, who's seven."

What's next? Are you going to marry her?

Spitz didn't answer right away. "I'd like to, but I gotta think things over."

I say do it. Sometimes you can think too much. You said she's the only one you ever loved. Snatch her up before someone else does!

Two Up in the Finals

The Beisst family and Julie were distractions for Spitz, pleasant distractions to be sure, but distractions nonetheless. There were the Bronze finals to think of.

The team was excited, confident, and focused. As proof, it

won the two games in Gallsun with some daring base running. In game one, Payday stole home in the seventh with what proved to be the winning run. Final score: Chum 3, Goldeye 2.

In game two, the score was tied 3–3 in the top of the ninth. Santa singled and Drum Drum walked. They both advanced on a double steal. But a pinch hitter for Amat struck out, and Payday popped up to the second baseman. With two outs, the runners were set to run on the pitch. French Fry hit a scorcher to short. It should have been the third out, but the ball took a nasty hop and hit the heel of the shortstop's glove and bounced into left. Santa scored easily, and Drum Drum just beat the throw home.

In the bottom of the ninth, Bule Penn came in to try to get the win for Amat. He gave up one run, but with two down and a man on third, he struck out the best hitter of the Goldeye. Final score: Chum 5, Goldeye 4.

While in Gallsun Spitz rented a car, and he and Compleet drove around North Woodside, admiring the lovely mansions and immaculate lawns. *What big houses! How many people live in a house that size? Ten? Fifteen?*

"No, not that many. As few as two, just the husband and wife, or perhaps five or six, including the kids."

The lawns! Look at all that grass, so green and going to waste! Why aren't animals grazing? The lawns look, well, they look unreal and kind of bare.

"The lawns are just for lookin', kid," answered Spitz.

Later the two went on board the big liner, *SS Enormorata*, which was taking on supplies for a cruise around the world. Compleet couldn't get over how big the ship was.

All those decks! How can a ship have so many? You'd think it would sink. And it's so long you can't see from one end to the other! Wow! You could stack hundreds of trees on the main deck or build dozens of boulder houses! What do people do when they are on the water in a big ship like this?

"The people are entertained and make new friends and eat

delicious food. It's a real adventure to be on a ship, and then visit a foreign country and see things you never saw before and hear people speak a language different from yours."

Spitz considered calling Julie while in Gallsun but decided against it. "It's best to talk to her face-to-face about the future," he confided to the bear.

The Perfect Ending

The plane with the Chum team, coaches, administrators, and the press landed at Cuspin Heights International Airport on Monday in the early afternoon. The fans were there in the thousands, cheering and shouting. In their room at the Three C's, Spitz and the bear saw a huge bouquet of flowers on a stand by Spitz's bed. Attached to the bouquet was an envelope. In it was a note. Spitz read it to himself and then Compleet.

It was from Ronny and was signed by all the Bruedocks and Kristy. It read, "Congratulations to Compleet and Spitz and the Chum. We all watched both games on TV and cheered often for you, Compleet. Sorry, Spitz, that you didn't get to play. Hopefully in game three or four you will get in the lineup.

"The family, and Kristy, have decided to watch the rest of the series on TV. It's a long drive, much of it in heavy traffic, from here to Cuspin Heights, and Grandpa and Grandma don't like long rides.

"Will the Chum take four straight? We hope so. Call when you get the chance, Spitz.

"Our love always, God bless. Go bear! (And Spitz!)"

Two more wins, and the bear, Spitz, and the rest of the team would have the rings, the recognition, the fans' gratitude and love, and the winner's share.

Game three was probably the most exciting game in the series. The Chum were going for a sweep, that is, their aim was to win the first four games. No one said it in so many words; no one had to. There was a kind of electricity in the air that seemed to come from the players, a sure-fire confidence, a feeling of destiny, a desire to quickly finish something that had been started. In the clubhouse, P.U. took a broom out of a closet and began to sweep around the shoes of teammates. Everyone smiled.

Walter "Muffy" Muffint took the mound for the Chum. Muffy was an enigma. When he was on, he was almost as good as Jammin; when he was off his game, he was awful. In early August, he had pitched a game against the Prumfort Porgies and allowed six runs in two innings. In his next outing, he allowed only one run in eight innings and struck out nine.

The Chum were waiting anxiously to see which Walter Muffint would show up. In the top of the first, he walked the first two batters, and some of his teammates thought, *Oh, oh, here we go again!* But he got out of the inning nicely when he struck out the next hitter, and Payday made a dazzling stop on a hard-hit ball and quickly relayed to Drum Drum who stepped on second and then threw to first for a double play.

From the second inning to the eighth, Muffy pitched superbly and didn't allow a run. He tired in the top of the eighth. Frog took him out after the first batter walked and the next singled. Gee Gee came on and got out the side after one run had scored on a hit up the middle. The Chum got the run back in the bottom of the ninth when P.U. homered to deep center. The game went into extra innings, tied one apiece.

Each team got hits in the tenth and twelfth innings but didn't score because of spectacular plays in the field. In the bottom of the fourteenth, the first batter for the Chum flied out to right. Compleet came to the plate, and the roar of the crowd spilled out into the streets around the stadium.

The bear held up on a pitch the ump called a strike. He thought it was low. The next pitch was a ball, high inside. Then the bear fouled off a slider. A ball evened the count at two and two. The next pitch was a fastball down. Compleet went down for it and hit it high and far. The fans, as if on a signal, rose to their feet. Out to left sailed the ball, a fast-traveling, tiny, white orb in the night sky, over the wall, over the bleachers, over the scoreboard, and out into the black night.

It was a walk-off home run—game three in the pocket! The bear ran the bases to deafening cheers. Led by Spitz, the players stormed out of the dugout and mobbed their hero, pounding him on the back, boxing his ears, and shouting praises. Every word was earned. Not often did a player win a Bronze game in extra innings with one mighty swing of the bat. Fireworks covered the dark night in blues, yellows, greens, reds, and purples. Across the top of the scoreboard, light bulbs of many colors flashed a giant "Number Three." Chum fans glanced at it with a deep feeling of satisfaction.

The Play

The outcome of game four was the talk of the town. On trains and buses, in coffee shops, at water coolers—everyone had questions to ask. Would the Chum sweep? Would Compleet smash another mammoth home run to win the game? Would the score be close and the game go into extra innings? Would the team choke, as it had done so often in past years? No one wanted to linger over the last question. The team was so close; how could it fail to win the Bronze?

The game, of course, was sold out; thousands were turned away. Scalpers were getting two or three thousand dollars a ticket, and buyers were thanking them for the opportunity to pay such prices! A few hundred persistent, lucky fans were able to squeeze into rooftop dining areas atop the three skyscrapers with a view of the inside of Tailors. Many stationed themselves outside the stadium so they could be near the action. Since they could hear the sounds within come cascading over the grandstand and out into the streets, it was almost like being inside. And of course they all had their boom boxes or small portable TVs or transistor radios or cell phones.

On the mound for the Goldeye was their ace, Gene "Dee Rock" DeeRouch. He had pitched a creditable game one. The

Goldeye were hoping for a better performance from him this time. The Chum pitcher was Tony Splinterrs, nicknamed Rail. He was tall, thin, handsome, polite, and a fierce competitor. His best pitches were a split-finger fastball and a slider.

The game was scoreless until the fourth. In the bottom of the inning, P.U. got a single, stole second, and came home on Santa's double. In the top of the seventh, the Goldeye pulled even on a triple and a single. The tension in the ball park was hard to describe. Everybody's nerves were frayed. To bring good luck to the Chum with the game up for grabs, many fans crossed fingers or toes, took out a rabbit's foot, or refused to move arms or legs or scratch an itching nose.

In the top of the eighth, with Rail still on the mound and a runner on second, the Goldeye cleanup hitter smacked a liner to left for a hit. The runner rounded third and headed for home as Ham fired toward the plate. P.U. got the ball on one hop, blocked the plate, and took a hard hit from the runner. But he held onto the ball, and the ump yelled "Out!" A huge cheer went up from the fans, and a collective sigh of relief echoed in the stands. On the next out, French Fry reinjured a hamstring making a diving catch. Frog and the trainer examined him on the field, and Frog decided to take him out. Spitz took his place in right and recorded the third out on a high fly to the warning track. It was Spitz's first appearance in the Bronze. Rail got a standing ovation as he came off the mound.

In the bottom of the eighth, Drum Drum managed a single but was thrown out trying to steal. Ninth inning! So many games won or lost in the ninth, so many hearts thrilled or broken! Who could predict the outcome? The fans were all emotion. A chant went up. "One, two, three … out, out, out … one, two, three … " and it increased in volume as the Chum took the field. The sound was earsplitting, the moment electric! The fans were reaching out to the players, urging them on, trying to tell them they would indeed prevail.

Then the chant changed. "Close the door, they get no more … close the door!" The umpire behind home plate stopped the game and stared at the fans in the right-field stands. Was he annoyed or was he just paying tribute to those fans who had endured such heartbreak over so long a time?

So long a time! William Taft was president (1909–1913) when the Chum last won the Bronze! The world was so much cheaper then. You could buy a new, upright piano with ivory keys for seventy-five dollars. Cokes were a nickel and a corn broom cost nineteen cents. Back then, men wore straw hats when they attended ball games.

The umpire behind home plate smiled. Maybe he was a Chum fan. The game resumed. On the mound was the Chum closer Bule Penn. He got the first Goldeye hitter on a grounder to Santa. Cheers rocked the stadium. The second hitter flied out to Compleet in right center. The cheers increased. The third hitter went down on strikes. The noise was deafening.

In the bottom of the ninth, the first batter was a pinch hitter for Penn. A chant started in right field, "Chum, Chum, get it done…Chum, Chum, get a run." But the pinch hitter went down swinging. A second chant started in the bleachers beneath the scoreboard and spread to the rest of the ball park. "One more, one more, get us one, we need no more…one more, one more." But Payday popped up to the first baseman in foul territory.

Spitz came to the plate. In the dugout, Compleet had paid little attention to the first two batters; he was wrapped up in his own thoughts. Before the first game of the Bronze, he and Spitz had been on a late night stroll. They had talked about the coming Bronze Series and how it would be great if the bear could win a game with a home run, and Spitz—his dreams were not so grand—could at least get some playing time and maybe get a hit and score a run. And here in the ninth inning of perhaps the last game, some of the things they had wished for had come true. Compleet had won game three with a home run in the fourteenth, and Spitz had finally gotten into a game.

But the drama was incomplete. It lacked a hit by Spitz and a run scored. Compleet moved to the top of the dugout and tried to get Spitz's attention. After strike one, Spitz stepped out of the batters' box and saw the bear looking at him, and signing, *Carpe diem! This is your moment!*

Spitz looked at a ball, down and in. He was charged up and felt like spitting tobacco juice on home plate but thought better of it. He chewed on his plug nervously. The next pitch was a fastball, a little high, but Spitz reached up for it and punched it into right field for a hit.

Now the run! Compleet thought. The fans began a chant. "Ham, Ham, wham it, wham it! Ham, Ham!" as he came to the plate. On the second pitch, Ham answered with a tremendous shot to left center. The ball rolled all the way to the wall and bounced away from the left fielder. Ham most likely could have ended the game with a triple and an RBI, but Spitz wasn't moving fast enough. The third base coach held Spitz at third; Ham overran second but got back to the base before the tag.

Two on and two out, and Compleet lumbered to the plate, dragging a bat in his right paw. The fans went wild! Their hero was at the plate. Yes, it had to be! He would hit a home run, maybe out to the stand of spruce in the river park beyond right field. The bear seemed larger than life. He towered over everyone, his muscles bulging. Every fan was standing and hollering. The chant started, "Home run, home run, the bear, the bear … home run, home run, we dare, we dare!" Again and again the chant echoed in the stands and out by the waterfall. Had baseball in Cuspin Heights ever known such a moment?

But Compleet had another idea, the play. When they had that talk about the Bronze, Compleet had signed how he would like to single Spitz home or bunt him home. He never signed he wanted to hit a home run with Spitz on base. No, that would take away from Spitz's running the bases; it would put Compleet in the limelight. The bear had had enough moments of glory in his brief stay with the Chum. He had already filed away, in the deep recesses of his brain, memories that would last a lifetime. He wanted so much to see his friend in the spotlight—a friend who had always been there in good times and bad. He had told Spitz if ever the right moment came along in the Bronze Series with him at the plate and Spitz on third, he would look in his direction and sign, *The play!* That would mean a bunt was coming.

Taking a lead off third, Spitz wasn't thinking about a bunt. Like everyone else in the stadium, he was thinking home run, or at least a double or single—any kind of hit but a bunt. Then he saw the bear drop his bat and with his paws sign, *The play!* Spitz shook his head back and forth. He was a slow runner. Almost everyone in the stadium knew it, including the Goldeye, who had seen him slowly move from first to third. A bunt was too risky; the bear had to put the team first. But as you know, dear reader, Compleet could be very stubborn at times. And this was one of those times.

The bear took a ball and then a strike. Again he dropped his bat and signed to Spitz. This time he looked away before Spitz could shake his head. Frog was standing at the top of the dugout with the rest of the team. He said out loud, "What in the world is he doin'? Why is he usin' sign language? Has he gone crazy?" The third base coach was equally puzzled.

Compleet took a second strike, and Spitz relaxed a moment. With two strikes, he wouldn't dare bunt. It was bad baseball; most managers would agree. A foul bunt with two strikes on the batter is an out. Yes, much too risky. But the bear was still thinking bunt. Two things were in his favor: he had developed into a fine bunter, which upped his chances of keeping a ball inside the foul line. And the infield had dropped back, not expecting a bunt. This meant Spitz had a chance; the infielder would have to take more steps to get to the ball.

One of the maxims in baseball reads, "Baseball is a game of inches." Like all maxims, it's true. If Spitz could keep away from the ball in the catcher's hand by an inch or two, he could score. And Compleet intended to give him those inches by bunting the ball along the first base line. That meant the catcher had to swing around with the ball to tag the runner, more so than if the ball came to him from the third baseman.

The bear looked down at third and nodded. "No, no!" said Spitz to himself. "He *is* going to bunt!" And bunt he did!

Sometimes we allow our hearts to win out over our minds. And who will say this is bad? This was more than an ash bat pushing a white leather baseball over infield grass. This was a thank-you note, a message with heart, a love song, a valentine, a big bear hug. This was about friendship, trust, and understanding between two ballplayers. This was Compleet saying, *Thanks, Spitz, for everything!*

When Spitz saw the ball slowly creep along the first base line, he took off for home. But his legs seemed to move in slow motion; the plate seemed so far away. His heart was pounding against his shirt, the sweat streaming down his face. His almost-forty body was trying to act like it was still twenty-two.

The catcher got the ball from the first baseman and spun around to make the tag. Spitz came in hard and slid wide past the plate as his hand reached out to touch it. The catcher dove for Spitz's arm, but Spitz eluded the catcher's hand and the ball by maybe an inch, until he had touched the plate. The ump's arms flew out from his sides. "Safe!"

Baseball, a game of inches. For Spitz and all who were cheering, it was a perfect moment in a perfect world!

End of game—end of the Bronze Series! The fans were unrestrained! Ninety years of frustration, anger, heartache, and tears—gone! The players mobbed Spitz and the bear, and some hoisted them to their shoulders. This took some doing. It required four robust players to get the bear onto their shoulders. Then the players, with Spitz and the bear in the spotlight, paraded around the field to the cheers and shouts of the fans. Fireworks lit the sky and shut out the night; a big "Number Four" blinked again and again on the scoreboard, followed by a huge "Bronze Champs at Last!" Loud, triumphant music filled the air.

No one wanted to leave the ball park. The moment was too joyous, the realization too intense; yes, the Chum were indeed champions! The party went on and on for over an hour. Fans danced in the aisles, lovers kissed, strangers shook hands with strangers. Some of the fans were crying, but they were happy tears. Many threw confetti or popcorn or taco chips or peanuts still in their shells. The fans chanted the names of the Chum players. They applauded as every player (except Compleet) in turn stepped forward and raised his hat or waved an arm. Compleet, when his turn came, simply stood there and looked at the fans and seemed to smile.

But joyous as the moments were, they had to end. The lights dimmed, a broad hint that it was time for all to leave. Dutifully, the fans poured out of the stadium, but not to go home, at least for most. This time might never come to them again; they had to try to stop the clocks. They jammed the restaurants, the amusement pier, and filled the parks. A long line of sedans, pickups, and SUVs drove up and down River Boulevard; drivers honked, passengers leaned out windows, waving, shouting, singing. Fire trucks joined the line and wailed, not a message to back off, stay away, but a message of delight.

After the customary clubhouse party and TV and radio interviews, the bear and Spitz returned to the hotel. In the lobby, all of the employees, including Helen (with Mai Tai in tow), cheered and reached out to touch them. In their room, Spitz fell exhausted on his bed, and Compleet sank to the floor. But neither slept; there was too much of the game to relive, too much to talk over. "You big, bad black bear!" said Spitz over and over, laughing. "With the entire world watchin', you bunt with two strikes! What were you thinkin'?"

I was thinking it was a good way to get you home. It worked, didn't it? It got you your moment of glory.

"Yeah, kid, my moment of glory." Spitz gave out a yell and threw pillows at the bear and a magazine that was on the table by the bed. Spitz's eyes were wide with delight. It was a time to remember, the dramatic ninth inning, the shouts and cheers of the fans, the slide into home plate, the victory walk around the field. When someone is on top of the world, the view and the feeling are indeed magnificent!

The Party Town

It took Cuspin Heights three days to recover from the shock— Cuspin Chum, Bronze Champions! Were the words true, wishful thinking, a dream? It had to be real; too many people had been in the stadium for game four. Too many people had read the headlines in the city papers and the papers in the suburbs.

In celebration, much of the city festooned itself. Along River Boulevard every lamppost, store window, and tree displayed banners, flags, or bunting. There was a victory parade from Tailors Station south to High Rock Park, with players, and team and city officials, in open convertibles or vans or pickups or flatbed trucks. There were marching bands and makeshift floats. Compleet and Spitz were in the lead team car, and further back were the Bruedocks and Kristy.

After game four, the five of them decided to go to Cuspin to help the bear and Spitz celebrate. When Ronny called the hotel, Spitz said he would help them get airline tickets and rooms at the Three C's. He and the bear would pay their expenses.

Spitz and Compleet met the four Bruedocks and Kristy at Cuspin Heights International a short time before the parade. The bear was overjoyed to see them again, but there wasn't much time for talk. There was time for them to drop off their luggage at the hotel and clean up a bit. Then off to Tailors in a cab to join the parade before it moved south.

At High Rock Park, the players walked into the park with cheering fans surrounding them, wanting to touch them, give them a pat on the back, or shake hands. Near Florets Fountain on a raised platform, the mayor of Cuspin gave a short speech, praising Compleet and other team members, the Chum organization, and the townspeople for backing the players.

As MVP of the Bronze Series, Compleet had to lumber up to the speaker's stand and receive the key to the city from the mayor. It was a monstrous key, and Compleet didn't quite know what to do with it. Spitz was standing nearby and walked over and took the key from the bear. Someone in the crowd yelled, "Let's hear a real bear yell!" Others clapped in agreement. Compleet felt embarrassed, but to oblige he let out a frightful roar. Everyone cheered!

Then Spitz, who saw that Compleet didn't know what to do next, spoke into the mike. "Thank you all for comin' out on this day of celebration. I'm the official voice of the kid, I mean, the bear. So if we can get him to use sign language to say a few words, I'll pass along what he says."

The crowd clapped and cheered in anticipation. Compleet, not used to speaking in public, hesitated, but Spitz smiled at him, and the fans kept silent as he organized his thoughts. *I can't tell you how happy I am to be here in this great city and to be a member of the team that has captured the Bronze. Every team needs a cheering section. And you fans are the loudest, the most grateful, and the most loving I have ever met!* Spitz repeated the message. Everyone laughed, clapped, or cheered. Compleet continued. *I don't know what else to say except... thanks for accepting me as a member of the Chum.* Spitz translated the bear's signing.

Loud cheers filled the air. Someone started a chant, and everyone joined in. "Compleet, Compleet...he gets it done...Compleet, Compleet...he makes it fun." Over and over, the crowd shouted the words "Compleet, Compleet...he gets it done..."

When the people quieted down, the mayor stepped up to the mike. "How about it, Compleet, are you going to come back next year?" The bear nodded, and everyone cheered.

"And win another Bronze for us?" asked someone near the stand. Compleet nodded again, and again everyone cheered.

Ham approached the mike and, as captain of the team, held high the huge bronze cup with its familiar medallions. As on cue, the sun came out from behind the clouds. The engraved bronze sparkled in the bright light. Ham passed the heavy cup from player to player, and a few gave a short speech while holding it. French Fry gave the best talk—short and to the point—about the loyal fans, savvy Chum management, and enthusiastic, skilled players, all of whom had a part in bringing the Bronze to Cuspin Heights.

Afterward Compleet and Spitz, pushing past adoring fans, located the Bruedocks and Kristy in the crowd and joined them. Then the seven squeezed into a team SUV and drove back to the Three C's Hotel. As Spitz drove west, Compleet signed to Ronny, *What door can I open with this huge key?* He held it out to Ronny.

"It doesn't open any door," answered Ronny. "It's just something that mayors do. They give these keys to very important people. And you're a very important person, that is, bear, in Cuspin Heights right now."

Clara tried to explain the key. "Compleet, giving the key of the city to someone means the entire city is open to the person. It's like the person can go anywhere, and the doors will open for him or her in love and gratitude."

Hm, thought the bear. *Why give a key to someone if he can't use it? Why not give him free meals or free taxi rides, things he can use?*

The next day, the Bruedocks and Kristy, Spitz, and the bear took an elevator to the Crow's Nest at the top of the Platt Building and a boat ride on the Muddy Muck. They walked along the prettiest part of the river within the city limits and visited the Flood Aquarium and the Museum of Models. Of course, they couldn't pass up a visit to Backlore Haven Zoo.

Twice during Compleet's suspension, he got permission from the court to visit the zoo. And he and Spitz visited Backlore a few times during the Bronze games. When the group reached the bear compound, Compleet began to purr in a deep voice. Honey B. appeared from behind a mound and answered his purr with one of her own. She hurried over to the section of the moat opposite him.

"Is that the sow you've fallen for?" asked Clint, smiling. Compleet nodded.

"She's a young, pretty thing," said Ginny.

"What a beautiful coat of dark brown, and there's a bit of black too!" exclaimed Kristy. "Her hair is so clean looking! I wonder how often she grooms herself."

Compleet didn't hear Kristy's comments. He was looking into

Honey B'.s eyes, trying to tell her he missed being near her. The two stood there staring at each other and grunting softly every now and then. This went on for the longest time. The Bruedocks, Kristy, and Spitz decided to leave the young lovers alone. They visited the gift shop and walked around the zoo looking at other animals. Later, Spitz went back for Compleet. He seemed not to have moved at all; the two bears were still staring at each other!

"Come on, kid, time to go. Throw her a kiss and tell her you love her."

Two New Families

S pitz and Julie saw a lot of each other after that first meeting at the Three C's and their night walk. They had much to talk over. Each wanted to know what the other had done since they broke up. Julie said when she read that the bear and Spitz had signed with the Chum, she became a Chum fan again. She had always liked baseball. Since she grew up in Spouler, which was northwest of Cuspin, she often attended Chum games until she married and moved to the East Coast. After her divorce and the sale of the house, she returned to Spouler with her two children. They moved in with her mom and dad, who had recently bought a house in a working-class neighborhood. The house was crowded, but Julie was glad her children could be close to her parents and get to know them better.

She always checked the Chum box score to see whether Spitz had been in the lineup. She went to a few games but never saw him at bat or in the field. She often spotted him in the dugout and thought of writing a letter or calling on her cell phone or showing up at practice before a game and asking for an autograph. Each time, she got cold feet. Suppose he was still on the bottle? Suppose he wouldn't talk to her because she had left him?

In the morning, on the day she met him at the Three C's, she said to herself, "Julie, you're acting like a schoolgirl! If you want to meet him, do something about it." While thinking what to do, she picked up a newspaper at a stand and asked the clerk if he knew anything personal about the star of the Chum, Compleet Bear. She said she was trying to get McOystre's address. She had never read anything about Spitz in the newspapers but a lot about Compleet. She learned they palled around and thought they might even live in the same hotel or condo.

The clerk said she must be new to Cuspin, that a while back there had been a scandal about the bear's drinking. Pictures of Compleet and McOystre in front of the bear's hotel got in the papers. He told her the two roomed together at the Three C's on East 93rd.

Spitz and Julie often took moonlight walks along the river and went to the best restaurants. Julie noticed that Spitz never ordered a drink. He told her he was off the bottle for good. She believed that this time he meant it.

That should have cleared the air between them. Julie wanted to remarry badly enough. Her kids needed a father, and she had a hard time making enough money as a personal trainer. Her parents gave her money now and then, but they had a moderate income and few savings. Most important, she loved Spitz. "I suppose, deep down, I have always loved you," she said to him one evening over dinner. "Even after I married, I found myself thinking of you at odd moments when I was doing some chore around the house or driving about town."

But there was one practice of his she hated: the tobacco chewing! She didn't want to be a nag, but she had to talk about it before they got married. She got her courage up and told him how she felt about tobacco. It was a dirty habit; it stained the teeth. And she hated to see him spit tobacco juice when they were walking.

"I'll make you a promise," said Spitz one afternoon when the two were sitting on a bench in High Rock Park. "I know my chewin's not good for me, although I do enjoy it. I know it's messy, that it causes bad breath, and don't help the teeth stay healthy. But let me get some real good chaws in before the weddin', and I give my word on a Bible I'll give up tobacco."

A Fall Wedding

And so the date was set for the nuptials. The church the two picked out was St. Zeffon by the River, one of the oldest churches west of the Appalachians. During their brief stay in Cuspin, the Bruedocks and Kristy had attended a service there. The bear and Spitz had tagged along. Spitz liked the music and the minister's sermon. When Julie saw the inside of the church, she commented on the fine, old-wood choir stalls and wainscoting. Compleet couldn't understand all the fuss. *Wood is wood*, he thought. *Good for scratching, that's all.*

At the wedding, Compleet was best man. He had to get court permission to attend since he still had to fulfill some of his thirty-days detention. He insisted on paying for most of the wedding, including Julie's dress. It was a lovely mauve damask cocktail dress with shoes dyed to match. Julie was in her midthirties, but on her wedding day she seemed ten years younger. Or so Spitz thought as he stared at her at the altar as sunlight entered the church and settled on her face.

In the congregation were some of the Chum players, and Fred Miltones, John Boslerts, Frogertee and their wives. Helen Achts was there with Mai Tai tucked inside her light coat. Dutch McOystre, who had back trouble and diabetes, had made it to the church. He said to almost everyone he met, "Only an earthquake and a tornado and a flood and a five-alarm fire happenin' all at once could have kept me away! He's my son, and he's got a Bronze ring on his finger! How many dads can say that, huh?"

The Bruedocks and Kristy were there, and Clyde and Joe Wathersmythe and their wives. The church was filled and about four thousand stood outside and along the nearby streets. Most had come to see Compleet or other star Chum players. Spitz knew few fans would be looking for him, but he wasn't upset. His daddy had made it to the wedding, and Julie would soon be Mrs. McOystre—the two things that counted the most.

The couple honeymooned at Manor Ridge in the Canadian Rockies. Compleet paid for almost everything—airfare, rented car, hotel, meals, and sightseeing. It was small payment for the many courtesies Spitz had extended to him. The snow was deep and the air invigorating. Julie was an accomplished skier; Spitz had never been on skis. On the fast slopes she got in some good runs, but mostly she stayed with Spitz on the flat trails. They did some snowshoeing and tobogganing.

At dinner one evening, Spitz said, "If someone had said to me last year at this time that next fall I'd have a Bronze ring on one finger and a weddin' ring on another, I would have said, 'Impossible!'" He paused and then added, "And to think I owe it all to a bear! He got me on the Chum team, and that meant I got a Bronze ring, and it meant you had no trouble findin' me. You never would have found me if I was still playin' ball in western Tennessee."

"So we both owe your bear friend a debt," said Julie.

Back in Western Tennessee

When Spitz and Julie returned from their honeymoon, they spent a few days with her parents, who had been taking care of her children. Then they drove with the kids to Tomtowne and rented a house. Where did they intend to live permanently? They weren't sure. Spring training was a few months away; they would have time to make up their minds.

Spitz helped Julie enroll Charles and Carly in a school near their house. In the days ahead, Spitz had a chance to get to know the two. He played computer games, board games, and baseball with them, and when the snow came, the three and Julie built a giant snow castle. Twice they all went to movies together and enjoyed snacks afterward. Spitz and Julie organized a birthday party for Carly, who turned eight in mid-November. Everyone in the neighborhood was invited. Spitz, who had never had a birthday party as a kid, probably enjoyed Carly's party more than some of her friends.

Spitz had been keeping track of the number of days left on Compleet's thirty-day confinement. When the time was almost up, he told Julie he would drive to Cuspin Heights and bring Compleet back to Tomtowne and then drive him to the farm. He had called the hotel a few times since the honeymoon and got a briefing from Helen, who was taking care of the bear as best she could. During the last phone call, he told Compleet, "I'll be in Cuspin in two days, so hang in there and think how much fun it will be when you're back with Ronny and the rest of the family." Helen was holding the receiver near the bear's ear.

Spitz bought an SUV off the showroom in Tomtowne and drove to Cuspin late at night when the traffic was light. At the Three C's, he woke up the bear so the two could have a joyous reunion. Compleet signed, *It was very hard without you. I was without a voice! But Helen or a bellhop brought meals up to the room. I used gestures to communicate with her, and they worked sometimes. I took a few walks but mostly stayed in the room.*

The bear looked at Spitz with a serious face and signed, *I want to take Honey B. back to the farm with me. I want to start a family.*

"That's fine, kid, but I'm surprised. I thought the two of you were just having a summer romance." Spitz knew that males are not part of a bear family. After a sow becomes pregnant, the male goes off on his own. When the female gives birth to a cub, she raises it without help. But Compleet was far from being an average bear. So it should have surprised no one he intended to mate with Honey B. for life.

After a short sleep, Spitz drove the bear to Backlore Haven Zoo to talk to the executive director. When told Compleet wanted to take Honey B. back with him to the farm, the director said the sow had been on edge for days after her scare at Tailors. Had her experience left a scar? Could she ever feel safe and happy outside the zoo? Spitz said the sow would share Compleet's boulder house; a fence circled the farm to keep the animals in and intruders out. Spitz told the director how much the Bruedocks loved animals. Ronny had been the bear's constant companion from the time the cub arrived on the farm until he joined the Tenn Nine team. Ronny still kept in touch by phone and letters. The family had been in Cuspin Heights for the victory parade. Spitz said Compleet wanted to start a family with the sow. Like Spitz, the director was surprised. But he relented. He knew the sow would be happier on a farm with her cubs and bear-man than at the zoo.

Honey B. was elated to see Compleet, but she became nervous when she got in Spitz's SUV. Was she going back to Tailors? She quieted down only when Compleet continued to purr in his deep voice and, at times, lick her face. The trip to Tomtowne was uneventful except for the few times honking horns got too near Spitz's car and upset the sow.

That night Compleet and Honey B. slept on a rug in the guest room. Spitz was in the room also to keep an eye on the two. It wasn't long before Charles and Carly crept into Spitz's bed. They had never seen a bear up close. Julie heard the children talking and soon joined them. There were four bedrooms in the house, and everyone was in the guest room! The McOystres were smiling—they were together again. But the happiest of all were two four-legged creatures sleeping on a rug.

The next day, Spitz, the bears, Julie, and the children drove to the Bruedock farm. Clint, Ginny, Clara, and Ronny were happy to have visitors and happy that Compleet and Honey B. would be staying with them for a few months.

The McOystres remained at the farm over Thanksgiving and the three-day weekend. Charles and Carly had a ball being around the animals and playing with the tamest ones. Carly took a special liking to Slo-Mikey, Autumn, and Carpenter. Charles was most interested in Desert and Andy. Ronny, when he was nearby, allowed them to ride Desert, but he kept a tight grip on the camel's halter. Carly and Ginny collected eggs in the hen house twice a day, and Charles and Carly helped Clara milk the cows. Spitz, Compleet, Ronny, and Julie often hit baseballs and played catch, and the youngsters sometimes joined them.

Honey B. and Compleet had little trouble moving into the boulder house, which served their needs with few changes. It should be mentioned Honey B. had put on considerable weight. The women folk noticed it, but out of politeness said nothing. But the evening before the McOystres were set to leave, Compleet stood next to Honey B. and announced he would soon be a father. She was due to have a cub, maybe two or three, sometime during their hibernation. Everyone clapped and smiled, and Spitz and Ronny proposed toasts to the young couple.

Afterward Spitz and Ronny talked about the news. "When did she get pregnant?" asked Ronny.

"I don't know," said Spitz with a puzzled look. "He didn't see her for the first time until late summer. And she was under close watch at the zoo."

"Strange," said Ronny. "Is he sure he's the father?"

"He sounded like he was. The kid's too smart to be fooled about such things. If he said he would soon be a father, then that's it."

They looked at each other but said nothing. Then Spitz smiled. "I'll be! Some nights the kid must have got into the bear compound. I remember his comin' back to the room real late sometimes. I just figured he'd been out walkin'."

Spitz never said any more about the pregnancy, and Compleet never offered an explanation.

The days between Thanksgiving and Christmas were perhaps the happiest in Compleet's life. Honey B. was always by his side, and the Bruedocks were the same helpful, friendly, considerate people they had always been. It was like old times on the farm. The only addition was Honey B. Kristy came over often. She, Ronny, Clara, Compleet, and Honey B. took long walks about the farm. Everyone noticed how contented Honey B. was; it was written all over her face. She had freedom never allowed her at the zoo; she was with her bear-man. And she would soon be looking after a little one, or maybe two or three.

At Christmas, Spitz and family returned for Christmas dinner and a short stay. The two bears joined all the activities, but everyone noticed they were listless and groggy. They would fall asleep at odd moments and struggled to pay attention to what was going on. So the Bruedocks prepared a hibernation dinner, which included turkey, seven sweets and seven sours, hot cider, and applesauce spice cake. When it was over, the Bruedocks and Kristy and the McOystres accompanied the bears the short distance to their boulder house. Compleet and Honey B. disappeared inside, and Ronny hung a sign outside the entrance. It read, "Do not disturb until spring. Just Married!"

Three Additions

For Compleet, this hibernation was different from the others. This time he had no nightmares, no memories of noise and lights and blood, no memories of his mom lying in a heap and not moving. When he dreamed of her, it was of pleasant times, of walking or loping with her and Sis through the dense woods at High Point and splashing in the cold lake. When he awoke from time to time, he looked at Honey B. stretched out next to him and went back to sleep, happy and at peace.

When he was ready to shake off his hibernation, he awoke one morning and heard soft, high-pitched sounds coming from near Honey B. He rubbed his eyes and saw three very small, bald cubs cuddled up to his mate. He was disappointed. *I thought they'd be up and jumping around and have a full body of hair. I guess I expected too much too soon.* Honey B. was awake and looked at Compleet with loving eyes. He crawled over and rubbed against her, as if to say, "Good job; they are just fine. And, hey, you gave me not one or two, but three young ones."

Later, when he went outside to get some fresh air, he saw Ronny and Clara nearby. He signed to Ronny, *Come see our new family.* When the two followed the bear inside the house and saw the three new additions, they smiled and told Compleet how cute they were. The bear thought they might be saying that just to please him; he thought the three were ugly.

They sure are skinny!

"Give them time," said Ronny. "Honey B'.s good milk will take care of that."

Have you been in contact with Spitz?

"He called a few times and wanted me to wake you, but I said it was best to let you wake up in your own time. I said you'd get in touch with him."

Call him when you get a chance and tell him Honey B. gave birth to triplets.

New Season and
a Hard Choice

It was three days before Spitz could leave training camp and fly up to Nashville. He stopped off in Tomtowne to see Julie and the kids before he drove to the farm. When he saw the newcomers cuddling up to Honey B., he smiled from ear to ear and gave Compleet a hard slap on the back and three cigars.

What are these for? Should I give one to each cub?

"No, no, kid! They're for you. Humans have this custom. The males give out cigars to celebrate a birth, in this case three births."

Should I eat the cigars?

"You're supposed to smoke them. I guess you better just put them in your house on a ledge as a reminder of the good news."

Spitz and Compleet walked out of the den into the sunlight. The smell of spring was in the air, and the earth was beginning to turn light green; meadowlarks and mockers and Tennessee warblers were singing cheerful tunes. Buds were everywhere. Compleet and Spitz both took deep breaths. "There's no season like spring, kid. Winter is behind us; it's time to think of baseball. The team's practicin' hard at Seedmount. We all missed you. How soon can you get ready to fly down?"

Compleet didn't answer right away. *I've got to tell you something important. But I don't know quite how to say it.*

"Spill it, kid. I can take it."

Well, humans talk about putting the most important things first. That's a good idea, and I've been thinking about the important things in my life, and, well, Spitz, dear friend, I've changed my mind. I'm not joining the team this year. I want to be with Honey B. and help her raise the cubs.

Spitz was stunned and didn't know how to answer. Compleet continued, *With players like Ham, Jimbo, Jammin, and P.U., the team can win another title without my help. But management may not renew your contract, and that bothers me.*

"I got my Bronze ring. A lot of better players then me can't say that. But you! Do you realize what you're givin' up? I know you could ask for a big raise, and Miltones would give it to you without thinkin' twice. Honey B. could stay on the farm, and the Bruedocks would make her comfortable. It just don't make sense you quittin' when you're on top!"

No, Spitz, I've thought it over, and I'm staying. I've already told Ronny what I aim to do. And when he told Clint, Ginny, and Clara, they said they were happy with my decision.

As soon as he left the farm, Spitz called Frog and told him what the bear had signed. "He what!" shouted Frog. "He's givin' up a career just like that? Why? If he stayed around long enough, he'd most likely break about every sluggin' record there is."

"I know," said Spitz. "I told him he was givin' up a good thing. But he's not that interested in a career like we guys are. It's his family he's thinkin' about. I give him credit for that."

When Miltones and Boslerts heard the news, they were dumbfounded. "That's what we get for not signing him to a new contract right after the series," moaned Miltones. He called an emergency meeting of the owners and Boslerts; they talked late into the night, trying to agree on a salary and other perks that would lure the bear back to the team.

When they had agreed on a package, Miltones said, "Let's talk to Spitz. The bear trusts him. He can get Compleet to come in for a talk. The only way we're going to get the bear to change his mind is to negotiate with him face-to-face."

When Miltones called Spitz and asked him to help arrange a conference with the bear and high Chum officials, Spitz readily agreed. After all, his baseball future was at stake as well as the bear's. Spitz was still in Tomtowne with Julie and the kids. When

Compleet had told him his plans, Spitz decided not to rejoin the team in Seedmount. Why should he return to spring training? If Compleet left the team, Spitz was sure the Chum wouldn't renew his contract.

For the second time in a week, Spitz drove down to the Bruedock farm to see the bear. This time he intended to plead with Compleet to talk to Miltones and the others. It wasn't necessary to plead. Compleet said he would be happy to talk to the Chum management. He owed the organization that courtesy, and he wanted to please Spitz.

The Money Game

Miltones, Boslerts, and other important staff were seated when Compleet and Spitz entered the room. Everyone immediately got up, smiled, and greeted both players. Someone offered them ham and cheese on rye or wheat and a choice of soda, coffee, or tea. It was obvious Miltones and the others wanted to put on a pleasant face, a helpful face. For the Chum organization, a lot was at stake.

Miltones looked at the bear standing in the middle of the room and said, "On behalf of the other owners, I want to thank you for coming here on such short notice, and I personally want to apologize for not offering you and your friend Spitz contracts last fall. We're sorry we let this matter drag; we intended to give you a big salary boost. You helped the team win the Bronze title and fill every stadium we played in during the last two months of the season and throughout the playoffs. You certainly deserve a raise, a considerable raise."

Compleet signed to Spitz, who repeated the bear's message. *Thank you for your kind words, but my mind is made up. I would rather stay close to Honey B. than play baseball. Since I helped you win a championship, I feel this gives me an out.*

"Of course," said Miltones, unfazed by the bear's comments, "if you would agree to a new contract, we would automatically re-sign your friend Spitz."

Spitz interrupted. "This ain't about me, Mr. Miltones. This is about the kid."

I'm sorry if you don't sign Spitz if I leave the team. But I know he would want me to do what my heart tells me. Spitz relayed the message.

Miltones persisted. "We intended to give you a big raise from 20 to 35 million. That's a lot of money. It would allow you to do so much good for yourself and those you love. And we would like, with your permission, to set you up with your own radio show and have you do spot commercials on TV, both with Spitz's help, of course. We can arrange for Honey B. to accompany you on road trips. If a hotel or motel has a policy that doesn't allow bears, the team will find a hotel or motel that does. We'll all stand behind you."

The bear didn't answer for a while; Miltones took that as a positive sign. Then Compleet signed, *Honey B. is a mother now with three small ones. She should stay on the farm and take care of them, and I should be there to help. I'm not interested in TV or a radio show. And yes, 35 million dollars is a lot of money.* Spitz repeated the message.

Miltones wasn't making any headway and he knew it. He played his trump card. "It's possible we could go higher, say forty, maybe even forty-five. I'd have to get confirmation on the higher figure from the other owners, of course."

Compleet looked down at the floor. Spitz, seeing he was embarrassed, got up from his seat, walked over to the bear and stroked his head. "It's okay, kid, stick to your guns. I can always say I played ball with someone that was offered 45 million a season and turned it down. Now that's a story!"

Spitz and Compleet took a cab to the Three C's Hotel. They planned to stay there overnight and catch a flight to Nashville in the morning. Helen was at the desk, and Mai Tai was sleeping nearby in a basket. Helen greeted them with a big smile and said it was good to see them together again at the hotel.

In their room, neither Spitz nor the bear said much. Spitz

knew his playing days were over. He had a lot to think about. How would he support Julie and the kids? Where would they live? Could he get a job as a scout or a coach with the Chum? Would he and the bear still see each other?

Compleet felt guilty. His decision had ended the career of his good friend. To whom did the bear owe allegiance? Was it to Spitz, the team, Cuspin fans, or was it to Honey B. and the cubs? *Oh*, he thought, *if only Honey B. could sign and understand English, she could give me some good advice.*

At noon the next day at Cuspin Heights International, Spitz and the bear boarded their plane. At the same time, Spitz was being paged on the loudspeaker. "Mr. McOystre, please come to the courtesy desk. Mr. McOystre, please come to … "

In the air, a stewardess approached Spitz. "Mr. McOystre?" Spitz nodded. "The airport has been trying to reach you. I have a message."

She handed him a small envelope. He opened it, pulled out a folded piece of stationery, and read the following: "Dear Mr. McOystre, The owners and John Boslerts held a meeting early this morning and have agreed to substantially increase our last offer. For the coming season, Compleet's salary would total 65 million dollars, and your salary would increase to 4.5 million dollars. If this is satisfactory, please get in touch with my office as soon as possible. Cordially yours, Fred Miltones."

Spitz's jaw dropped. He kept looking at the figures and said to himself, "Did I ever in my wildest thoughts expect to earn 4.5 million a year in baseball or anywhere else?"

Compleet signed, *What is it? Is Miltones offering me more money?*

"Right, kid, but you'll never guess how much."

How much?

"Sixty-five million! And I'd get 4.5 million! Kid, you can't keep turnin' down money this big. You could hire ten vets to stay with Honey B. and the cubs and tend to them. You could set up a special fund for the Bruedocks, and they'd never have to worry about money."

Let me think this through.

Spitz was content not to say anything more. This was a big decision for the bear; no one could advise him. At the Nashville airport, Julie picked up her husband and the bear. Compleet asked Spitz to get in the back with him. On the way to Tomtowne, the bear signed, *You're right, Spitz. This money is big. I was thinking about Honey B. in that small space in the zoo. I mentioned it before, buying big chunks of land to create reserves for wild animals, like the safari parks, game reserves, and national parks in Africa I heard about.*

"Here's your chance. Take the owners' offer, sign a contract, and 65 million is yours."

By the time Julie pulled into the McOystre's driveway in Tomtowne, Compleet had made up his mind. *Spitz is right. This money is big, too big to ignore. With it, I can make sure the Bruedocks never have to fret about money, and I can set up my nature parks. Ronny and the others will keep Honey B. and the cubs safe and comfortable when I'm not at the farm.*

The bear signed to Spitz, *Before you drive me to the farm, call Miltones and say we accept his generous offer.* Spitz smiled, made the call, and spoke briefly with Miltones. Then he drove the bear to the farm, stayed an hour to chat with the Bruedocks, and returned to Tomtowne.

Miltones made a brief statement to the press shortly after he got off the phone with Spitz. Soon all Cuspin Heights knew of the bear's decision. Chum players and the tens of thousands of fans who had known of the bear's wish to retire (courtesy of TV and radio news flashes) all let out a deep sigh of relief. Frog, Boslerts, and Miltones couldn't stop smiling.

Defending Champions

The Chum held a special news conference with Miltones, Boslerts, Frog, Compleet, and Spitz on stage. Miltones presented the bear with a huge check, almost as large as the bear himself, made out to Compleet for 65 million. The owner smiled and reached down and patted the bear's head. Flashbulbs popped. Compleet felt foolish holding the huge check. He thought, *What am I supposed to do with this? I thought management would pay me with regular checks and not all at once.*

Later he asked Spitz about the huge check. Spitz answered, "Do? Don't do nothin'. It's only worth somethin' to a dealer in baseball stuff. Miltones did that so he could brag about all those zeros. Or maybe so the old folks watchin' on TV could read everything."

Compleet's huge salary (a baseball and sports record) was the talk on every radio and TV station in the country and on stations around the world. Chat rooms on the Web were jammed with messages, many questioning how someone could spend 65 million and still have time to have a life. Newspapers from coast to coast carried the news on front pages, as well as lengthy comments on the sports pages. Cuspin papers all ran banner headlines.

Reaction in the baseball world was mixed. Some thought it all right for an established all-star player to get that much but resented a second-year player, and a bear to boot, getting such a huge raise. The Chum players greeted the news with delight. After all, it was hard to be jealous of a teammate that had played his heart out in the postseason and was responsible for victories in Bronze games three and four. In part, their rings were a gift from the bear. If all went well, Compleet would lead the team to another championship and put another Bronze ring on the players' fingers.

The opener against the Troefield Trout had been sold out for months. It was no surprise most of the seats had gone to the same fans that had followed the team for years. But something had changed. On game day, the Chum players were quick to pick it up. The fans were, well, more relaxed, more confident. The smiles and the jokes came easy; there was a holiday spirit in the air. The long-suffering faithful didn't have to wonder if this would be the year. Last year was the year! This year the team was the defending champion! And if someone had asked any group at Tailors whether the Chum would repeat, the answer was predictable, a resounding, "Absolutely!"

Though he had missed spring training, Compleet was in top shape. After he agreed to Miltones's offer, he and Ronny worked out every day: running the bases, catching flies, hitting, and calisthenics. Spitz too kept in shape. He jogged and lifted weights. During the game, the team was still in playoff mode. Compleet had two home runs and a double, Ham and Jimbo each homered and singled, and Jammin threw a five-hit shutout. The Chum won easily 9–0. Fans nodded to one another. All seemed to agree this would be the pattern; the Chum would have a stellar season and breeze into the playoffs and maybe sweep again in the Bronze. With Compleet in center, Ham and Jimbo hitting home runs, and Jammin throwing shutouts, another title was a sure thing.

The first month of the season went well for the Chum. By the second week in May, they were firmly in first place in the Coral Division, four games ahead of the Flagfish. Spitz and Compleet again shared a room at the Three C's Hotel. Julie decided to stay in Tomtowne. The kids liked their school and had many friends. Honey B. and the cubs were still on the farm; everyone concerned agreed it was the best place to raise the sow's young. Clara had suggested names for the triplets: Tom, Terry, and Tracy. Compleet liked the names.

Almost every week, Clara sent Compleet photos of the cubs taken while they played, walked or loped, rested, ate, or slept. The bear kept the pictures in envelopes inside his locker. Before game time, he would take out one of the envelopes and look carefully at the pictures. He told Spitz it inspired him to play his best. It especially hurt not being with his family. He knew that during the cubs' first year they would grow and change a lot.

Compleet decided this season would be his last—one more

championship for the Chum and then retirement. His huge salary would allow him to pursue his dream of buying up outsized areas for wild animals. Wanting to help the bear, Miltones enlisted the aid of the Chum financial staff and the top money managers in and around Cuspin Heights. They got the bear started with high-grade stocks, tax-free municipal bonds, high-quality corporate bonds, choice real estate, treasury issues, and various foreign investments.

Not forgetting those who had befriended him, the bear bought Clara a new pickup, Clint a new tractor, rake, and combine, Ronny a Porsche, and Spitz a silver and gray Bentley. He purchased insurance on the Bruedock property and individual policies for the four Bruedocks. He promised to take Ginny, Clara, Kristy, Julie, and Helen Achts on a shopping spree, perhaps around Memorial Day. He bought a season pass to the Chum home games for Helen, a box seat in the lower grandstand behind first base. For himself, he bought a classic Stutz Bearcat, for show, really, since he had no license. He took out an insurance policy on himself and made out a will with Ronny and Spitz as the beneficiaries.

A Near Fatal Incident

It was a brisk evening in late May. Feeling restless, the bear decided to go for a walk and asked Spitz if he wanted to join him. During the game earlier in the day, Spitz had sprained his ankle in a collision at first with the runner. "I better stay here, kid, and rest the ankle. I'll still be up when you come back. Take your time and enjoy the night air."

Compleet walked over to River Boulevard and through Michel's Park to the river. He found the cool air refreshing; his fur bristled at the soft touch of the wind. The full moon lit up the water's surface. After a while, he doubled back to the boulevard and turned north. He passed joggers and shoppers and some workers on their way home. Everyone recognized the bear, of course, but they were polite enough not to bother him.

The bear passed Mullet Amusement Pier, which was aglow with lights, and entered Muddy's Park. He found a comfortable patch of grass in a quiet area. Lying down, he looked up at the sky; the moon and the stars seemed to be looking right at him. He thought how lucky he was. He had a family now, a Bronze ring on his paw, the affection of a city, and enough money to do just about anything he wanted. Next season he would be retired and could spend his time with Honey B. and watch their three young ones grow. He would teach them the fundamentals of baseball. Perhaps one or two would have the skills to play for the Chum. They might even become more famous than their dad. It was exciting and a joy to think of the possibilities. If he tired of being inactive, he would get more involved in his nature parks. He was certain of the future; he expected all the pieces to fall into place.

The sound of a woman shouting broke the bear's reverie. He

stood up on his hind legs to get a better view and saw a young woman pointing at a man who was running away from her. He was holding a pocketbook by the strap. Compleet got down on all fours and walked quickly toward the woman. She saw him approach and recognized him as the Chum center fielder.

"It's you, Compleet!" she said in a surprised voice. "I need help. That man stole my handbag," she said, pointing. "My credit cards, driver's license, and money are in it."

The bear held up a paw as if to say, "I'll get your bag back." He started after the thief, who had a big lead. But Compleet, running on all fours, almost closed the gap by the time the two got near the boulevard The thief ran into traffic to avoid the bear. Because cars were backed up and at a standstill, he scurried between cars and got across. Compleet also tried to cross, but the cars had begun to move, and he was hit by a driver who didn't see his dark figure until it was too late. The bear flipped and landed on his head.

Traffic came to a stop again, but this time because of the bear lying in the road. A number of onlookers called 9–1–1 on cell phones, and soon police cars and an ambulance were at the scene. Two medics strapped the bear onto a gurney and with help from three policemen lifted him into the ambulance. Compleet had a flashback of his mom lying in the road. He thought, *No! No! Please, not me. Honey B. needs me ... the cubs.*

The medics wanted to take Compleet to Backlore Haven Zoo. Since it was after hours at the zoo, a medic asked the police to make calls so the main gate would be open, and a doctor would be at the zoo's hospital.

Spitz learned about the accident shortly after the ambulance reached the zoo. The doctor at the hospital knew from sports reports that Compleet and Spitz were roommates at the Three C's. He called the hotel, and the desk clerk rang Spitz's room. The doctor told Spitz he had taken X-rays and found swelling of the brain. He thought it important to operate to reduce the swelling and wanted Spitz's permission. Spitz gave his okay and then drove to the zoo. Before he left the Three C's, he called

Ronny and Julie. Ronny said the family already knew about the bear's accident from a radio broadcast special. Spitz told Ronny the bear needed an operation, and he would call again as soon as he had more to report.

At the zoo, Spitz waited at the hospital over three hours in a small side room. When the doctor spoke to him, he said the operation had gone well. The bear's condition was guarded, but the doctor thought Compleet had a good chance to recover fully. The bear was in a coma. The doctor wasn't sure how long it would last.

A Guarded Condition

The letters of condolences and love poured into the zoo's hospital. TV and radio sports stations kept their listeners posted on the bear's condition. Attendance at Backlore Haven tripled because Compleet's fans were hoping to get a glimpse of him. But they could only read a daily report of his progress posted on the hospital's front door.

Spitz visited the bear every day—in the morning if he had a day game, in the early afternoon if he had a night game. Sometimes teammates went with him. Miltones, Boslerts, and Frog visited when the team had an off-day. Miltones told Spitz that players' insurance would pay all doctor and hospital bills as long as the bear was at Backlore Haven.

Spitz called Ronny often to report on the bear. Tests on Compleet continued to show improvement. There was still some swelling in the brain, and the bear's heartbeats were way down. The doctor was puzzled and said it was almost as if Compleet had gone into hibernation. Spitz said he talked to the bear even though he got no response. And he always said a short prayer. When the Chum were on the road, Spitz called the hospital every day.

Three weeks after the accident Compleet was still in a coma. The doctor had decided not to do any more tests. He would let nature take over. There were signs the bear was fighting to regain consciousness. He sometimes moved a leg or turned onto his side. Now and then he emitted a soft sound, almost like the sound of the wind on a still summer day.

Ronny and his family wanted to be nearer the bear. Ginny thought the Bruedocks might be able to rouse the bear with kind words and prayer. After work one day, Clara drove into Tomtowne to the town's nursing home. The bear was still highly regarded by the town and its team. The Tenn Nine players had all signed a big get-well card and sent it to Backlore Haven Zoo. Clara spoke to the director to find out if the home had a vacancy. She said her family wanted to transfer Compleet to Tomtowne. The director said there was space. He could convert two rooms at the end of the east hall into comfortable quarters for the bear. Clara wanted to know the monthly cost.

Ronny called Spitz and told him what Clara had found out. The cost was high. Spitz said the bear's private insurance would pay something. He wasn't sure if Compleet's policy with the Chum would pay anything. No matter. Spitz said he would pay the balance; he knew Julie would give her approval. Ronny protested. His family should also pay. "No," said Spitz, "Clint and Ginny and Clara are saving money to send you to college. Julie and I have extra money. Let us help."

When Spitz told Frog about the Bruedock's plan, Frog mentioned it to Boslerts, who informed Miltones. After a meeting of the owners, Miltones called Spitz and said the Chum organization would pay for Compleet's air transport to Memphis and would arrange for a vet to check on the bear at the nursing home two or three times a week. Frog arranged for Spitz to have three or four days off to accompany the bear.

At the Memphis airport, Clara and Ronny were waiting in Clara's new pickup. Clara cried when she saw Compleet on a gurney, motionless and with his eyes closed. Ronny put his mom's hand on the bear's chest so she could feel a heartbeat. "He'll be fine, Mom," said Ronny. "You'll see." Clara drove slowly all the way to the nursing home so her driving wouldn't jostle the bear. Spitz stayed with Compleet in the covered back end of the pickup. It took a while to get the bear comfortable at the nursing home. The director told Clara not to worry. He would make sure a nurse or someone with first-aid experience would look in on the bear every hour around the clock.

Spitz stayed in Tomtowne with Julie and the kids for two days. On the morning of the third day, Spitz, Julie, and the kids drove to the farm for a short visit with the Bruedocks, and then to Memphis so Spitz could catch a late afternoon flight up to Cuspin Heights.

With Compleet in nearby Tomtowne, Ginny arranged for one or more of the Bruedocks to visit the bear every day. She told them to talk to him as if he understood, and pray. Sometimes the Bruedocks prayed in the bear's room, sometimes on the farm, alone or with other members. Prayer and talking to the bear would bring him around. Ginny was convinced it would work.

Ronny's Promise

Perhaps no one was as deeply upset and saddened over the bear's accident as Ronny. And now he had to deal with Compleet's coma. If the bear were convalescing and could use sign language to talk to him it would have been okay. But there was no exchange of thoughts and feelings between the two. Ronny talked, and the bear just lay on his bed, unresponsive and helpless.

Spitz had told Ronny about the bear's special dream, his nature parks. And Ronny learned that Miltones had helped build a portfolio for Compleet. There would be a lot of money to establish the parks. The bear's parks became the third topic Ronny always talked to Compleet about, along with news of the Cuspin Chum and Honey B. and the cubs. On his phone, Ronny spoke often to Spitz to tell him how the bear was doing and also to get information about the Chum. He told Spitz he hoped Compleet would come out of his coma sooner if he heard news on those topics closest to his heart.

And he knew nothing was closer to the bear's heart than the sow and cubs. On the farm Ronny often stuck a small notepad in his pocket so he could jot down some amusing incident to tell Compleet, like the time Tracy tried to catch a fish and ended up with a mouth full of water. Or the time Honey B. heard some stray dogs bark and huffed (a signal of alarm to the cubs). The three cubs immediately climbed the nearest tree, but Terry lost his grip and fell, knocking Tom and Tracy to the ground.

When Ronny visited the bear he sometimes went by himself in his new Porsche. Sometimes he invited Kristy to go with him. He always started his one-way conversation with Compleet by telling him how much he missed him on the farm, how every time he passed the boulder house he thought of the bear.

When Ronny talked about the nature parks, it was more about family than about the parks. At the end, he used almost the same words every time. "You got us a new barn; Gran'pa, new machinery; Ma, a new pickup; insurance for all of us, and more. The family owes you a lot. Your nature parks, your dream? We'll help you realize your dream. I promise."

An August Surprise

Clint and Clara began to wonder if the bear's coma might continue indefinitely. Only Ginny and Ronny were upbeat. "Any day he could snap out of it," said Ginny on a number of occasions.

"I thought he understood what I said," announced Ronny one day during the second week in August. "It was his expression. It wasn't blank. And when I held his paw, his claws moved as if he were trying to grasp my hand. It was more than a reflex, I know it."

I t was the morning of the twenty-third of August. One of the nurses at the home was talking to the bear, as she and the other nurses were instructed to do, and wiping his hair with a damp cloth to bring out the shine. Suddenly, Compleet opened his eyes and let out a deep grunt and began to purr. The nurse had never heard the bear utter more than a whisper, and his eyes were always shut. She was so startled she fell backward and let out a surprised ahh. Two of the staff who had heard the commotion ran into the room. Their jaws dropped when they saw the bear with his eyes open and heard him emit deep, soft sounds.

The director called the Bruedocks. Clint answered the phone. When he heard the exciting news, he called Ronny's school and left a message and then called the Three C's to alert Spitz. McOystre informed Frog and got permission to fly to Nashville as soon as he could schedule a flight.

That evening the Bruedocks and Kristy and the McOystres visited the bear. Ronny held one paw; Spitz, another; and the others crowded around Compleet's bed. "We're so happy you've come back to us," said Ginny. "How do you feel?"

The bear answered, but it took him a long time to make his signs. *I'm tired, but… when I'm able… able to get out of bed and go outside in the sun… I know I'll feel better.*

"We're all here to wish you well," said Ronny. "Do you recognize everyone?"

Compleet looked carefully at each face on his left. *I'm not sure who the young woman is*, he signed, looking at Kristy. *The face is familiar, but…*

"That's my girl," said Ronny, smiling. "That's Kristy."

The bear's face brightened when he heard the name. He continued to scan the faces and then signed to Julie. *Ma'am… have we met?*

"I'm Spitz's wife, and these are our children, Charles and Carly," she said, pointing to them. "Some time ago Spitz and I, and Carly and Charles, spent a night in our guest room in Tomtowne. You and Honey B. slept on a rug."

"Do you remember that night?" asked Spitz.

I… don't know.

"Honey B. and the cubs are fine," said Ronny. "The cubs have gotten a lot bigger since you last saw them. When you get your strength back, I'll drive you to the farm to see them. I love the Porsche. Thanks, Compleet. I'm so grateful." The bear nodded.

There was more talk, but everyone could see the bear was tired. Spitz suggested they say their goodbyes. "He'll be here for some time," he said. "And I know he wants to see us. We can tell him all the news he missed."

Outside, Julie asked, "Do you think his memory will come back?"

"I'm sure of it," said Clint. "He remembered most of us. Compleet has a lot of fight in him. In time he'll be as good as before the accident."

The Road Back

The contusions had healed, but Compleet still experienced pain and was troubled by moments of forgetfulness. Three months in bed had left his legs weak and his whole body sore and soft. But he was determined to get well. Regular visits by the Bruedocks and Julie and her children helped keep his spirits up. Twice a day he took walks about the property with one of the orderlies. He used the home's treadmill every day. The residents often watched him and were amazed how someone so big could maintain his stride and keep from falling off. He remained at the nursing home five more weeks before he felt strong enough to be on his own. There was still some pain and memory loss, but he was confident he could deal with it.

The evening before he left, the staff presented him with gifts—one was a knitted scarf, another was a carving of the bear in profile—and the chef baked a cake for the occasion. On it, in green icing over white, were the words, "To Compleet Bear, Star Center Fielder for the Tenn Nine and Chum. Best of luck from all of us here at the home." The staff sang songs, and many of the residents joined in. The director said how sad he was the bear was leaving, although it was good that Compleet's health had improved so much in recent weeks. He had been a morale booster at the home. One of the great stars of baseball was in their midst.

The Bruedocks picked up the bear the next day and returned to the farm. Ronny was driving Clara's pickup. As soon as Compleet got out of the pickup, Honey B. detected his scent and loped over to him. The cubs followed her but had difficulty keeping up. The reunion was heartwarming. Ginny and Clint had tears in their eyes. There were so many grunts and purrs and licking of faces!

The cubs just stood there not knowing what to do. They saw

this large black bear and their mom all lovey-dovey. After a time, Compleet looked at the cubs and started to walk toward them. The three were scared and felt like running, but their mom gave no huffs that told them of danger. So they stood there, nervous. Compleet licked each one and gave them some playful pushes or slaps. Honey B. joined them, and the family played together for a long time, while Clara and Ronny took pictures of the historic occasion.

Compleet was well enough to walk about the farm and play with the cubs. But he had headaches and pain at times in his hind legs and back. His memory still failed him at odd moments. But he wasn't complaining. He was back on the farm with the Bruedocks and Honey B. He could watch the cubs grow. Next year Ronny would go off to college and make everyone proud of him. In the off season, Spitz would be close by in Tomtowne. His baseball career—short as it was—had netted him many rewards. And with planning, his nature parks would become a reality. The future looked bright—brighter than ever before.

Epilogue: "Whatever Happened to ... ?"

I see that I haven't many pages left, but I would like to tell you what some of the characters you have met did in the months and years after the great bear's accident and partial recovery.

Ronny

He attended a first-rate agricultural college, got engaged to Kristy in his junior year, and married her a month after graduation. As a college student, he was able to help Spitz—and Compleet when he had fully recovered—with the nature parks during college breaks and in the summers. After he and Kristy married, they built a house on the Bruedock farm. In the early years, work with the nature parks kept them away from home for long periods. But during spring planting and harvest, the two always returned to the farm. Clint could still help with many tasks, and during spring planting he always put in a full day in the field.

During the bear's convalescence, Ronny and Spitz established the first two nature parks, in South Dakota and the western part of North Carolina. Spitz ran both parks until Compleet felt fit enough to help. After his graduation from college, Ronny took over the one in North Carolina. One of Clint's sayings was, "You help the locals first." Ronny told Compleet and Spitz what his grandpa had said, and all three agreed to hire only local help. Some men and women acted as guides. Some built cabins, work-stations, and administrative buildings. Some checked fences for breaks and fed and watered the animals in dry spells and during the cold months. Some were sent to school to become bookkeepers, managers, publicists, veterinarians, or breeders.

When the first two parks had been stocked and operations were under control and running smoothly, Compleet, Ronny, and Spitz decided to expand. They eventually established parks in five other states. Ronny set up a summer program for youngsters who wanted experience in handling large animals. And over a period of five years, two hundred young men and women attended college under scholarships paid for by the Nature Parks Foundation. After graduation they were assigned to one of the parks full-time; following a long apprenticeship, five were named as park superintendents.

Ronny and Kristy started a family soon after they married. Eventually they had four children: Christopher, Carrie, Cindy, and Cassie. Ronny insisted the first names begin with a *C* in honor of the bear.

Fred Miltones

Because Compleet's salary was huge, the Chum organization had taken out a special insurance policy on him. It stated that in the event of the bear's death or debilitating injury during the baseball season, the Chum would be reimbursed for salary paid out. From the start of the season to late May, management had paid the bear about 19 million.

When the Chum organization was reimbursed, most of the owners wanted to use the monies to make repairs to Tailors or sign players, including a replacement for the bear in center. Miltones, who felt otherwise, reminded his colleagues of the great good the bear had done for the team and Cuspin Heights. He had been responsible for a boost in attendance at home and away; he had given the team a new spirit and had led it to the Bronze title. In appreciation, Miltones said they should donate the money to the bear's Nature Parks Foundation.

There was much haggling, but eventually Miltones got most of what he wanted. At a news conference, he handed Spitz, who substituted for Compleet because the bear was still in the nursing home, a check for 15 million dollars.

Miltones kept in touch after Compleet and Spitz left the team.

With his wife, he eventually visited every nature park. Each year at the end of the season, he threw a big party for team members and their families. Compleet, Spitz, and Julie were always invited and almost always attended.

Clara

She took business courses on line from a Midwestern university. After she got her degree, she took over the finances of three of the nature parks. She never remarried, although she had a number of offers. She helped run the farm when her son and daughter-in-law were busy at this park or that one. And she looked after Honey B. and the cubs when Compleet was at one of the nature parks on business and Ronny and Kristy were absent.

Frog

He continued to manage the Chum for four years after winning the Bronze, but the team never won another championship. When Compleet left the team, his absence affected the players; a certain ethic, energy, and identity disappeared. The year the bear was injured the team played well enough to get into the playoffs, but it lost to the Horstead Haddock in the Neptune League finals.

After the fourth year, the Chum didn't renew Frog's contract. Frog decided to retire so he could live at a slower pace and spend more time with his family, especially his grandchildren. He ordered a special case made of maple to hold his Bronze ring and displayed the ring in its case in the den, together with memorabilia he got from the bear and other team members. Whenever he and his wife had guests, he removed the ring from the case and showed it off and told a story or two about one of the four Bronze wins. He was proud to say he was the only person in the In-The-Sea Association who had managed a bear.

Spitz

While the bear was recuperating in Tomtowne, Spitz finished out the season with the Chum. He spent most of his playing time in the dugout. Memories made every game painful. In the locker room, he often imagined he saw the bear standing next to his locker. In the dugout, he would see the bear in the on-deck circle, about to take a turn at the plate.

At the end of the season, Boslerts told him the club had decided not to renew his contract; he was a free agent. Briefly, he thought of trying to sign with another team. But after talking to Julie about the future, he decided to retire from baseball. He was forty; he didn't have to worry about money. Since he was needed to help run the nature parks, they became his next big challenge.

He and Julie had a house built in Tomtowne; they also bought a stately old house in Cuspin in Splendor Park West for Julie's parents. After two years of marriage, the McOystres had a son. They named him Morgan, but Spitz always called him Dutch because the boy looked so much like Spitz's dad.

Charles and Carly took a liking to their half-brother; and Morgan, since he was so much younger, idolized his brother and sister. All went to different colleges and chose different careers. Charles became superintendent of the nature park on the Upper Peninsula in Michigan. Carly's love was skiing. As a preteen, she took lessons from a pro at Vail. A few years later she was racing against skiers twice her age. Her aim was to win a medal at the Winter Olympics in 2022. Morgan became a veterinarian and joined the staff at the Lincoln Park Zoo in Chicago.

Helen Achts

After Clara had spent a year managing the finances of the three nature parks, she realized she had bitten off more than she could chew. She couldn't carry out her duties as chief financial officer of the parks and help run the farm at the same time. She complained to her son that she needed help. Ronny told Spitz of the problem.

Spitz thought immediately of Helen because she had a way with animals. He suggested Helen move to the farm and take over most of Clara's duties. Wanting a change, Helen agreed.

She and Clara were about the same age and became good friends. Mai Tai continued his strange fascination with bears and was usually seen in the company of Compleet, Honey B., or one of the cubs.

Joe Wathersmythe

The principal owner of the Tomtowne Tenn Nine never forgot the bear. When Compleet and Spitz joined the Cuspin Chum, Wathersmythe read all he could about the bear in the newspapers and sports magazines. When Compleet was moved to the nursing home in Tomtowne, Wathersmythe and his wife often visited him.

Wathersmythe had a vision; someday he would find another Compleet. If one bear could play ball that well, why not others? When the Tenn Nine club folded because of poor attendance, Wathersmythe set out to realize his dream. He hunted bears not only in the U.S. and Canada, but in South America and Asia. He followed up on every lead, no matter how farfetched it seemed. He hunted not only black bears, but grizzlies, brown bears, Kodiak bears, polar bears, spectacled bears, sloth bears, and sun bears.

But he never heard more than a grunt, a huff, or snapping of teeth from a bear. He never found a bear that understood human language. He never discovered a bear that could use sign language. He never came across a bear that could play any sport— baseball, soccer, football, volleyball, lacrosse, rugby, or cricket. He never found a bear that could box, hit a tennis ball, or a golf ball. In short, he came across bears that could only be bears! He had to admit to himself, Compleet *was* unique! There was not another bear in the whole wide world like him!

Was Wathersmythe disappointed? Yes, but he was also glad and proud. He had been the first to sign to a contract the only bear in the world that could play baseball.

Matti Gimcrack

A short while after Spitz and Compleet visited Matti to thank her for rescuing the bear, she decided to pack up and leave

Troefield. *Better to get away*, she thought. Her job was a dead end. She wanted more meaning in her life. And she wanted to meet a good man.

She moved to Wheatland, a small town northeast of Troefield, and got a job as a receptionist in the office of a small business. She made some friends and had one romance, but it lasted only four months. One evening she passed a sign in the window of a drugstore about a church social. She decided to attend and met a man she was attracted to. He was rough looking and reminded her of Spitz. He was well mannered and had a sense of humor. He told her he worked as a driver for a trucking outfit.

They started to date and found they had a lot in common. They got engaged and soon afterward tied the knot. Although it was a small wedding, Matti invited Spitz and Compleet to the wedding and reception. After talking to Julie, Spitz decided to attend. The bear declined, fearing his presence would upset youngsters at the church and reception.

Spitz stayed at the reception long enough to dance with Matti. He asked, "Are you happy?"

She gave him a wide smile and said, "Yes … I found a good man."

Honey B. and Cubs

When Compleet left the nursing home and returned to the farm, Honey B. noticed how unsteady and slow moving he was at times. And at night she often heard him moan in pain. She imagined he had been injured in a fight, like the one she witnessed at Tailors. Sometimes she moaned with him to show her support. And she grunted and purred for long periods when he was with her to show how happy she was. He was always attentive, and he played with the cubs often over the course of a day. Honey B. had never seen a male at Backlore Haven stay close to his sow or play with his offspring. She realized how different her bear-man was.

After Compleet made a full recovery, he spent long periods visiting one or more of the nature parks to help Spitz or Ronny or one of the apprenticed park superintendents. Honey B.

thought he was playing baseball. Since he always returned, she grew accustomed to his routine.

As the cubs grew, the Bruedocks, and later Helen and Kristy, were eager to see whether any of the three had some of Compleet's traits. Whenever the cubs were nearby, Clara, Helen, Kristy, or Ronny talked to them and looked for signs that they understood what was being said. Tracy acquired a sizable vocabulary and was a superior athlete. Ronny decided that when the nature parks no longer took up so much of his time, he would work with her on vocabulary and baseball skills. He was hoping she had in her some of her dad's talent. As for Tom and Terry, they turned out to be, well, just plain bears!

Compleet

It took a year for the bear to recover fully from his accident. He was patient. He was surrounded by those he loved. Why hurry? Why worry? He and Honey B. took long walks in the woods, waded in the stream looking for fish as snacks, and swam in the pond during the hot months. In season, they went berry picking in the south end of the farm. In the woods they hunted for nuts. Often the cubs, Mai Tai, or one or two of the wild ones would follow them. At night, Compleet, the sow, and cubs snuggled together in the boulder house.

When he was at full strength, Compleet took pleasure in visiting different nature parks to help out or merely to watch the animals graze, engage in mock fighting, or run with abandon. He had given them the freedom to wander over vast stretches of land. That was their delight, and that was the bear's triumph.

Every summer, Compleet, Honey B., Tom, Terry, Tracy, Ronny, Kristy, Spitz, Julie, and often Clara and Helen, and Charles, Carly, and Morgan took a trip to the nature park in South Dakota for a two-week vacation. Over the main entrance was a large wooden sign: "Enter, friend. The earth belongs to all God's creatures." Although everyone had a ball, the main purpose of the visits was to allow the three cubs to experience the joys of the open prairie, the wide, clear skies, the rolling landscape, the lively, warm winds, the miles and miles of land just there for playing and running and exploring. The experience wasn't exactly freedom because the three were closely watched, and their movements were restricted. But the cubs got great pleasure from their time out in the open.

Each year, close to the date of their starting out on the drive to the park, the three bears grew restless in anticipation. Ronny and Spitz would smile when they noticed how enthusiastic the cubs were. And when Compleet was at the park watching the sow and the cubs at play, and he looked up at the clear skies and out at the undulating countryside, he could only think how lucky his life had turned out. A long time ago in Muddy's Park, he had told himself all the pieces would fall into place. It had taken longer than he wished, but, yes, the pieces were in place. His life had come full circle. At High Point, his mom had given him and his sister a loving, secure upbringing. Now it was his turn to give love and attention to the cubs and Honey B. He knew he wouldn't fail. Failure was a word the bear didn't understand.

Endnotes

Turning Pro as a Solution

1   That is, using sign language.

2   Italics indicate Compleet is using sign language or is thinking. Because sign language doesn't translate into standard English sentences, I have smoothed out the bear's signing for you, dear reader. I have inserted words where called for, found the right word for the context, and used a recognizable order.

A Different Kind of Ballplayer

3   American Sign Language

4   Pidgin Sign English

Year Two with the Tenn Nine

5   In truth, he had just turned four.

New Ball Club, New Town

6   Spitz was thinking of the giant sequoias and coast redwoods. In Sequoia National Park, the famous General Sherman Tree is 305 feet tall and measures 36½ feet around the base! Some coast redwoods are taller but not as wide at the base. The tallest known tree in the world—a coast redwood—is 379 feet high!

7   Abe and his wife, Mary, had four sons, but only one lived long enough to become an adult. Willie died in 1862 at age eleven.

8   In those days, presidents wrote their own speeches and letters. There are five originals of Lincoln's Gettysburg Address—all in Abe's handwriting! Each one is worth a ton of money because the wording of the Gettysburg Address has become so famous. Incidentally, Lincoln made a big error in the address when he wrote: "The world will little note, nor long remember what we say here…" We do remember, Abe!

A Setup

9   -o ending is the singular; -i ending is the plural.

10   Bud Abbott (the straight man) and Lou Costello (the funny one) were popular comedians on radio and in motion pictures, especially in the 1940s, and on TV in the 1950s. Their comic banter, "Who's on First?" is a classic and can be heard/seen in the Baseball Hall of Fame in Cooperstown, New York.

11   It's short for "All-points bulletin."

Separating Fact from Fiction

12   French words that mean "famous scandal."

Baseball and Lovers

13   The name given to the female of some animals, like bears.

The Bronze in Sight

14　According to Shakespeare, Julius Caesar said, "Et tu, Brute!" ("You too, Brutus!") as he fell to the floor outside the senate chamber. Caesar had just been stabbed by conspirators, including Brutus, supposedly his friend!

Caesar didn't say, "I came, I saw, I conquered it all." Those words, minus "it all" and in Latin, may have been on a banner in a triumph (great victory parade). Or Caesar may have written them in a letter in reference to one of his campaigns. *The Oxford Dictionary of Quotations*, 3rd ed. (Oxford University Press, 1979).

e|LIVE

---

listen|imagine|view|experience

AUDIO BOOK DOWNLOAD INCLUDED WITH THIS BOOK!

In your hands you hold a complete digital entertainment package. Besides purchasing the paper version of this book, this book includes a free download of the audio version of this book. Simply use the code listed below when visiting our website. Once downloaded to your computer, you can listen to the book through your computer's speakers, burn it to an audio CD or save the file to your portable music device (such as Apple's popular iPod) and listen on the go!

How to get your free audio book digital download:

1. Visit www.tatepublishing.com and click on the e|LIVE logo on the home page.
2. Enter the following coupon code:
   2e9f-61c9-7bab-5767-934c-d94f-b47a-e7e9
3. Download the audio book from your e|LIVE digital locker and begin enjoying your new digital entertainment package today!